To Claurice, who listens patiently to the stories of others,

Joanne Cutting-Gray

TELLING LITTLE,
TELLING ALL

JOANNE CUTTING-GRAY

Copyright © 2018 Joanne Cutting-Gray.

All rights reserved. No part of this book may be used or reproduced by any means, graphic, electronic, or mechanical, including photocopying, recording, taping or by any information storage retrieval system without the written permission of the author except in the case of brief quotations embodied in critical articles and reviews.

Archway Publishing books may be ordered through booksellers or by contacting:

Archway Publishing
1663 Liberty Drive
Bloomington, IN 47403
www.archwaypublishing.com
1 (888) 242-5904

Because of the dynamic nature of the Internet, any web addresses or links contained in this book may have changed since publication and may no longer be valid. The views expressed in this work are solely those of the author and do not necessarily reflect the views of the publisher, and the publisher hereby disclaims any responsibility for them.

This is a work of fiction. All of the characters, names, incidents, organizations, and dialogue in this novel are either the products of the author's imagination or are used fictitiously.

Any people depicted in stock imagery provided by Getty Images are models, and such images are being used for illustrative purposes only. Certain stock imagery © Getty Images.

ISBN: 978-1-4808-7018-5 (sc)
ISBN: 978-1-4808-7017-8 (e)

Library of Congress Control Number: 2018913009

Print information available on the last page.

Archway Publishing rev. date: 12/22/2018

"A few escaped destruction & came back to tell the tale.
... There is more power in telling little, than telling all."
—Mark Rothko

Prologue

In the highest mountains of Arcadia, there once lived a huntress, Atalanta by name. She was born to a disappointed father who wanted a son. He exposed the baby in the wilderness where she was found by Artemis, virgin goddess of the hunt. Artemis, who had pitied the defenseless babe, assumed the form of a she-bear, suckled her, and gave her to be raised by hunters. Atalanta grew into a beautiful woman famed for rustic appearance, skill in hunting, and fleetness of foot. She pledged her chastity to Artemis, and, living in pure maidenhood, took part in hunts, slew the Centaurs, and ran footraces that she never lost.

Now it happened that a monstrous boar was destroying crops and wreaking havoc on cities. A young man named Meleager, hearing of Atalanta's skill with the bow and spear, asked her to join his search for the beast. The two roamed the forest together until they came upon the brute whose enormous tusks and sharp teeth had struck fear in the people. Atalanta plunged her spear deep into the beast's side, then, as it rose to attack her, Meleager felled it and gave her the pelt for having struck the first blow.

The myth lay dormant for centuries and then, without rhyme or reason, sprang to life in a modern city.

Backlog

The heels of art historian Helena Gandolfi clicked sharply on the marble floor of the museum. Her footsteps were driven by a seismic event in the art world that elsewhere went unnoticed. She stopped abruptly in front of an orange and maroon Rothko from 1952 whose soft-edged rectangles seemed to undulate with life. "It's the deep breath before the plunge" she sighed to herself, then abandoning the canvas reluctantly, continued down the hall. At the door of the board room office she stopped and was about to knock when it opened as though waiting for her.

Board member Felicity Hardcastle, a thin woman with an earnest, sallow face, invited her in. As Helena stepped inside, she saw another person behind the desk. It was a striking man with incisive eyes and a forehead crowned by silver curls. He rose like a cobra from his chair. "You know Dr. Zaron of course," Felicity said of the surgeon-cum-billionaire-art-collector whose presence insinuated trouble.

"Of course," Helena answered with a knowing smile and held out a hand. Talon-like fingers grasped it as sharp eyes took in her black dress, shapely legs, and high-heeled pumps. Pointing to a chair in front of the desk, he invited her to sit down while he remained standing. An attempt to intimidate? As her eyes swept the room, they searched less for a thing than a mood. She read it in the stiffness of Felicity's demeanor toward Zaron, whose presence reduced the light-filled space to an obdurate thing. The mood was the opposite of possibility. She saw it in the way Zaron swayed ever so slightly and the muscles in his cheeks contracted. Having made his upright impression, he sat down again behind the desk and stared at Helena.

Felicity meekly accepted a subordinate role alongside the desk and declared in a soft quavering voice, "Dr. Zaron has informed me there's reason to believe that the last, missing painting by Mark Rothko has been found. As you know, rumors have floated for years that he gave a work to distant relatives in 1970. Two sisters, just before he died. We, that is Dr. Zaron and I, believe it's in Atlanta. Rothko's last, and maybe his greatest masterpiece." On edge with excitement she continued. "If we can get it before a museum with a large endowment, we can purchase it for millions less. We know that once the word is out, the price will skyrocket."

Zaron, meanwhile, stared off blankly into space tap tapping on the desk with the fingers of one hand. It was the demeanor of a man too busy searching his mental filing cabinet to brook circumlocution. Felicity meanwhile, rattled nervously on, offering nothing of substance or use.

Helena sat wondering what place art had in the discussion. These two made it sound like a commodity with a market price. Didn't they know that art is a tsunami that sweeps everything in its path?

When Felicity's quantum jitters subsided, she looked expectantly at Zaron, who leaned forward, alert now that the preliminaries were over, and addressed Helena as his sole audience. "What we're discussing must be kept in absolute confidence until the painting is in our hands. And of course, we would want *you*," he gave Helena a patronizing nod, "to authenticate it." With total confidence, he described the market value of the painting and rattled off figures. It was the language of deals made in back rooms and money passed under tables. The surgeon whose business was to cut up and reassemble human objects jabbed his words into the air like thrusts of a scalpel. What Helena heard was her own threat to his ambition. This meeting was a tactical strike against her. Were *he* to get his hands on the Rothko, it would be a trophy like a stuffed rhino head.

She confronted them as one booted and spurred and ready for battle. Slashing through the subterfuge, she had pointed words for Felicity. "I know what *you* want. What I'd like to know is what you two don't want me to know."

Felicity's thin face wilted, but Zaron took the question in stride. "The question could be asked of *you*." His contempt was easy and he rode it hard. "What do *you* know that you don't want *us* to know?" He paused dramatically. "We think *you* know who has it." His poker face told little of what he was really thinking, though it was enough to tell her all. He was a man so habituated to deception that he believed his own lies.

She recalled the monumental blue-grey painting listed in the catalogue raisonné of works on canvas simply as "#835, Untitled, Whereabouts Unknown" and measured what she would say next. "Why would you think that?"

He was not one for equivocation. "The whole business is obviously entangled in your relationship with Reginald Foxcroft and his daughters." The English Sir Reginald was a wealthy Atlanta collector and old friend of Helena who had been searching for the painting for years. "We think you might offer it to him rather than *us*."

Helena passed over his hubris. "Us?" she repeated. The inflection implied that he wanted the painting for himself. She already knew why. For him art was everything Mark Rothko loathed and strove against.

His smirk acknowledged a point scored. "Not even Sir Reginald could afford it if the word got out—unless the purchase is arranged under the radar of the market. A Rothko that sold for eighty-seven million in 2012 would fetch hundreds of millions today. The museum doesn't have that kind of money, but I would arrange the purchase and lend it to them." He exposed two rows of perfect teeth in a grin that assumed the matter was settled.

"Naturally." Helena underscored the irony. Zaron had inherited millions from his father, the former Russian oligarch, money launderer, and swindler, and was well-known to practice his father's arts. "Let's see if I understand correctly. You want me *not* to tell Sir Reginald what you think I know, in case he beats you to it." She continued—not that she expected to be believed. "I don't know the whereabouts of the painting." She watched Felicity's taut face crumple in puzzlement as Zaron sneered in disbelief.

"Then how do you explain these?" He threw a sheaf of glossy photos on the desk. Helena sifted through them as he watched like a bird of prey. They were the recto and verso of a large blue and grey painting. There was no need to examine them. They were images of the 1970 Rothko.

"What do you expect me to say about a bunch of photos? That they are what you presume they are? You can't know that from photos. They could easily be fakes."

Zaron's lip curled in disdain. "Do you deny having seen them before?" He had spoken in the grand manner of one who is right without ever having been in the wrong.

"Of course, I don't deny it. I see hundreds of photos of purported masterpieces. That's my job." Hearing herself say it and seeing how it was heard strengthened her resolve.

"Who gave them to you?" Zaron commanded tersely, unaccustomed to being challenged.

The demand reassured her of his intention. "I'd be only too happy to tell you, but I don't know. Such things come to me anonymously from time to time." He was about to unleash another stinging comment when she raised a hand in protest. "I didn't come here to be basted and grilled by you two. What you want is for me to make sure that the lost painting, if that is what it is, will go to—what did you say? —'us.'"

A flush erupted on Felicity's cheeks while Zaron's teeth clenched threateningly. "Dr. Gandolfi, I'd hate to think what the University would do if you resist cooperating with us." He had promised pieces from the famous Zaron Collection to the University and implied that if Helena didn't do as he asked, her job in the Art Department would be in jeopardy. It was his way of operating—by insinuation and threat. "Especially," he went on, watching her face for traces of knowledge, "if they knew you were involved with a stolen painting."

Against this accusation, she raised another. "I'd hate to think what the University or this museum might do if a board member" —she stared pointedly at Felicity— "or a trustee" —she turned her laser eye on Zaron—"puts personal interest above the institution." It was rumored that he bid for paintings against the very museums on whose board he served. On hearing this, Felicity blanched and glared suspiciously at Zaron, who passed the glare on to Helena.

"As a matter of curiosity," Helena asked, "why do you want the painting?"

"Isn't it obvious?" He answered with the air of a man handed back the false banknote he had tried to pass. "It's a masterpiece."

"Yes, but what does that *mean* to *you*?" It was an odd question for a woman like her to put to a man like him, but she had been summonsed under false pretenses.

"What does that mean?" He hurled the words back with violence.

"Do you judge it on its own merits or because someone told you it's great?"

He regarded this as touting her expertise. "I see by your question you want to intimidate me."

"Not at all. A man who seals every chink in his consciousness can't be intimidated." She gave back his stare with amusement. "Apparently you, a great collector, have no faith in the power of art to transform life."

He didn't understand the remark at all and took it as a trick. "Does anyone think works of art change lives?"

She marveled at the gap in his thinking. "Plato must have thought so. He banished the poets as the terror and ruin of the city." Before he could respond, she got up with a warm smile and stood in the doorway, her eyes fixed on him like an insolent and powerful goddess. Then with a nod she left.

This meeting took place in the midst of a war. When it began, if we can say when anything begins—but for all that we need to go back. If not to the beginning, at least to a place where, after the fact, truth can be seen as having left its mark. For it is not only amid things and persons that we live and speak. It is in a world transformed by events.

1

Phineas McGinley, overweight and emphysemic, sat at his computer staring blankly at the screen. From time to time he glanced nervously at his office closet. His mobile dotted and dashed signaling a text. He ignored it. It whistled an email. He ignored it. It chirped like a cricket. He picked it up, recognized the caller, and laid the phone back down. Real estate agents were constantly receiving messages that required answers. But there was more to it than met the ear. Without knowing, Finny had a serious case of a modern malady. Being fundamentally bored, he escaped into idle curiosity about who might be calling about nothing significant. Until today. Today he noticed—and was too distracted to be distracted. The cause was an anonymous email that said, "You are the receiver of stolen property. If you don't return it you will be in danger." His big-boned face, splotched and puffed from Irish genes, too much whiskey and fried food, crumpled into a worried frown. Who sent the email and what was he to do about it?

In a job that demanded slick surfaces and an air-brushed appearance, Phineas McGinley was an anomaly. Unruly ginger curls and twinkling eyes made him look more like a leprechaun than a business man. Though he wore custom-tailored clothes, his body never aligned with the tailoring. The pants tended to hitch up, the shirts to crumple, and the shoes to scuff. Yet he sold more million-dollar pieces of real-estate than anyone in Midtown Atlanta. Success in business, however, had not transferred to success in love, as attested to by two short-lived marriages and messy divorces.

Finny had adored his sister Kate and mourned her terribly when she died. He was a loving uncle to his orphaned nieces Sandra and Justine, but he couldn't abide Kate's arrogant ex-husband, Sir Reginald Foxcroft. The feeling was mutual—which is why he suspected that the threatening email had come from the self-important collector. He grumbled, with a guilty look at the closet, "I was a fool to accept that damned paint splotch!"

It happened in the way things do that are completely unforeseen. Unlike younger agents who stored their lists of sales and clients in the cloud, that demonic version of paradise, he still kept paper files and personal notes locked in the office closet. From time to time he searched it to resurrect the names of people he had met during four decades of selling houses. People and houses. He still thought of his transactions in personal terms. Several months earlier, he had come across the names of two reclusive Russian-Jewish sisters to whom, forty years ago, he had sold his—and their—first house, a bungalow in Druid Hills. They were already old maids when he met them and treated him like a nephew more than an agent. Despite his lack of expertise and social skills, they encouraged him to persist at a job in which he thought himself a failure. He had never forgotten their kindness and called from time to time over the years to see how they fared. Some weeks ago, one of them had called to tell him that her sister had died and asked him to stop by.

It was the first time in forty-odd years he had been inside the house. He was astonished to find the unchanged and nondescript cottage filled with small paintings and prints. An eclectic but insignificant collection, he concluded, his knowledge of art limited to what he had picked up from hanging around Kate, his nieces, and their stuffy father. After a tour of the house that was bursting at the seams with the stuff, the now ancient remaining sister announced that her sibling had wanted to give him a painting to remember her by.

Imagine his disappointment then, when from among the pretty landscapes and quaint old portraits, she proudly offered him an enormous unframed canvas with two giant blue-grey rectangles, the colors and shapes smudged and unfinished. They told him nothing. That was all. Worse than nothing. He tried politely to refuse. It was too generous. He really had no place to hang it. No way to transport such a large painting. It might be better off in a museum. What could he do with two worthless blue blots? But she insisted that it was an important work given to them by a very great artist. She even removed the wood holding it together so he could transport it, and gave him a long cylindrical canister to put it in. Finally, he had no choice but to accept.

As soon as he got the thing to the office he stashed it away in his closet until he felt free to dump it. Then the remaining sister died and left behind what turned out to be a fortune in art. That's when it dawned on him that the blob might really be worth something. With that idea in mind, he searched the High Museum and discovered a similar canvas in orange and purple by a painter named Mark Rothko. While he was looking at the thing that was nothing, who should happen upon him but Kate's bristling and insufferable ex-husband? Foxcroft acted offended, as though he, Phineas McGinley, polluted the work just by looking at it. That made him begin to wonder if the painting in his closet might be by the same artist. He had only actually seen it that one time at the sister's house, as briefly as politeness allowed, but its presence still troubled him. When he was supposed to be working, he found himself thinking about it. He felt as if in shutting it away he had denied some sort of truth to the world. As if some living thing was hidden in the closet, like the spirit of the living God inside the Ark of the Covenant threatening to annihilate any who dared look at it. He had to get rid of it, Rothko or no. He could no longer bear its concealed presence or hide from himself that he was hiding from it.

———◆———

The voice of famous soprano Victoria Vargas soared through

the rehearsal hall: "*I wish my heart to offer Thee, / Offer Thee my care, my all. / I wish my all for Thee could be / In this world, for Thee so small, / Oh, in Thee I do not fall. / Thou, more than earth and heaven, all.*"

The chorus joined in. "Stop!" the celebrated diva cried and scowled at the director as if *he* had interrupted *her*. It was the third time she had disrupted the rehearsal, and surreptitious glances told the tale. As accomplished as Madame Vargas was, she was also haughty, difficult, and self-important.

The choral director, dark of eye and deep of thought, absorbed the angry glance as one absorbs a blow, without flinching. "Let's take it from 'Oh, in Thee,'" Jonah Hartman said smiling. The smile, if Victoria cared to read it, understood her impatience. Flashing eyes and a heaving bosom said she did not care.

"Remember Victoria," he added gently, "Bach has taken you on an arduous path through dangerous and difficult lines. But you're not alone. The chorus is with you." The admonition tilted away from her, the soloist, toward the chorus.

A toss of her head expressed indignation. The others were mere amateurs, while the world knew *her* as the *true* professional. As Jonah, her husband, raised his baton, she gave him a look that said, "You'll pay for this."

Jonah Hartman understood his volatile Latina wife, or thought he did. Professional opera singers both, they had dedicated themselves to their art and built their careers together. But he had given up his career as a soloist to devote himself to helping other singers sing. Apart from the occasional concert, he now taught voice at the University and was the new director of the Atlanta Symphony Chorus.

"If you can stay until 10:30, we'll take a break and come back to Victoria's solo in twenty-five minutes," Jonah proposed. Normally the once-a-week rehearsals ran from 7:30-10:00, but tonight the music was so demanding they needed a break. Since the 1970s the all-volunteer, 200-member chorus had garnered a stellar reputation. Its dedication to the art was so complete that singers moved to Atlanta just for a chance to take part. And now with a world-class singer-conductor at the helm, the chorus was eager for the challenge of a staged version of Bach's *St. Matthew Passion*.

"I did everything perfectly," Victoria snapped as the couple walked through the lobby on their break. "The problem is the chorus." She really meant the problem was Jonah. Instead of being grateful that he had given up his career for hers, she was disgruntled and condescending, as if his sacrifice had degraded her. A frown conveyed her annoyance—until a familiar figure appeared at the end of the lobby. Shaking her black mane, she thrust back her shoulders, and smiled at the handsome young man, well-coifed and smartly clothed, with slim muscled body, and mischievously expressive eyes. Bartram Gandolfi was a narcissistic, brilliantly talented virtuoso, who at the age of twenty two—he was now thirty—had become the ASO's principal flutist. He was a darling of the public and a nuisance to everyone else, including fellow musicians and his mother, art historian Helena Gandolfi.

"Bonsoir, Cherie," he cooed, bending over to kiss Victoria's ring-encrusted fingers and lifting playful eyes to hers. "Beautiful as always." When a smile and heave of breast gave him the looked-for response, he dropped back into self-absorption. "I'm doing a solo concert at Spivey Hall tomorrow," he offered, as if other people spent their time admiring him.

"Can we also count on your golden flute for the *Passion*?" Jonah asked. Bartram had been known to cancel a performance when something better came along.

Eyes still on Victoria he answered, "Of course. I would never miss playing for the lovely Madame Vargas."

The choral director tactfully ignored this bit of flirting. Where Bartram swaggered, Jonah held back with a natural, even austere dignity. It was not just the dark curls, the smoky eyes and the chiseled features—nose like the prow of a ship, a deeply cleft chin, and muscular, controlled lips—that expressed him. It was an intense presence. When he entered a room everyone became alert, as if he exerted an electrical charge. And unlike those who insisted on making themselves noticed, he had a way of peering seriously from under knotted brows that immediately concentrated attention. He now gave Bartram one of those looks and the young man's face fell. Then recovering himself, Bartram smirked with secret knowledge. "I'm glad I ran into you two. My mother would like to attend one of the rehearsals." The eyes rolled in mock disdain. "Bach is her favorite."

"Certainly," Victoria replied, assuming for herself the director's authority.

Jonah concurred. "Your mother probably knows the *Passion* as well as the chorus." Helena Gandolfi had impressed him with her musical knowledge and she never missed a performance.

"Mother knows *everything* about the arts," Bartram remarked smugly, wrinkling his nose. Disparaging her assuaged his conscience, since she, unlike he, was dedicated to art without self-aggrandizement.

The remark puzzled Jonah. Helena Gandolfi was famous for identifying lost and misattributed works of art, so why should her son scoff?

Bartram's eyes crinkled dismissively. "Now she's searching for a lost Rothko."

"Rothko?" Jonah asked, interested. It was Victoria's turn to roll her eyes.

"Collectors have been looking for it for years. Mother's writing a book on him. If you give her half a chance," he warned, in a mixture of condescension and pride, "you'll hear all about it."

As this topic did not make her the center, Victoria broke in, "We really must go."

They parted, and the couple made their way to a nearby coffee bar, she, fuming still that Jonah had insulted her in front of the chorus. He meanwhile was preoccupied with the *Passion*—how to get the chorus to sense the reflection of the piece, to live the words, to inhabit their parts. It was a leap for modern secularists to internalize Baroque Lutheran spirit. He glanced at Victoria. How was he to get *her* to stop acting her role and start living it—in the rehearsal room *and* at home? Her 'passion' was all about the self rather than sacrifice. But the shyness of intimacy prohibited telling her this, especially as listening implied a willingness to hear the truth.

They sat down with their coffees and she complained as if they were still discussing her solo, "If the chorus doesn't get my entrance right, the audience will boo me."

He tried to make a joke of it. "No Victoria, they don't boo singers here. Only in Milan." Unamused, she snorted, and turned her body away from him in protest. They finished their coffees and made their way back to the rehearsal in moody silence.

When they reentered the room, the chorus fell silent and gave Jonah their full attention. If the first impression that had commanded their respect was his fame, that was soon replaced by awe at his fidelity to the music. He had a European air about him that was formal and polished and at the same time warm and attentive, and he trained the chorus as if they were professional singers: diction, phrasing, pitch, rhythm, tone color, movement, an unparalleled standard of excellence.

"The next section has been interpreted many ways," he resumed. "But let's sing what Bach actually wrote. Everything is there in the score. We'll see where it takes us." With an affectionate nod, he shook his lion's mane of curls and raised his baton. The glorious sound of "Receive me my Redeemer" filled the room.

After rehearsing her solo Victoria had to leave promptly for a concert in Chicago. The chorus applauded her politely and she, a hand cupped beneath her bosom where the heart was supposed to be, blinked back false tears as if it were a standing ovation. A far different response came later when the rehearsal ended, and the room erupted in enthusiastic applause for their director.

He was the last to leave symphony hall. As he walked through the plaza of the art center, he stopped and looked up at the surrounding buildings, benevolent monoliths with lighted windows that winked hypnotically into the open space below. Atlanta was not yet his place, he, wanderer from elsewhere. His had been the European cities where he had performed and from whose older cultures he had drawn strength.

In ancient worlds, where half of life was spent in the dark, the eyes were drawn irresistibly to the stars. But to the eyes of the modern urban dweller, no longer bounded by the stars, the bright dome of a city is there to push back the darkness. And when the city no longer illumines the wayfarer's path beyond the end of the street, how does he find his way back to the stars?

As he walked the few blocks to his Ansley Park condo, his reflections expanded to the place of art in the American city. And what place for the artist who wishes to care for more than possession and progress? He stopped a moment and listened to the silence behind the humming noise of the city. A distant echo passed through him like a prayer: *"I wish my heart to offer Thee, / Offer Thee my care, my all."*

By one of the strange coincidences that foretell a future, the line from the *Passion*, "*I wish my heart to offer Thee*" was playing in the ears of Sandra Foxcroft, MD as she walked down the Zaron wing of the Hospital. The ASO was doing the choral work in the fall and she wanted to know it better before the concert. She switched off the earbuds reluctantly and dropped back onto the plain of the everyday. Her team with its own arias and responses was waiting for her at the nursing station. Physicals done and histories taken. Check. Records reviewed and tests ordered. Check. Referring physicians contacted and therapies suggested. Double check.

"Stop!" An imperious voice commanded. "What were you doing back there?" The man belonging to the booming voice pointed at her. "There is no need for me to see my patient again," Dr. Ouruk

Zaron, the Chief of Surgery persisted loudly. "The idiots in charge," he meant Hospitalist Sandra Foxcroft and her team, "have ordered a procedure that was completely unnecessary."

"Dr. Zaron . . . Sir," Sandra answered in a soft monotone, the unstressed "Sir" slightly ironic.

The man for whom the hospital was named was an outstanding surgeon-philanthropist—from a distance. At closer range he was a demanding tyrant who expected everyone to genuflect. He continued to berate the young internist. "I'm too busy to waste time with an uninteresting patient." A patient was "uninteresting" if he required too many insurance forms, had too many complaints, or didn't respond well to treatment—unless *she* was young and pretty. Dr. Sandra Foxcroft, 33, tall, slender, long brown hair, dark intense eyes, was interesting, but not given to genuflecting.

The surgeon, handsome, gifted, arrogant, and perfectly aware of the impression he made, suspected, without proof, that Dr. Foxcroft disliked him. He may have been unmindful of those around him who were not rich or important, but he was not unmindful of Sandra. Perhaps because no matter how hard he tried, he had been unable to break through her professional reserve.

"I will inform the patient and his family that you refuse to see him and will note that in the chart. Sorry to have bothered you," she replied with a cool dignity. It made the man, usually so oblivious, reconsider his demand.

When knowing looks passed among her team, Zaron began to regret that he had an audience. "Oh, all right. I'll see him. But only if *you* attend me," and off he sauntered, expecting her to follow.

Instead she turned aside and called her sister Justine. No answer. She was protective of her younger sister. Their mother had died ten years ago when Justine was thirteen, and she, the twenty-three-year-old big sister, took on the role of foster mother. Kate, their mother, had been a warm, gracious southern lady who bestowed unstinting love on them and their father, the vain and haughty collector, Sir Reginald Foxcroft. In a moment of aristocratic weakness, or so he thought, he had married an American "commoner" and produced two half-breed daughters who were indifferent to his own native distinction and wealth. After his wife died, he preferred his art collection to the company of his daughters, and at that point Kate's friend Helena Gandolfi stepped in as surrogate mother. She and Justine had remained close, but the medical school years had set a distance between her and Sandra.

When Sandra finished her shift several hours later—after attending the Chief of Surgery and listening to him pontificate on his genius and her dereliction—she heard a voice behind her.

"I teach you the overman. Thus spake Zaron-thustra. What have you done to overcome him?" It was Russell Baramore, her fellow hospitalist and partner, arriving for his shift. He flashed a brilliant smile and ran a hand over closely cropped black hair.

"You heard."

"Hospital gossip travels faster than a speeding scalpel."

"It was the deeply-committed-surgeon act played for the benefit of a patient who groveled in gratitude. A rebuke to me. I'd dared to suggest he might not be Albert Schweitzer. Then he did an odd thing," she frowned, still puzzled. "He asked me if I'd heard anything about the lost Rothko. Out of the blue."

"Well everyone knows he lusts for it. It would be the capstone of his collection. The publicity alone would make him world famous, not least because it would be worth millions."

"I need to warn Justine," Sandra said guardedly, almost to herself. Russell raised an eyebrow but said nothing. He knew better than to interfere where Justine was concerned. She was like a small planet with a little too much gravitational pull for his taste. Why someone 23 and on her own should still need Sandra's watchful maternal eye was a mystery—and an annoyance. "Well if you get wind of a small Rothko for sale like so," he grinned and made an eight-inch square with his hands, "let me know." And so they parted, he to his shift, she to her car, where she tried, again unsuccessfully to reach Justine.

Sandra's concern for her sister reflected their differences in age and temperament. In appearance they were similar—slender and fine featured, with high-cheekbones, full lips, and a straight, almost regal carriage. Both were considered strikingly attractive, with dark hair and arresting dark eyes—one pair candid and direct, the other pair guarded and mysterious. Except the older impressed one as perhaps more beautiful than appealing, and the younger as more winsome than beautiful. In temperament they shared the same thoughtful intensity toward the world, though in different registers: one detached and cautious; the other engaged, adventurous, and sprightly. A reserve of quiet dignity inherited from their British father invited others to take them seriously. In the case of Sandra because of ten additional years and a position of authority. In the case of Justine, despite a youthful fragility, a composed self-possession. Differences aside, however, their one unchangeable constant was an absolute and affectionate reliance on one another.

On the way home from the hospital, Sandra tried to convince herself that Zaron's mention of the Rothko was just an offhand comment, as Russell had said. But then Russell always wanted to normalize things. Feelings tamped down by reason. Differences harmonized. Everything leveled to the everyday. But hadn't she opted for leveling too? Love insured against risk, and without rapture. The words in her headphones haunted her: *"I wish my heart to offer Thee, / Offer Thee my care, my all."* Would these words ever be hers?

By another strange coincidence, Helena Gandolfi was humming the same chorale, *"Thou, more than earth and heaven, all,"* in her office at the University. Her son had been playing it on his flute this morning and it brought Augustine to mind. "For man's thought will confess you and the rest of this thought will solemnly celebrate you." Art and knowledge as celebration. Like what she did as a historian: celebrate works of art. Turning from Bach to an article in *Art Forum*, she bent her silver head intently over the page and began to read. When her sharp gaze was fixed on someone or something it would not let go. Her friends associated her with the polished, reflective surface of the finest sterling, or even a rare and pure quicksilver. Lively, laughing, intimate, mocking—she had the power to attract even when resisted. In another time, her singleness of mind might have founded a holy order or a female knighthood, but today it found its vocation in art.

There was a timid knock on the office door. A small, heart-shaped face with a pair of enormous brown eyes peeked in. When the eyes met Helena, they glowed with pleasure and a smile broke like a wave over her face. Helena beamed back at the girl who was like a daughter to her. Justine Foxcroft had the effect of spreading delight to everyone—everyone, that is, but her father. Batting her eyes and smiling, she was fetching. With a light grace, she glided smoothly into the room, chin up, back straight. "How much she has absorbed from the dance," Helena thought, remembering the little dancing girl who had once hoped to be a ballerina. She might have succeeded too, if an ankle injury hadn't permanently ended her training. The old discipline was now combined with an airiness that made one think of Saint-Gaulden's sculpture of Artemis. The slender goddess balances with one leg on point, the other leg extended back airily as she readies to launch an arrow from her bow.

Though sociable and gamine, Justine was not superficial. Immediately after college she had applied for a job at the telephone company. Despite her lack of experience, she persuaded them to hire her, in no small part due to her charm, but even more due to her intelligence and quiet dignity. "Give me something that no one else wants to do," she had said. So they gave her a task that others had found impossible: convincing delinquent clients to pay their bills. With an engaging yet precise half-British voice and the sheer power of personality, she eventually won over even the most recalcitrant deadbeats. But for all her fine qualities, Helena reflected, she had yet to be tested.

Today she had come, she said, to ask Helena about a painting which raised a question: Why come here to the University, rather than come to her house where she might run into her roguish son. Justine adored him and Bartram adored being adored. Helena concluded that Justine had something else on her mind.

"Uncle Finny," Justine began breathlessly, "is giving me a painting that he thinks may be important. He's asked me to keep it safe and not tell *anyone*." Uncle Finny was Phineas McGinley, Atlanta realtor and brother of her late mother. "He knows I'm here. He said that you'd know what it is and would keep it secret." Her face was earnest, grave even.

"How did Finny get it?"

"Some elderly spinsters gave it to him."

Helena started. It had been rumored that Mark Rothko gave his last painting to two sisters who were distant relatives. Perhaps the same? Before pursuing that idea, she needed to know other things. "Where is the painting now?"

Justine glanced around the room cautiously and whispered, "In . . ." A stentorian knock interrupted and the door opened peremptorily. Helena was surprised and not entirely pleased to see Justine's father, Reginald Foxcroft, family friend and lover, past-tense. He was a tall, long-limbed, man with a rather dry, polished manner as if he had been rubbed too hard by life.

"Stop whatever you two are doing," he commanded sternly. His watery brown eyes gazed at Helena with the discontent of one ready to rehearse her wrongs.

"Regie darling," Helena trilled in her theatrical alto and held out a hand.

Regie darling winced, and "Helena" slipped from his lips as he kissed her hand. His gesture was a reproach for an appellation he detested. Then to the point, "I know perfectly well why you're meeting," he said with a voice as brittle as matter subjected to stress. "I ran into Justine's uncle at the High. Gawking at, of all things, the yellow and orange Rothko." Justine's coffee-colored eyes grew larger and her face paler.

"Why shouldn't Finny look at the Rothko?" Helena mused. "It's one of the museum's finest works." She studied Regie thoughtfully. His face, marked by disappointment more than by lines, hinted at vulnerability, but under a seasoned veneer.

"Don't be disingenuous, Helena. I know why you and my child are meeting!" A baleful glance at Justine was not without affection. Of his two children, he preferred the fey younger to Alexandra—Sandra, the solemn older. "You two know something about the lost painting." He made it sound like betrayal. It was unnecessary for him to add—his face said it all—that the painting ought to be with a famous connoisseur: himself. This he followed by a denunciation of everyone unworthy of such a work, including his former brother-in-law Phineas McGinley, Dr. Ouruk Zaron, the international art market in general, and the Atlanta museums in particular. And, lest the point be insufficient, he added one more: "In the right hands, the painting would confer the prestige once only accorded to aristocrats and popes."

While he was speaking, Helena was busy with observations of a subtler kind. Regie's impassive face was only a guise of detachment. The corners of his mouth pulled down too tightly, and his shallow breathing betrayed controlled anger. She was a close observer, professionally famous for detecting the secrets of artistic style and had even proven a work wrongfully attributed to Titian to be a Giorgione. With an eye for the painter's smallest, scarcely conscious shorthand—fingers, nails, earlobes, or in the case of contemporary works, edges, colors, and the picture plane itself—she discovered where an artist gave himself away. The technique also applied to people.

"And you came all the way from Buckhead to tell me this?" She had always a clarity of mind, to say nothing of a dry humor. "How kind of you, Regie dear. But why should you object to my meeting with your daughter?"

"Do you deny she's here to talk about the missing painting?" His baritone darkened accusingly and he glared at Justine.

"Certainly, I don't deny it," Helena said disingenuously. "The *Chuck Close* painting of her mother, your dear belated wife, is still safely stored at home in my closet." She addressed Justine confidingly: "I'm so glad you've found a place to hang the portrait, the one by Chuck Close," she emphasized the words, "I know it's been missing from your life."

Having immediately caught Helena's subterfuge, Justine exchanged a troubled expression for one of delight. "I have missed it. I'll pick up mother's portrait tonight after work, if that's all right."

Regie looked disdainfully from one woman to the other. "I see where this is going." Moving majestically to the door, he grasped the knob firmly. "I will find you out. You can't keep a secret this big," and fumbling with the door let himself out.

The two women looked at each other knowingly. Though they had succeeded momentarily with their charade about Chuck Close's portrait, Helena cautioned, "If your Uncle Finny gives you what your father seems to think you have, the Rothko, you must treat it with care. Photograph it thoroughly for your records, front, back, and sides, and make several copies of the photos. Remember, you can't put a thing like *that* in a safe deposit box." Then anticipating the next question before it was asked, she described the methods for storing a large, valuable work of art, none of which were available to Justine.

"What should I do?" Her face clouded with concern.

"Hide it where no one can find it."

"Where?"

"We'll talk about it tonight."

"Tonight?"

"When you pick up your mother's portrait."

2

In the midst of the modern city, traces still of ancient myth, lost, forgotten, a goddess darting like a star, flashing through the trees with raised spear and wild countenance. To some, the fleetfooted huntress Atalanta, figure of the human imaginary; to others, an ordinary young woman dashing through the park.

The day after the Bach rehearsal Jonah took a walk in Piedmont Park to reflect on his marriage. The central park, with a diverse terrain, multi-layered tree canopy, and dense landscape, offered a respite from busy city life and the routine of habit. He proceeded west on an open expanse of park that swept gradually uphill through a twisting avenue of trees. Beyond, tall buildings gleamed like a mountain range anchoring the vista of the park. The pyramids, columns, needles, and helixes like heads and wings of legendary creatures, things left out of everyday experience by the modern city.

He chiefly saw that his life—his and Victoria's together—had been less a past rehearsed than a search for something overlooked. Not looking for a cause exactly. How identity a point of departure? Does anyone know the beginning until after the fact, when beginnings seem ordained? The cause assigned after the effect?

He had been called to a vocation that places impossible demands on one impossibly small thing: an apparatus of muscle and cartilage that vibrates when air passes over it. Twenty years of discipline, skill, and dedication had produced a gleaming tenor that in full throttle could raise hairs on the back of the neck. He started singing in an opera chorus, and went on, often frustrated and rejected, to minor roles in out of the way places. His big break came in Zurich where he also met his future wife. They were young and idealistic. Music was their common ground of life together. But soon enough their success fueled ambition and opened a gap between. By the time Jonah took time to think about it, their paths had diverged. Yet it might not have happened if he had kept his eye on his own career.

They had been in love, but there had been three in that love, them and music. That much they had gotten right—until ambition intervened. He thought he had solved it by retiring early from the stage. But it had the opposite effect. He set that thought aside as one lays aside a book and goes on to other things.

In the rehearsal last night, the chorus had breathed life into Bach's libretto with strata of heavenly sounds. Now in the spring landscape of the park he could almost *see* the music as a striving for perfection itself. Perhaps better, he could, *hear it* in a texture of natural harmonies—the soaring notes of birds interwoven with earth and sky as the score echoed in the words of the chorale: *"Who gives clouds, air, and winds / Their paths, course, and track / will also find ways, / Where your feet can walk."* When had the green been this green? When had light through the trees made density so transparent?

Unbidden, his thoughts returned to the topic laid aside: Victoria. Self-love and the appetite for flattery betrayed even her work as an artist. The first time she appeared in a major opera house as the consumptive courtesan in *Traviata*, she triumphed. But with increasing success, she relied more on technique and began playing herself rather than her roles. An ominous moment came when she sang Violetta again several years later in Zurich. Instead of bringing the audience into the spell of the music, she made them adore her. The golden calf of self became a substitute for the love of music—and for their love. Though she still responded in kind whenever he said, "I love you," the words had taken on an empty grudging tone.

What did she understand, he wondered when she sang, *"I wish my heart to offer Thee?"*

◆

After their meeting at the University, Justine began to worry about Helena's warning. What if the painting she was about to receive really was the missing Rothko, as Helena had surmised? How was she to keep a masterpiece safe in her tiny apartment? For one thing, her father would do his best to get it. "Hide it where no one can find it," Helena had said. Hide a painting that large? That important? "You can't roll it up and tuck it away in a cardboard tube," Helena had also said. Easy for her when *she* had a humidity-controlled closet in her house. There was always Sandra, but she was never at home and besides there was her partner, Russell. Could he be trusted? She mulled over all these things while she drove the company car back to work, then changed into running clothes and headed for the park.

Running liberated her from worrying about the painting. As she breathed in the smells of growing things, grass, trees and shrubbery, passersby turned to look at the wisp of a girl whose running feet barely touched the ground. From the openness of her face to the nimbleness of those feet she appeared energetic and fearless, as if the purpose of her being were to light the darkness. Some might even have seen a modern young goddess flying by.

Her attention was arrested in flight by a man in the distance. Walking slowly, deep in thought. As the figure got sharper she noted him tall and broad shouldered with chiseled features. She always noticed how people walked and even read their character in the angles and rhythms of their movement. Unlike casual strollers, or those too preoccupied to see anything, this man seemed alive to his surroundings. Caught up in observing him, she missed a sudden rise in the path, stumbled, and fell—hard, arms and legs in a sprawl.

He was immediately at her side. "Are you hurt?"

"Only my dignity," she laughed, accepting an extended hand. "Thank you," she said gratefully with a smile that would have melted a glacier.

"I watched you running. You seemed to fly through space like a dancer. It's that amazing ability that seems to defy gravity." He searched for the idea, "as if earth and air changed positions." What he didn't say was how she had impressed him as thought itself, free and unburdened.

Her eyes widened in surprise that he understood so much. "I wanted to be a dancer, once. Just now I wiped out like a dancer!"

He nodded as though he understood her shorthand. Then a remark that made him an enigma. "We don't run with our feet but with our desire. You must have been thinking earthward at that moment."

She grinned with appreciation that he understood, then remarked, her eyes twinkling with mischief. "You also come to the park to think."

That surprised him. "Walking here clears my head. Gets me in tune."

The expression echoed her own thoughts. "In tune?" she repeated. "It works for me too. Like a work of art."

"You're an artist then?"

"Oh, no! I have no talent for paint, just a love of painting."

"I can hear the park *sing*, but how does a painting get you *in tune*?"

"By coming from elsewhere and taking me outside myself to someplace new." The strange answer to an even stranger question was offered lightly and in all seriousness.

The barest of smiles said he grasped her thought. "That's what music does for me."

"I *thought* you were a musician!"

"And how could you think that?" he laughed, shaking his curly head.

"You move to a rhythm as you walk. As if you were singing it."

In fact, he had been walking to music from yesterday's rehearsal. "I didn't know that a walk revealed so much," he replied, diverted. "But of course, it would to a dancer." He looked down at her amused, like a god captivated by an engaging mortal.

Her eyes held nothing in reserve and grew so large they seemed to swallow her face. "The smallest gestures give us away don't they? As the smallest brush strokes give the artist away."

"You *are* an expert then."

"No, but I learned from an expert. My second mother. Perhaps you've heard of her. Helena Gandolfi?"

"You know Helena? She's a colleague. And she also loves music." He held out a hand. "Jonah Hartman. I direct the Chorus for the Symphony and teach voice at the University. See how right you were?"

With, if possible, a face more radiant than before, she took his hand. "Justine Foxcroft." A slight frown said he had heard of her father, and not favorably.

"I'm his daughter—from a distance," and laughed delightedly.

He urged gently. "And you say Helena Gandolfi is your second mother?"

"When my mother died Helena stepped in. She's a mother and a friend."

"Helena is a wise woman. You're fortunate to have such a friend."

They chatted together animatedly, each delighted with the other. Her expression suddenly turned serious. "Do you like modern painting?"

The non-sequitur amused him. But her sober face made him take the question seriously. "Painting . . . music . . . even this park seduces us."

"And do you like" . . . she hesitated only a second, then rushed ahead, "Mark Rothko?"

It was the second time in two days that name had been mentioned. "Yes, very much," he replied but without asking why. He was more interested in the flash of an idea on her face than in her question.

A daring idea had crossed her mind. "Perhaps I'll stop in to see you, Mr. Hartman, the next time I'm at the University."

Sandra Foxcroft, still in her scrubs and weary from the long day, headed home from the hospital. After twelve hours, twenty two patients, two team meetings, a staff conference, and Dr. Zaron, she was ready to collapse with a glass of wine and her feet up. She parked, then hesitated to face an empty house. At work she was the fixed entity, the defined quantity, Dr. Foxcroft. Yet at home, the rational, practical person cast a shadow over just plain Sandra. On a whim she decided to recover the person stifled in the doctor and go for a walk.

All day she listened to patients and diagnosed their diseases, while ignoring her own dis-ease. Medicine was supposed to heal the body, but the body healed was an abstract object, not the flesh of the feeling body. In college and medical school, she had lived under the regime of the medical body. The burden of her job was taking bodily measurements, diagnosing disease, and living day after day with its alienating effect. It had forced her into a strait jacket of thinking.

As a child, she had learned the art of listening from her mother. "It's a matter of attunement," she had said, "like attending to an instrument to discover its timbre." That took a different discipline than medicine. Not acquiring knowledge of an object, but responding to a silent song.

At the entrance to the park and with her cell phone left behind, Sandra felt her burden lifted. For the first time in a long time no one had to know where she was. It affected her as being someone else, someone who, by receiving everything around her close at hand, felt herself feeling herself. It was magical. As if the spring landscape beckoned her with its splendor. Her heart began to sing the words she had heard in her headphones, *"Thou more than earth and heaven, all!"* How unlike the hospital. But when she tried to attend to the beauty of the park, her thoughts wandered to something she didn't want to think: Ouruk Zaron. He made a blot in the landscape. Why had he brought up the lost painting out of the blue? What did he want? And why her? To find out if she knew anything? Had heard anything? From whom? Her father? Helena?

A night several months ago sprang up in memory where the subject of Rothko had come up. It was at one of those events for high-class hedonists at the High. Zaron had spotted her with Russell in the crowd. After looking her up and down as an object for his pleasure, he grudgingly acknowledged them both with a slight nod. He wasn't about to come to them, so Russell had suggested they go to him. Russell craved admiration and yearned to become a collector on the scale of Zaron and her father. It made her wonder whether he only dated her because she was the daughter of the famous art connoisseur.

Zaron, suave and elegant—and aware of the fact—was enjoying being admired. But as soon as she and Russell reached him, he began complaining, "The Kapoor and Kelly are fine, but why on earth did they put Rothko in the exhibit?"

"You don't admire him?" Russell asked innocently.

He assumed the look of false concern for one who ought to know better. "It only highlights the embarrassing fact that they have just one."

"Actually they have four," she corrected. "Two are early works."

He waved a hand dismissively. "Early works don't count. They're worth less on the market."

"You think a painting has to be quantified to be valued?" She knew better than to take him on, but he was provoking. Having grown up with art as her native place and household god, she took umbrage at the man's crassness. He cared more for the prestige of collecting than the works themselves.

He smiled condescendingly at "little Alexandra" as an innocent of the higher order of knowledge. "You're too busy grubbing with disease to understand the relation between art and the market. Until there is a market, there is no art."

"Doesn't that reduce the work to the one with the measuring stick?" She grinned through gritted teeth. Then before he could respond, walked away, leaving Russell to contend with him. The man always stirred aggression she didn't know she had. Later when Russell accused her of making him look like an idiot, she realized that she was just a prop to make him look good before people he admired.

She was musing on all this in the park when a tall, dark-haired man approached over the hill. His expression, thick brows over penetrating eyes, was so concentrated and intense that she stared. His eyes widened, aware of someone looking. Their gazes met, in an exchange so transparent, so unguarded it pierced her soul—if such a thing is imaginable in the modern world. She felt exposed, even assailed, so given over to the unexpected that it took a struggle to regain her equilibrium. Then her protective grin appeared and instantly the spell was broken. His face that had been open closed in on itself.

He turned away and she had a wild impulse to call out to him, if only he would turn back. He did not turn back, and she felt abandoned as she watched his strong back receding up the path. She wanted desperately to run after him and say something. But say what? Why had she broken the spell between them? What was she afraid of? He was just a man who caught her eye in the park, a momentary attraction, that's all. But when their eyes first met, words from the *Passion* burst in on her, "*I wish my heart to offer thee.*" Russell would never look at her like that. Brought down to earth again, she walked on in a daze until she found herself at the other end of the park, where there, sitting on a bench was Justine.

"I was wondering if you were ever going to notice me," Justine said, tickled. "Where are you going in your scrubs?"

Instead of answering she asked, "Have you eaten? Let's get a bite somewhere." They crossed the street to an artsy restaurant near *Trader Joe's*, where Justine chatted enthusiastically about an interesting man she had just met near the Oval. "He's the Chorus Director at the ASO. And he knows so much about the arts." If she had really been listening, Sandra might have wondered if it was the same man she had just met. But, preoccupied, she wasn't listening. The man who had made her feel not just looked at but *seen*, so filled her thoughts she didn't taste her pasta or notice an upholstery spring of the booth poking sharply into her thigh.

Justine looked at her archly and laughed, "You haven't heard a word I've said."

"Sorry." She regarded her sister attentively, recurring to the unpleasant encounter with the chief-surgeon. "Listen Justine, if you ever run into Dr. Zaron, don't tell him anything, anything at all about you or me or father." She hesitated then went on more insistently, "and *nothing*," underscoring the negative, "*nothing* whatsoever about paintings, any paintings. Don't even say who you are. In fact, avoid him if you can."

Justine stared at Sandra in silence. She had learned long ago from their mother when to listen and when to keep quiet. Shadows under Sandra's eyes and lines of worry puckered her lovely face, prompting Justine to lean over and gently touch her hand. The gesture captured a lifetime of affection between sisters so alike and so different.

3

Helena opened the door of her house in Ansley Park, threw the car keys on the foyer table, kicked off her heels, and poured herself a bourbon. The house in its earlier incarnation when she and her husband Carter first lived here had been a typical craftsman cottage. After he died she had an architect transform the cottage—to the chagrin of her neighbors—into a contemporary home with clean lines, loads of glass, and a minimalist Zen garden. As a CD began playing "*Come ye daughters, help me lament,*" she sank into a sofa, put her feet up on a hassock, and sipped her drink. Her eyes traveled around the room, an open yet intimate all-white space highlighted by tall windows, a creamy stone fireplace, and a thick white rug over a black polished floor. The monochromatic color scheme created a background for the contemporary art works that lined the walls.

The music and the warmth of the bourbon let the disorder of the day slip away. She closed her eyes, brushed aside a silver lock that fell over her forehead, and leaned her head back into the cushions. A lifetime of reflection was inscribed on the face with the high cheekbones, prominent nose, and full mouth above a sharp chin. Wit sparkled when the grey eyes were open and was hinted at when the eyes were closed by lines radiating from the corners and a natural curve of the mouth upwards. She was an exemplar of the adage that the world is a comedy to the one who thinks, a tragedy to the one who feels. That is not to say she was unserious about a dark threat, for she saw with sober lucidity that she was engaged in a war. She knew all about art wars—forgeries, copies, authentications, restitutions—all the wars between art and the marketplace. She had known it all, but never had she had to fight those battles in person. For the first time she was obliged to acknowledge how insidious the enemy had become. Not always a person, but the pervasive unthinking of the modern age.

Listening to Bach cleared her head and let what needed to be thought come to her. She needed to see around several corners and find a way to show her young friend around them. If Justine had indeed stumbled on the lost painting, how was it ever to be properly cared for? It would be tempting to take over the painting herself. Justine would probably be relieved. But there was a snare in that arrangement. The expert in the middle of writing a book on Rothko can tell too much. Can blur the distinction between the timeless, impersonal quality of art and personal "appreciation." Reduced to the commonplace, appreciation is an opinion of taste—"I know what I like." That panders to the individual and its interests. For people like Ouruk Zaron, and to a lesser degree Reginald Foxcroft, possession of the Rothko would aggrandize *them* at the expense of the work itself. Infinitely worse, it would diminish art as an event that can sweep the self away as a tsunami can sweep away a city in its path.

A ringing doorbell brought Helena back to the moment. She opened, gave Justine a hug, and welcomed her into the living room. "Have you eaten? Can I get you anything?"

"No thank you. I met Sandra in the park and we had supper together."

"How is Sandra?" It was some time since Helena had seen the older sister, and longer still since she detected in her the same zest for life as in Justine.

"Fine, I think. You know Sandra. It's hard to read her." Sandra had always been serious even as a teenager and especially after their mother died. But since medical school she had folded up in herself, like the hidden-dimensions of quantum physics. Justine excitedly changed the subject. "I met the most interesting man today in the park."

"Oh," a silver eyebrow arched into a wing. A rival to supplant Bartram? Though Justine adored him, Helena had no illusions about her son's being right for someone so self-effacing. Justine would wither under Bartram's egotism.

"He's the chorus director at the ASO and has the most amazing eyes, like tamped-down coals about to burst into flame."

Helena's grey eyes opened wider. "You mean Jonah Hartman?"

"Yes!"

"He's a colleague." If Justine had struck up an acquaintance with Hartman, who taught voice at the University, that would be a blessing. He was a man who could guide her. A thoughtful, intelligent teacher, patient with students and peerless in musical knowledge. *And,* not insignificantly, a man who had chosen to abjure power. She searched her young friend's face for a sign of a sexual attraction and finding none added, "I'm glad you met him. Jonah is a man you can trust absolutely. And I don't say that lightly."

Justine's face blossomed with delight. "I knew it. Sometimes you can know without knowing why."

"Asking why does tend to stifle wonder. But I need to warn you about something, Justine." Helena looked at her intently. "Not Hartman. It's Finny's painting. You've seen the soft-edged Rothkos often enough to know one when you see it, haven't you?" Justine nodded. "Even if the painting Finny gives you doesn't look like a Rothko, be careful. There is someone out there who would do anything to get his hands on it, Rothko or no. He suspects *you* already. You are your father's child."

"Who?" Justine's eyes grew into two round discs.

"Dr. Ouruk Zaron."

Justine turned pale. It was the second time that day she had been warned about the man. "The surgeon who built the Zaron Wing at the hospital? *Sandra's* Dr. Zaron?"

"The same." Helena had been leaning forward intently to make her point. Now she relaxed into the sofa cushion again. "Let me tell you a story of why I think he is so dangerous. Zaron's father, Alexi Zaron, saw art as a means to wealth and recognized that people will pay anything for a masterpiece. He sold his first 'lost Rembrandt,' a fake he acquired on the art black market, for four million dollars. Then he bought several authentic masterpieces. He also bought at bargain prices art collected by celebrities who were ignorant, kept the best pieces, and sold the rest. He collected relentlessly by avoiding the commercial levers of major art and using back channels that feed off the markets like New York. When he had a significant number from Rubens to Van Gogh, he offered them for public view, first in lesser-known museums, then larger ones. Slowly they became known as the Zaron Collection."

"And what about his son," Justine asked, "the surgeon?"

"He continued in his father's footsteps, using the prestige of painters' inscriptions to inflate works of inferior quality and adding significantly to the collection. Several years ago, he promised part of it to the High. It was his way of getting a powerful seat on their board. He was even able to install an unqualified and irresponsible board member to help him acquire for himself pieces the museum was interested in. That's of course unethical. Only then, when his reputation was assured, and the works had become household names, did he get interested in modern art—Rothko in particular. You know that contemporary art is the current cachet in terms of economic value and market status. For Zaron, art is not just about money and prestige. It's about power that he would use to put others in his debt. He's no fool. Once scholars began to write voluminously about Rothko and museums like the Phillips Collection and the Tate Modern devoted entire rooms to him, he saw what a commercial prize the late lost Rothko would be."

Justine listened with interest, then concern, and finally alarm. Each registered on her face in a changing stream until all settled to a depth and she became utterly grave. "But why did Zaron choose Atlanta?"

"Because the city is raw material he can mine and form in the shape he pleases. Atlanta doesn't have a deep history in the arts. Like most modern cities, it's a scene of random expansion. Commercial kudzu consuming natural habitats and traditional ways of life. In this environment, an art predator like Zaron is at home."

"Then I must get the painting somewhere absolutely safe," Justine declared.

Helena was on the brink of explaining how to keep the painting safe, when a key turned in the lock and Bartram entered. Expressive eyes in an elegantly shaped face, crowned by a shock of well-coiffed hair, radiated an insouciance that could disrupt any room or conversation. They now confronted two sober pairs of eyes. "My, my, you two look as if you've been discussing something dreary. Zurburan's portrait of St. Agatha?" The allusion was to the Spanish painting of the saint with her cut-off breasts on a platter. When they didn't laugh, he added to Justine, "Or has Mother just forced you to listen to her *complete* recording of the Bach *Passion*?"

This brought a smile to Justine's face but not to Helena's. Bartram lived with her out of convenience. It had been her suggestion, as he was often out of town performing. Why maintain a separate apartment when she lived a few blocks from Symphony Hall and her second floor was unused? Convenience however had had its drawbacks. A self-centered, thirty-year old celebrity son as flat mate did not mesh well with a contemplative habit and character. Especially at a moment like this when she was tempted to be severe. Nonetheless she resisted. His frivolity might be just what was needed to lighten the mood. "Bartram, how convenient that you're here. You can help us transport the portrait of Kate to Justine's new apartment." Her tone said she wouldn't brook refusal.

It must have been fifteen years since Helena had recommended that Sir Reginald have the girls' mother painted by Chuck Close. It was one of his monumental portraits that used a grid and geometric shapes to build up features, color cell by color cell, pixel by pixel. Kate and her daughters had loved it, but Foxcroft, who admired the painter and owned several of his works, thought the work undignified. It was all right as a portrait of an American, even an American president from Arkansas, but not the wife of an English gentleman.

Helena saw at once that Bartram would resist helping if she left him a way out, so she added flattery. "You have a good sense of space and placement. The Chuck Close might look wonderful in a gallery but will be harder to place in a small room where it hits you in the face."

Before he could respond, Justine thanked him, "Oh I'm so glad you can help, Bartram. You'll know exactly where to hang it."

Bartram agreed with a smirk and Justine glowed from head to toe. In her clear, melodious, half-British voice she sang, "Oh Bartram, dear Bartram, you are so kind." Because she never taxed him, it was easy for him to remain smug and complacent. But this time she inspired him to *be* the better person she imagined. All this led to a conversation about the portrait in which he took a genuine interest.

While Bartram made a speech about color in art and music, Helena watched Justine. Rapt with concentration, her large eyes grew larger taking everything in. She listened to others as if she were hearing them for the first time. It was the secret to her youthful freshness that age would never stale. Still, Finny's gift could very well test her. And she might need testing, especially where Bartram was concerned. Justine's unquestioned admiration, indeed flattery, brought out the worst in him.

Helena left them together and went to the kitchen where she gazed into the Zen garden and brooded on the safety of the alleged Rothko. If Justine kept it, she would be exposed to Zaron and her father. But if she, Helena, played shepherd, it would only attract the art wolves. Who could she turn to? She went through a list in her head and came up with two possibilities. One was Sandra and the other, a long shot, Jonah Hartman, whom Justine had just met. But one problem at a time. The immediate task was transporting the Chuck Close to Justine's apartment as publicly as possible.

She remained in the kitchen until only Bartram's voice was audible. His usual song of himself required her return to the living room. Justine looked up joyously from their tete-á-tete as she entered, but Bartram, having lost his adoring audience, turned sullen. Helena announced gaily, "It's time for Justine's mother to come out of the closet." Justine giggled, and Bartram gave the smirk that passed for a smile.

As they rolled the dolly with the large portrait from the art closet into the living room, Justine asked, worried about their being seen, "Shouldn't we take it out the back way?"

"Absolutely not! We want to annoy all those scandalized by modern art! Bartram, bring the van around. We'll take it out the front door as conspicuously as possible." A short ride later they were at Justine's apartment building in the Fourth Ward. There was only one wall in the apartment large enough for the portrait, but it was lined with furniture. Justine looked to Bartram for a solution.

"The portrait will dictate where everything goes," he explained confidently and began pulling furniture away from the wall.

When the massive portrait was at last hung, it dominated the room, even crowded it. The small, bold circles and squares produced the contours of Kate's face in a shifting interplay of associative colors that leapt from the canvas and filled the room. The three stared at the effect, then opened a bottle of champagne and clinked their glasses: "To our dearly beloved Kate."

"To Kate coming out of the closet with Chuck," Bartram quipped. Champagne loosened a mood that had gradually become convivial, and an hour later at midnight they were still marveling at the portrait. Yet when mother and son finally left, Justine remained alone with the threat that Helena had described. The portrait of Kate had been a ruse to ward off trouble. But what if Finny's painting should really turn out to be the lost Rothko?

4

Shortly after Phineas McGinley encountered Foxcroft at the museum and received the threatening email, he assumed that the latter had sent it. It was then he decided to give the painting to Justine. No one would suspect her, a young single woman at the telephone company, of having a valuable painting—if it was valuable. At least he would be rid of it, without its falling into the hands of his ex-brother-in-law.

But what if the email came from elsewhere? The threat kept coming back: "You are in danger." He lay awake nights worrying about it. The painting itself encouraged paranoia. It was as if those blue-grey rectangles were a pair of accusing eyes. Of what? Why? How was he to get it safely to his niece? Someone might be watching him. A seven-foot metal tube couldn't exactly be hidden in his back pocket. Then he had an idea. One evening alone in the office, he unlocked the closet and gingerly took out the tube. The metal felt hot to the touch. Even after laying it on the floor it radiated an invisible power like gamma rays. In a rush to get it out of his presence, he took an extra-long garment bag, bought for the purpose, and laid it open on the floor. With shaking hands, he placed the tube inside and hastily zipped it shut. Then cautiously opened the door, whisked the bag down the stairs, out the rear entrance and into the back of his SUV. Furiously he drove to Justine's apartment as if pursued by demons.

"Uncle Finny," Justine sang joyously as she opened the door to her favorite uncle. He entered with the long bag and carefully laid it on the living room floor. "What's that?" she asked.

He looked about nervously and closed the front blinds before answering. "Something for you. You're not expecting anyone, are you?" His gravelly voice, ruined by cigarettes, sounded shaky.

"No, but what . . .?" she stopped mid-sentence, watched as he unzipped the bag and slowly, almost reverently removed a long metal tube. "That's not . . ." she didn't finish as he kicked the garment bag aside and opened the tube. Sucking in his breath as if to hoist a great weight, he carefully drew out a canvas and unrolled it on the floor. "It is!" she exclaimed, dumbfounded. Her eyes were like brown spotlights lit from within. Finny stood mutely in fear and loathing, his head turned away from the censorious painted eyes while Justine stared mesmerized. Layers of blue and silvery grey swirled on the floor like inverted storm clouds over the deep. At first the rectangles appeared as a horizon where the sea meets the sky in metal greyness. Then the dark-blue grey became choppy and aggressive, until it turned docile and assumed a silvered look, as if wavelets were stroking the unformed edges. "But what will I . . . how will I . . . where can I keep it?" She gave him a doleful look that turned her bird-wing brows into black hooks.

He glanced around the room, noticed for the first time the portrait of Kate, and peeked at the unearthly canvas he had been avoiding, as though getting the idea of it without really having to see it. Even supine, the rectangles shimmered with the unseeable. It was as if the flatness of the canvas made a window of the floor opening into a forbidden void. So uncanny was the sensation that he was tempted to raise the canvas and look for a hole into the abyss. Absurd of course. Nothing there. Less than nothing. Just the floor.

Justine remained bent over transfixed, tears making wells of her eyes. "Oh, Uncle Finny," she cried, "It runs right through you like a ray of light." She had lived with art all her life but never had a painting done such a thing to her before. When she looked up at him, her face shone with an illumination that caused him to back away. Where she saw light, he saw darkness. Grabbing an afghan off the sofa, he threw it over the painting to blot out its eyes while she stood over it, crying softly. "We're like shackled prisoners brought from the cave into the sun. We can't bear the light."

He stared, uncomprehending. "What cave?" he was about to ask, until rusted gears and grinding wheels brought Plato's allegory to his mind for the first time in fifty years. The strain of the unused machinery was too great and he mumbled woefully, "Do you have any whiskey? I really need a drink." His eyes bugged in terror and his face blazed crimson as if he were strangling. She didn't have whiskey but fetched him some Kir that he swigged in one convulsive gulp. Then he took her by the hands solemnly, "Look, Lass, roll this thing up and put it back in its tube. Hide it in your storage locker. Don't tell *anyone* you have it. Not anyone. Especially *not* your father." Then to prevent Justine from asking the questions written on her face, he rushed hastily out the door.

It was the beginning of Sandra's week off. For seven glorious days, she could forget about the hospital, complaining patients, grumpy staff, and Ouruk Zaron. Those who knew Dr. Foxcroft at work would have been surprised by her at home. The cool, low key internist inhabited a house of vibrant color. Red, her favorite, present everywhere, often below the radar in accents: a lamp shade here, a throw pillow there, trim on a hassock, covers on books, small appliances in the kitchen, a bowl of tulips on the coffee table. In clothing too, whether the red t-shirts worn at home, or the red accessories worn with her other favorite color, black. Justine joked that she would wear a red wedding dress were she to marry, or red scrubs if she could.

In the living room was a striking picture of a dark-haired female remarkably like Sandra bundled up against the wind in a bright red coat. The print was *Brisk Day* by Alex Katz. Its bold simplicity evoked with a few broad strokes the most profound humanity from an entirely generic face. The print was a clue to Sandra's character. Her passion, cloaked in the protective garment of the practical and rational, all crammed into the color red.

After cleaning the house and doing the laundry, Sandra still had six days and 12 hours before her next shift. The house in order, now she must put herself in order. She peered into the bedroom mirror like Alice's looking glass and saw not the doctor, Sandra, but another Sandra. It had been so long since she'd taken time to look, really look at herself, that the experience was uncanny, as if all past Sandras were infinitely receding. Was it just a few years ago that she was in medical school, idealistic and excited about the future? Then residency and a plunge in the submarine for four claustrophobic years. When she resurfaced, seasoned, disciplined, and tough, she eagerly joined the Zaron wing as a full-fledged hospitalist. And now? Though she loved medicine and found satisfaction in her skill, something was missing, like a memory that wasn't forgotten because it had never been remembered. Often, she referred patients to rehab for relearning mental skills, but where could she go for renewal?

Patients survived because of her, but for what? To live cautiously and avoid risk by taking pills? That would be avoiding living itself. Overseeing the medicalized body had made her forget the demands of her own flesh. She could feel the abstraction, the leaving herself out, omitting the desiring, loving person. In short, herself. So here she was, without definition, lacking even an object of desire. It was an old question. What does woman want? But the generic, *woman* is as empty as the generic *what*. And what is it empty of? What's missing? What does the singular Alexandra Foxcroft want? Apparently not any so-called thing. She could escape these thoughts at the hospital. But alone, thought intruded like a chill creeping into her chest. Then again, there was the man in the park. Would he answer to her desire?

The words she had been listening to over and over on her earphones came to mind: *"I wish my heart to offer Thee, / Offer Thee my care, my all."* Was this her desire? To go on desiring infinitely? That certainly was not the God she had been taught. He was another "it," another Father, whom, thinking of her own father, she didn't particularly care for. The chorale, *"Thou, more than earth and heaven, all,"* celebrates the beyondness of things. Even herself beyond herself. Is that what she really desired?

Then the phone rang.

"Sandra, Justine. I've got mother's portrait and thought you might want to see it."

"The Chuck Close?"

"Yes," the excitement in her voice was palpable.

An hour later, Sandra was in Justine's living room staring at the portrait that overwhelmed the tiny space, crowding out everything.

The portrait smiled lovingly at her as if it shared a secret. The effect, one looking, the other looked at, was the inverse of looking at herself in the mirror. It was as if their mother were close by in another room. It had something to do with the way she had inhabited whatever she loved. It had kept her surroundings from passing into ordinariness. Justine had the same attentive openness. Sandra watched her gracefully rearrange a small vase of flowers discovering its proper place. Then with a look as mischievous as a child's Justine pointed to the portrait. "Do you see anything special?"

Sandra gazed again at the geometric color patches that gave a kaleidoscopic effect to the portrait. Her mother's smile, like the Cheshire cat, floated, detached from eyes that seemed to lower and rise inscrutably. "I'm not sure what you mean. It's as though it painted her vitality and her love rather than a face."

Standing there, the three together invoked the deep past. Their mother had made life an adventure that did not include their father. Even he seemed to inhabit the room, but as an alien presence. He had once loved their mother, but a withered heart withers everything. Kate had tried to make things work, and when they didn't, chose for their father what he couldn't choose for himself: separation. Relieved, he had fled from the three women as if from a fatal disease. Then, after their mother died—he didn't attend the funeral—the sisters distanced themselves from his dead world of money. So began a completely new life together. They deserted Buckhead and got a modest apartment in Druid Hills near the University where Sandra entered medical school.

Their father assumed that the rift was a temporary, youthful rebellion. And lest others should think he had abandoned his daughters to penury when he was disgustingly rich, arranged trust funds for them. But he didn't reckon with the radicality of their break. They refused. How could they? How could they not?

The sisters' reverie in front of the portrait was broken when Justine renewed her question, "See anything else?"

Sandra applied her doctor's squint and lightly stroked the canvas refamiliarizing herself with its surface. "No, nothing new. Why? You've made it work, especially with the way you've rearranged the furniture."

Suppressing a grin, Justine said, "Bartram rearranged it. It was he who 'hung' mother." She giggled at the joke.

"Ah yes," Sandra replied in an ironic voice, "Bartram." She had always disliked the man, so full of himself, as she had always wondered what Justine, ordinarily a better judge of character, saw in him.

Justine observed as much and changed the subject. "You remember that man I told you about, Jonah Hartman? The man in the park?" Sandra nodded absently, eyes still on the portrait but recalling the man *she* met in the park. "He's a friend and colleague of Helena's. I have a client to see near the University so I thought I'd look him up this afternoon. Why not come along? You're playing the music from the *Passion* in your headphones all the time. Why not meet the man who will direct it? He's wonderfully interesting and knowledgeable about the arts."

"If you don't mind, I'd rather not." Sandra laid a hand on

her shoulder affectionately. "I like to avoid the University on my week off."

The smile remained, but a trace of disappointment showed in Justine's eyes. The sisters hugged each other goodbye affectionately, and as the door closed behind Sandra, Justine looked up significantly at the portrait and said, "Well Mother, it seems to have worked. She didn't see what you're hiding."

5

With the keen sixth-sense of a con man, Dr. Ouruk Zaron was always on the lookout for art acquired cheaply or on the sly. So when the estate of two reclusive Russian sisters was offered for sale, he went to investigate. Inside the tiny house every inch of space was covered with art. A minor collection, not worthy of his interest he thought—with one exception: an empty wall in the dining room where a large painting had once hung. Gambling that he was onto something, Zaron bought the house and its entire contents. It didn't take him long to deduce a painting fitting that empty space was the one given away by the sisters just before they died. Or that the man who had it, Phineas McGinley, was uncle to the daughters of his greatest rival, Sir Reginald Foxcroft. Under another name and by proxy, Zaron offered to buy the painting from McGinley. He refused. But that wasn't the end of the affair.

Shortly after Justine showed the Chuck Close to her sister, Sandra received a certified letter from a law firm. It asked about a "large modern painting 6 x 5 feet that she or her sister may have acquired recently" and offered to buy it for a client. Thinking they wanted to buy their mother's portrait by Close, and not knowing of the painting Finny had given Justine, Sandra tossed the letter in the trash and forgot about it.

A short time later, Justine received a letter from the same law firm. But unlike her sister, she did not toss it in the trash. Her letter said that she "was in possession of a large painting 6 x 5 feet that belonged to an anonymous party as part of a recently acquired estate." The firm threatened: "If she didn't return it she would be sued." This sent Justine into a tailspin. Helena and Uncle Finny had told her to keep the painting safe and hidden. And she had. What should she do? She must consult Helena. So with photos tucked in her bag, she stopped for lunch at General Muir's Delicatessen near the University, intending afterwards to drop in on Helena at her office.

Jonah Hartman was alone at the same restaurant when Justine entered looking distracted. Even preoccupied she appeared airy and graceful as if her body was the very source of mobility. It was "the running girl," as Jonah had called her playfully. He waved a hand inviting her to join him. With a perfunctory hello and a half-hearted smile, she sat down and lapsed into a troubled silence. The two had become friends since they met in the park some weeks ago. Friendship, unexpected but fortuitous, had happened at just the right moment.

This is how it came about. One day shortly after their meeting in the park, there had been a knock on Jonah's office door. "Come in," he had answered. A lovely face with a set of enormous brown eyes peered in. Jonah tried to place the girl with the amazing eyes and marvelous smile.

"Remember me?" she said in a liquid, melodious voice. "We met in the park? Justine Foxcroft."

"The running girl." He smiled. He had forgotten what at the time seemed unforgettable, and seeing her again, had wondered why. She had the rare capacity of vitalizing a mood that moments ago had been pedestrian. "Well running girl, sit down please," he gestured to a chair. Sweeping her full skirt gracefully beneath her legs, she sat posed like a dancer. "What can I do for you?"

"I was between clients close by and took a chance of seeing you." He looked surprised and she explained. "My job is to go around to delinquent clients and convince them to pay their accounts."

"And I bet you're good at it," he laughed, unable to imagine anyone not falling under her spell.

"Well yes, I am. Isn't it *wonder*ful?" she said gratefully, crediting the wonder and not herself. Then she pulled a book from her bag and handed it to him.

"What's this?"

"A gift, for rescuing me in the park." It was a book about Mark Rothko. "It's signed by the artist. My father gave it to me a few years back and I'd like you to have it." Her simple offering revived a spirit sagging from a troubled marriage. He thought: "She can't know that she just rescued me."

She had searched his face as if she could read his thoughts. "I can usually tell by looking into a person's eyes whether they're trustworthy." She clarified: "You can discover character when you catch a person off guard the way I did with you in the park the other day. People you know hide what they think because you know them so well."

He observed the openness of her face while they talked. She was one of those people who seemed to hold nothing back. In her openness, he had seen what does not come naturally: That another can't be reduced to me and my concerns. In really seeing her, he rediscovered his own openness to the world.

And here at General Muir's, some weeks later, was the same girl who had lifted his spirit then, now looking woebegone. "Something's wrong running girl." He put a hand on his cheek thoughtfully trying to imagine what it was. "I remember that you were quite serious about a painting."

She held back a second, then, as if there were no going back, pulled a letter from her bag and handed it to him with brimming eyes.

He read it silently. "I don't understand. Someone is suing you because you supposedly have their painting?"

"Yes." She hesitated, and the dark lashes made a sweep over the large eyes. "I think I have it . . . *the lost* Rothko. I can't tell you how because I promised not to. But it's not theirs!" came out in a soft wail.

He put a large hand over her small one resting on the table. "The letter from the law firm is a fishing expedition. A bluff. They hope you'll panic and tell them what they want to know."

"What do you think I should do?" she pleaded.

Her intelligence, youth, and want of guile made him want to help. "Do nothing. Keep the letter. Show it to Helena." It was the calm voice of authority lined with affection.

Encouraged, she reached into her bag again and passed him another large envelope. In it were a number of 8 x 10 color glossies. He sifted through them slowly. They showed two rectangles in dark blues of similar intensity scumbled with white. This blue-grey work was calmer and simpler than the severe negativity of Rothko's black and mauve paintings. It had a covert complexity. They brought to his mind the colors in music, like a chorus singing pianissimo.

He handed them back. "I'm not an art expert. How do you know it's a Rothko?"

"I don't. Helena would. But if she knew for certain I had *this* painting," she looked around anxiously and pointed to the photos, "and if she knew it was the lost Rothko, it could threaten us both." Her saucer eyes were asking him to believe her. "She herself told me this." She leaned toward him across the table and said in a soft voice, "There are people who would do *anything* to get their hands on it. The threat from the law firm proves it." She left it to him to fill in the blanks.

He nodded, thinking along with her. Anyone else might have scoffed at the idea that a painting could generate criminal interests, but he understood the rivalries and power struggles among people who staked their lives on the arts. "In becoming commercial," he muttered, "art, like music, has become cutthroat." He frowned, shaking his head. "Like the acid thrown in the face of the dancer in Moscow." Then he changed the subject. "Helena is coming to a rehearsal of the *Passion* tonight. Would you like me to give the photos to her?"

Her eyes brightened. "Would you? The person behind this"—she pointed to the letter from the lawyers—"might try to get his hands on the painting before it can be authenticated." She paused, lowering her eyes, then slowly looked up into his. "I know it sounds foolish. But I think someone is following me. So if *you* would give Helena the photos tonight, it wouldn't connect the envelope with her or with me."

He regarded her thoughtfully, "And if Helena should say it is the missing painting—she can't know for certain from just a few photos—then what?"

"I don't know. I'll know what to think and do when it happens."

Grasping both her hands tightly in his, he looked at her severely with knotted brow. "Call me anytime of the day or night if you are in real danger." The insistence in his voice and demeanor said the words were not given lightly. She nodded solemnly, sighed regretfully, and looking at her watch said wearily, "Sorry. Must go. An appointment."

"Am I to contact you or you me?"

She considered. "Call me after you give these to Helena. She'll have to see the actual painting, whatever the danger."

"And what about the photos? Do you want them back?"

An idea popped into her head. "There are three sets. If I keep one and give you one and she has one they'll be confirmation that the painting exists." Aware of the burden she was putting on him, she held out a graceful hand. "I can't thank you enough for your advice and what you've agreed to do for someone who's nearly a stranger."

"People who care as passionately about art as we do aren't strangers."

She beamed. "Well then, friend, till we meet again." She kissed him on both cheeks impulsively and glided gracefully out the door. He watched her move with a light, tripping grace and recalled again his first view of her running in the park. It brought to mind the story of Atalanta tempted with the golden balls by Aphrodite. And what of this modern Atalanta? She might be tempted to retreat from a challenge, but would she be distracted? He barely knew her but thought not. At least not the girl, woman really, who unafraid, could take on the burden of a great painting and convince delinquent customers and a new friend to answer to her.

Afterwards, he returned to the University, and sitting at his desk thought of Victoria who was away for another performance. If he told her about the photos what would she, who claimed to be as passionate about art as he was, say? She'd laugh mockingly like Carmen at Don Jose and say how silly he was to be taken in by an insignificant chit of a girl. They could talk for hours about the finer points of their discipline, for days about the interpretation of a particular work and still not be attuned in spirit. She had done an interview recently for one of the local TV stations, looking glamorous as she spoke with glowing eyes and a fetching accent about her art. She seemed taken outside herself, dedicated, a handmaid to her craft. Everything she said that day was what he also felt, what he wished they both felt. But when she came home with a scowl on her face, out spewed angry remarks about the interviewer, the TV station, and the stupid people for whom she had to say stupid things. And he despaired at the gulf between them.

His thoughts returned to the photos. The blue-grey rectangles invoked a world of figures fading ambiguously into a silvery-blue sea. How explain that we can love what we cannot hold in a clear idea? The painting was like that. It pointed to something beyond the knowable. As when one hears a silent voice, a call. He had just heard it, not in Justine's plea for help. It came from the painting itself. A call to him to save it for the sake of art's truth. The thought reinvigorated him, and when his student tenors arrived for class, he gave himself to their music as if the world depended on it. For it did.

Ouruk Zaron strolled with long, straight legs across the marble floors of his mansion admiring his private collection. Sleek and muscled, with the restless energy of an animal barely tamed, his flashing eyes, sharp nose, and sensuous mouth gave him the assured look of mastery. He passed before a Rubens he had acquired in exchange for a mediocre painting by the artist his father had given him. *He*, unlike his father, prided himself on the ability to see the difference between a masterpiece and the off works that even the greatest artists produced. The elder Zaron had often overpaid for minor pieces and even fakes, as though they were bargains. *He*, however, could recall to the dollar what he paid for *his* acquisitions and how he had squeezed, finagled, and in some cases cheated to get them.

He moved onto one of his favorites, *The Rape of Proserpina*, and smiled, exposing strong, white teeth and thickly curved lips. The voluptuous daughter of Demeter had flowing black hair over naked breasts and a scarf in danger of slipping off her sex. Her arms were raised in supplication as Pluto, dark god of the underworld, with eyes sharp as arrowheads and hair like tentacles across her shoulders, grasped her by the waist. Her proud disdain was the same as Zaron's sultry mistress when she first caught his eye. He smiled pleasurably at the memory.

As if in response, a warm female body pressed against his back. As her arms encircled him teasingly, a mouth breathed provocatively into his ears, "Is that your way of having me again?" He turned and looked into coal black eyes as they shone with possession and triumph. Jet hair fell in becoming disarray around her exquisite face and shoulders as a diaphanous gown fell open at the front to reveal her sensuous body. She kissed him hungrily as he lowered her to the floor for a second time.

When it was over, she kicked off the heels. With gown and shoes in hand, strolled naked down the hall, the diva backstage after a performance. He watched her disappear, then turned again to Proserpina. The painting brought another dark-haired beauty to mind: Sandra Foxcroft. He had tried to picture her naked under her scrubs but could never imagine her adequately until he saw her

Joanne Cutting-Gray

at the High Museum dressed in a red sheath. But however much he lusted for her, he was not sure, that *that* Proserpina would ever stroll naked down the floors of his gallery.

A half hour later his reigning goddess emerged from the guest house by the pool, perfectly groomed in a halter top, harem pants and high-wedged sandals. Her arms, neck and ears were wired in gold jewelry, the glittering rings on her right hand reducing the simple wedding band on her left to insignificance. He was waiting for her at the bar next to the cabana. "Drink?"

"Champagne, thank you."

He opened a bottle and filled crystal flutes. "To my latest acquisition," he said, tilting the glass toward her. She laughed theatrically as if it were a joke, knowing it was not. All his women were prized possessions lusted after and acquired like his paintings. He preferred masterpieces unavailable on the market, especially those that belonged to someone else. The latest acquisition was not only beautiful, talented, and haughty, but half of a famous couple, lending a frisson of excitement to his success. He had won the high-strung, temperamental beauty with no one the wiser. That preserved his reputation, and her frequent travel kept the affair from going stale. His driver would pick her up when she flew in—earlier than her husband expected—and whisk her here to his mansion for a few secluded days and nights together. He had ensconced her in the guest house where he never intruded, giving her privacy as well as a place for the expensive wardrobe worn only for him. At the end of her stay a private limo took her home to the unsuspecting husband as though she had just flown in.

As the two lovers sipped their champagne, the setting sun reflected off the long formal pool nestled among five acres of woods and gardens. The secluded house might have been in the countryside rather than the rolling hills of old Atlanta. In the early part of the twentieth century, it had been built by a well-known local architect. Of classic design, it had a large, three story central core, matching wings on each side, and included an Italian balustrade, grand staircase, and Corinthian columns. Behind the mansion this formality was softened by a canopied patio that protected the couple from the late afternoon sun.

As Victoria's long fingers and polished red nails tapped impatiently against the champagne flute, she asked peevishly, "Well we've made love twice, had lunch, and admired your paintings, what do you have planned for the evening?" She was, in the parlance, high maintenance and skittish. Gardens that brought images of Versailles with furnishings as luxurious were not distractions enough.

"I thought we might watch a football game in the theater," he answered in dead pan. Her dark eyes widened in horror. He laughed. "Or maybe you'd like to wallow a bit in Spanish television and then watch a live performance of the New York City Ballet." The famous Latina had a soft spot for shows in her native language and raised a perfectly arched brow coquettishly. But ballet was another thing. She liked it too, but not as he did. He loved the ballet more than he loved his paintings. As a lonely child he had watched old videos from the Bolshoi to escape his random upbringing. It was the only art he could ever truly lose himself in.

"Why not invest in a ballet company rather than paintings?" she taunted. "Think of the dancers who would lust for this"—she gestured widely across the park— "while you lust for them." He held back a retort and they fell into a negative silence accompanied by a low rustle in the giant maples. She goaded him, "Tell me, are you still saving your testosterone for that mysterious painting? What do you think? Will Foxcroft get it?" Amused, she watched him turn grim.

"What have you heard?" he snapped. Words were now becoming stones to hurl at each other.

His anger left a delicious taste in her mouth. "A musical friend of mine seems to have heard something about it."

Rumors about the painting had been on the wing like flocks of crows, most of them false, and if truth be told, promulgated by the surgeon himself. It was one of his tricks to flood the art world with rumors so that time wasted chasing them diverted attention from his current schemes.

"Who?" he snapped.

"Oh, I can't say," she lied. "He asked me not to tell." In fact, Bartram Gandolfi hadn't told her anything, but she wanted Zaron to think he had. He grabbed her wrist tightly and the champagne flute fell with a crash on the pavement. "Ouch! You're hurting me," she cried, twisting the hand from his grasp and clutching the wrist against her breast like a broken wing.

He was not a stupid man. He guessed that she had heard something indirectly. His mind clicked through a list of names and stopped at the letter G. "So, you talked to Gandolfi did you?" He grinned like a tiger baring its fangs, and a flicker of fear glinted in her eyes.

"The art historian?" she asked disingenuously. "She's not musical," and tossed her head dismissively.

His face hardened into granite. He understood the power of association. Gandolfi's son *was* musical and may have picked up something from his mother. When he spoke again he had regained his bedside manner. "You've been very useful, Vicki," he deliberately used the nickname she disliked, "in more ways than might have been expected."

6

Nine pm: A knock at the door of a penthouse. Whoever ventured fifty stories up to see Sir Reginald late on a Sunday night had to be full of admiration. Why else would one dare come? What, therefore, did Russell Baramore want? The internist entered wearing scrubs and a friendly smile that did nothing to soften Sir Reginald's irritation. "Sorry, to come unannounced. I wouldn't have intruded except for something urgent and confidential."

He stretched out a strong hand to the dapper figure, formally casual in smoking jacket and tasseled slippers. Foxcroft, smoothing his mustache with his left hand, but keeping his right in his pocket, looked the younger man up and down critically.

"I came from my shift at the hospital." Russell dropped his hand and took in the surroundings: a dizzying expanse of glass thrusting into the Buckhead nightscape, fireplace two stories high, and sleek monochromatic furnishings. The walls were covered but not with the paintings in the famous collection. Instead the space was commandeered by monumental works that Russell didn't recognize.

Sir Reginald guessed what he was thinking and responded offhandedly, "The reflected light here is too strong for most of my paintings. I keep them elsewhere." He sat down and lit a cigarette without asking Russell to take a seat. That left Russell standing in the middle of the floor staring at the lighted cigarette and wondering what point he was making. Was it the intrusion, his coming in scrubs, or was it racial? Foxcroft seemed to guess, and having made his point, rang a bell on a table and begrudgingly offered Russell a seat. It wasn't race, as Russell suspected, but class. The aristocrat took umbrage at anything that smacked of the bourgeois, and that included the intrusion at his front door on a Sunday evening of someone "in trade," even a physician.

The retainer who had answered the door reappeared, strikingly beautiful and tall with almost white hair, and gold-brown eyes in a nearly pallid face. He moved across the room, graceful and intense as a dancer across a stage, without acknowledging the others. Russell stared admiringly at the elegant figure.

"Olas, will you serve us some wine please? Claret." The young man exited without a word. "Now, what is this about? I was in the middle of my reading." He gestured with long slender fingers toward an open book, binding side up, on the coffee table in front of him.

"It's about the lost painting. I learned something recently I thought you should know." Russell spoke with authority, elbows on the chair arms, hands and fingers interlaced thoughtfully. The abruptness of this plunge into so-called polite conversation and Russell's less than subservient demeanor affronted the older man's sense of manners. And Russell's obliviousness only made it worse.

The irritated aristocrat asked crossly, "Why do you think *I* should know? Did Alexandra send you?"

"No, but it was she who told me."

The young man reentered sylph-like with a wine bottle and two glasses and set them on the table. Foxcroft waited, eyes half-lowered, until he left. Then the eyelids raised like a pair of blinds, "Go on."

"Sandra told me that Zaron asked her about the Rothko. And for some reason I don't understand she said that Justine should be warned."

At the mention of Justine, something appeared in the older man's eyes, just a flicker, then the venetian lids lowered again. "I fail to see what this has to do with me. I have no idea why Alexandra should want to warn Justine. Or are you telling me because you think *I* know."

Russell's authority reasserted itself. "I'm not here only about Justine, although I thought you might be concerned about your daughter. The point is Zaron. He seems to know something and thinks that Sandra knows something. That can only mean he thinks *you* know something and told *her*."

"I . . . I know nothing." He raised his hands in protest. "And since you are intimately acquainted with Alexandra, you also know that she doesn't confide in me." He reached for the open book and turned it over. The gesture may have been to close the book properly, but it served as a reminder that he was being interrupted.

Russell got up from his chair, his dignity ruffled. "That's my whole point. I thought since you haven't been in touch with Sandra lately" —he tried to put a good face on it— "you'd want to know what concerns her and what Zaron is up to."

"But you haven't told me anything about Zaron." The older man sniffed dismissively. "Except that he asked Alexandra if she knew anything about the painting. According to you," he shrugged, "she doesn't." He saw from the angry frown on Russell's face that he had overplayed his hand and moved to make amends. "Are you in a hurry?" he asked in a dignified but false note. "Have some of this fine Claret." Before Russell could decline, his glass was filled.

A half hour later, the Claret bottle now empty, he left looking pleased with himself, as Foxcroft with a similar expression on his face sat staring out the window, not reading.

◆

Peachtree Street was almost deserted after the Monday night rehearsal. Jonah was the last to leave symphony hall. He ought to have been pleased that the rehearsal had gone so well, but all he felt was an unexplainable angst. Perhaps it was because Victoria was away again advancing her *career*—the word tasted like sawdust in his mouth. Music had once been a vocation for them. More than a vocation. In those days it had been life itself. It still was for him, yet something was terribly wrong, like a violin off key. The music they had just rehearsed said it all: *"For me the untrue world hath set / With lie and fable, many a net / And trap in secret places."*

As he walked along under a sky as brooding as his thoughts, two women emerged just ahead from a fashionable bar. Their laughter echoed down the empty sidewalk. One was short and middle-aged, the other tall and younger, with an outline and bearing that in the shadows suggested beauty without the delineation of features. She was vaguely familiar like the half-forgotten resonance of an aria. The two were talking animatedly and barely noticed him. As the younger one drew near, a street lamp illumined her for just an instant. A lightening flash—shock. Things rushed at him, too many to make sense of. Only when she passed did he realize that it was the woman from the park. As he gazed at her receding back he was flooded with perceptions. She was walking arm and arm with her friend in a manner that revealed a natural gracefulness. Close up, in street clothes, she appeared quite slender. Her hair, pulled back from her face before, was now long and loose around her shoulders. He recalled the blinding jolt when their eyes met in the park. It was the strange experience of not really seeing anything except a bursting forth that submerged everything in sight. Something in her profile now hinted at a contradictory quality—warmly familiar yet unapproachable. Was it her laughter and open smile, or the quick way she gestured with narrow hands and long fingers that suggested a lively intelligence?

As she faded into the distance he wondered regretfully, "Why didn't I recognize her sooner? I could have nodded at least and said hello. The idea was silly. "Hi. Remember me, the man you didn't meet in the park one day?" The self-parody opened an interior argument: He was married to a woman he loved, for whom he had altered the course of his life. He had chosen stability and security over upheaval. Why jeopardize all that for the imaginary?

A romantic illusion? Hadn't he seen enough in his profession of flirtations, exploitations, casual affairs, and painful breakups—the fruits of vanity? And yet walking swiftly now, he was filled with an overwhelming sense of loss. What had happened twice wasn't attributable to causes and reasons. Was it temptation or was it a gift, unforeseeable and incalculable?

"It was him!" The recognition came as Sandra put the key in her lock. It swept over her in one infinite moment of regret. "The man from the park! Why was I so slow to recognize him?" A stranger passes on a street or brushes against you in a crowd and is instantly forgotten. Yet on some level she *had* registered his presence, his intensity of concentration, almost a will drawing her toward him—then she diverted her attention. Now, too late, his image flooded her. The same eyes that had gazed at her in the park—like storm clouds across a plain. The same cloud of dark curls and sculpted profile, strong back and set shoulders. Remembering, she could almost feel his repressed energy of thunder in the distance. Regret caught in her throat. A gift given twice—and refused.

A set of keys was on the foyer table. Russell was back from his shift and undoubtedly in bed asleep. She didn't want to go to bed even though she was tired. Slipping out of her heels, she sat in the living room without turning on a light. Darkness held the image of the man in presence just as the all-too-real Russell in bed would banish it.

As she stared out the window into the lights of the city, they winked at her folly. How absurd to fantasize about someone she hadn't even met. Reason told her he could be anybody—drug-dealer, psychopath, jerk, surgeon (perish the thought), or worst of all—a married man. Cold reality tempered her imagining. She had no appetite for illusions. Hadn't she observed it often in others? There was her mother's illusion that their father was a better man than he was. Her father's illusion that money and a title set him apart. Her own illusions about family, medicine, and, in a world that conflated it with sex, love. Even now she clung to the dream that family could be reinvented, that medicine could be about helping people, that the cure was love. But after yet another obese patient with diabetes she had, not experience, but weariness—too tired to cook, read, or have sex. Real experience needed, not the brute facts of everyday, but possibility—the possibility arising from chance—like an unexpected event with a stranger. But she had tricked herself into avoiding the unexpected. Words from the *Passion* welled up like tears in her mind, *"For me the untrue world hath set / With lie and fable, many a net."* With heavy footsteps, she climbed the stairs to the bedroom, looked at Russell sprawled and snoring in the tangled sheets, and went to sleep in the guest room.

◆

Phineas McGinley had a sick feeling in his stomach, a nameless anxiety that he couldn't escape. After giving the spooked painting to Justine—mysteriously alive and suggestive of death—he thought he'd stop feeling accused. Yet even busy with clients he felt responsible and wherever he turned accusations followed. They were working on him from afar like a kind of cosmic microwave background.

It all came back to him—when it wasn't obscured by anxiety. The bitter truth of forty years in real estate. People don't know what they want. They don't really want show kitchens, spa baths, formal dining rooms, vast lawns and mortgages greater than they can afford. They just want *to appear* that they do. They're too busy to cook, too tired to clean, too financially stretched to enjoy. Even after forty years he didn't understand why. That would have taken more imagination than he or his clients had. His imagination had been closed, altogether sealed, and now something had happened. The frightening experience, the bewildering brush of alarm. Threatened with something that didn't fit the world of buying and selling—a work of art—he was lost, adrift, confounded. It was unpleasant.

But he resisted. Absurd to be worrying about a painting, he told himself—the himself who wasn't convinced. Responsibility had grabbed hold of his pants leg with its teeth and wouldn't be shaken loose. "I don't know what to think. But if I know I don't know, then what's the good of thinking?"

He had to spread the uneasiness to another, to Justine. But he didn't want to see her at home and confront *it* all over again. Billows of anxiety piled up until he could resist no longer and called her. "Is it secret? Were you able to put it away somewhere safe, Lass?" he asked, relieved to shift his anxiety to her.

"Yes, Uncle Finny. I found the absolutely *perfect* place for it." Her voice was full of mischief.

He waited for her to say more and when she didn't, added, "I hope giving it to you wasn't a mistake. I didn't want to burden you." That sounded defensive and called for something more. "But then you know so much more about art and all." He heard his words as cowardly.

She reassured him. "Don't worry, Uncle Finny. No one would ever suspect I have a priceless painting in my humble apartment."

"Priceless?" The word stirred a new interest and a generosity tamped down by fear. "Listen, if you need my help, you know, if something comes up that smells like trouble, anything at all, call."

"I will Uncle Finny, I promise." She hesitated as if wanting to say more. "We're not alone you know." She wasn't just thinking of Jonah or Helena, but of the world, the *we* given by the work of art.

That startled him. Who was this *we*? He wondered but didn't ask.

Afterward, peeved with the division in himself, he declared stoutly, "I'm going to watch over her!" And so began his nightly mission as part of the greater *we* to patrol the streets around Justine's apartment.

7

Elated, worried, or both, Helena was at her desk with a dozen photographs propped in front of her. There was little doubt it was the lost Rothko. The colors and size were exactly the same as "#835, Untitled, Whereabouts Unknown." The same interaction between the rectangles, dark above and light below. Except the color value was reduced where the darker blue distorted the light in the way that gravity bends it. That's its power. It breaks through the seeable, bends it out of shape.

The real concern was not about the photos of the recto but the verso. The stretcher and cross bars where Rothko usually signed his name and the date were missing. There was no other evidence of an inscription, not even on the tacking margins. And yet he was known not to sign a painting that was a gift, so the inscription could be missing if he had in fact given the painting to the sisters.

Authenticating a painting was never easy, and she was skeptical of the dogmatic, almost religious belief in science that authentication implied. A work of art was not a so-called *made* thing, or a scientific object. And the material subsistence of a painted *thing* doesn't make it art. Leonardo's *Last Supper* may be a ruin that has lost most of its original materiality, but that doesn't diminish its power.

Forensic evidence and similarity of technique were not necessarily proofs of authenticity either. Rothko used a mixed medium that varied from canvas to canvas—oil, turpentine, egg, powder, water and varnish—avoiding repetition, always inventing. His rectangles could be shiny or matte, thin or clotted, cloudy or luminescent. The brush strokes, even in the largest paintings, might be uniform and small, so any consistency of appearance was superficial. And unless there was a documented history or provenance of the painting after it left the artist's studio and it was listed in an annotated catalog raisonné, there would always be room for doubt.

The expanding possibilities made her giddy. It led her to reflect on how art experts in good faith preserve, classify, and evaluate. The process itself blocks the force of the work, substituting knowledge for experience. She recalled Rothko's well-known hatred of art historians, experts, and critics. He was right. It was an indictment of the insistence on aligning the work with what is already known. "But in whatever way you paint a large canvas you are within it," he had said. His large canvases engulf and overwhelm the viewer, so they can't be fully comprehended. No unifying it under a concept and mastering it. One doesn't command, one *receives* a Rothko. So how, when she knew so much and could tell all, was she to leave knowledge and consciousness behind and stay open to receiving?

Olas Lindgard rode his bike south on the eastern beltline toward Zaron Hospital. The landscaped and well-used bike trail, retrieved from an old rail line, had recreated the urban scene. An outdated sprawl tied to the automobile and clogged freeways had been superseded by a walkable, bikeable environment that eventually would circle the city. Olas parked his bike and took off his helmet and goggles. His blond hair shone brightly in the sun and set off the shiny cycling gear that adhered to him like a second skin. The finely wrought features turned heads as he strode purposefully through the hospital entrance and down the corridors like a young Greek god. He passed the visitor's lounge, passed the nurses station, passed the patient rooms, until he reached the door marked

"Chief of Surgery," and entered. "Olas Lindgard," he said compellingly to the receptionist on guard. "He's expecting me."

"He . . . he'll see you," she stammered, awestruck by the gorgeous vision that whisked past her and through the door.

Behind an imposing desk, Dr. Ouruk Zaron stared at the epitome of male beauty and frowned. "You work for Reginald Foxcroft?" he asked, dropping even the pretense of manners.

"Yes, Sir," the young man snapped, legs astride like a soldier.

"Does he know you're here?" The upper lip curled into a suspicious sneer.

"No, Sir."

Zaron relaxed a little, "Why have you come?" Then added testily, "I'm a busy man."

"Sir Reginald heard that you approached his daughter about the lost Rothko."

"Who told him?" He hurled it at him like a projectile.

"I don't know."

Zaron, staring hard, "How is it you don't know? Weren't you there?"

"I was in my room. I overheard them."

"So you eavesdrop on your employer do you?" He sniggered, pleased at a discovery that might prove useful. He pressed, tapping a hand impatiently on the desk: "Was it a man or a woman speaking?"

"I can't say."

After a wary silence, "You can't? Or you won't?"

"It's better not to know some things."

"You mean you don't *want* to say."

"It's *better* not to say."

It occurred to Zaron that he had found another man like himself. "If I did say something to his daughter," he pressed his palms together, "and mind you, I don't say I did, why would you be telling me what I already know?" He cocked his head and stared at the young man archly.

Olas glanced around the grandly appointed office as if searching for the answer. "A hired retainer doesn't make much."

Zaron's flint-colored eyes glinted at this bold revelation of character. Far from doubting the young man, he believed him in believing him to be as false as he was. It's not that Zaron himself *denied* the truth, but that he assumed it in falsifying it and putting a lie in its place. In some dank chamber of his soul he wanted to love the truth, to lay hold of it, but only in his own way—as falseness. And since he assumed everyone was a liar and hated the truth, he turned the falseness he loved into its opposite so that when he lied, he lied truly. "I expected there was something. Everyone has his price."

After their thicket of words, they came to a quick agreement.

Olas retraced his steps down the busy corridor. Once again, heads turned at the sight of the young Apollo in shiny cycling gear. Among the medical staff at the nurse's station, Dr. Russell Baramore recognized him as the man from Sir Reginald's and a frown puckered his brow. A thousand suspicions rushed upon him. Why is *he* here? Did he recognize me? And where has he been? Did he tell Zaron about seeing me in Foxcroft's penthouse? Overhear us discussing the painting? A spy then? Yet when the young man passed without a flicker of acknowledgment, he felt at once relieved and strangely disappointed.

"Who were you staring at?" Sandra asked. She had seen Russell's umber skin shade at the sight of the young man.

Russell shrugged his muscular shoulders, "No one," and changed the subject.

"It is!" Helena asserted emphatically when she saw the thing itself open on the floor.

"I knew it!" Justine rejoiced.

Helena had arrived at her apartment at night in dark glasses, her head swathed in a scarf. Once the door closed behind them, she wasted no time. The long metal tube was opened, the canvas withdrawn and rolled out on the floor. She gasped, dumbfounded. For five long minutes, she stared without moving. Then, still wrapped closely in her scarf as in her thoughts, she examined the canvas from all sides with a jeweler's pocket lupe and a UV light, spending as much time on the back as the front. When for the third time she searched the back and checked the tacking margins, Justine opened her mouth to say something and was silenced by a raised hand.

At last, Helena acknowledged her and uttered the two, fateful words, "It is!"

"I knew it!" Justine cried out for joy. She hugged Helena tightly.

Smiling gravely now, Helena slowly unwound her scarf, unwinding her thoughts more to herself than to Justine. "He's softened the corners, erasing the hard edges. Yes, and those," her fingers pointed to an edge, "are the old nail and mounting marks. And *there*," pointing to the lower edge, "the stain is so thin you can read one color through another. It gives the work a power of inseparability. Like the force carriers that bind things together and occupy the same place. Gluons," she said.

Justine stared at the painting considering it all. "The layers are its music, aren't they? Like polyphony where the voices sing on top of each other."

The remark brought Helena back from her musings. "Where, how did you come to see that?"

"Jonah Hartman said something like that when I showed him the photos."

"Ah, he would. Yes, he knows. He's one of us," she said enigmatically, and returned to her semi-private dialogue with the painting: "It refuses to satisfy the desire for a visible image. It stops us." She nodded slowly in agreement with her own thoughts. There were paradoxes enough to hold them in silence for a time.

Finally, Justine ventured hesitantly: "Now that you know it's the lost work, will you please take it with you?" She realized what a relief it would be to give it up.

Helena shook her head slowly, solemnly. "No, that's the last thing I must do," she said, making the contradiction gentle.

Justine only partly understood. She was hoping to return to familiar ground where less was required of her. "Isn't my part done? I can't be the bearer of something so valuable, and it's not practical to keep it in this apartment. Especially as I'll have to hide it in the same place I did before." She glanced involuntarily at the portrait of her mother.

Helena looked as if Justine were just entering her field of thought. "The practical thing, the realistic thing would be for me to take it. But the practical and realistic have no place here. What seems practical is shortsighted."

Justine tried one last time to make her case. "We're heading into summer. Shouldn't it be in a controlled environment? Safe?"

"Yes, it should. But not yet. We can't play it safe. Play safe and you never discover anything. You have to trust to chance. If I took the painting, there would be a greater chance of its being discovered too soon. Physically safe, but not safe for posterity." Then she added with an even deeper gravity, "The world is blind to the danger." Justine's eyes widened into brown globes. She stared at the painting, resisting, then sighed, surrendering at last to the thing given to her to do.

Helena echoed her inner voice. "Even if we don't feel part of an epic—nothing feels epic anymore, not even wars. But there is such grandeur here." She pointed to the painting on the floor. "We won't know what part we've played until afterwards. You must keep it awhile longer while I think where it can be stored, safely. It's a lot to ask. There is no one else."

8

"There is no one else." The words called for precaution, and Justine began for the first time living in anxiety. Helena had warned her that the painting would become a burden. Now it weighed on her, even deciding things in her life. She who once joyed in the moment, suffered from forebodings. On the way home from work one day, a sedan with darkened windows seemed to be following her. As she turned on Freedom Parkway it turned. She turned on Ralph McGill, it turned on Ralph McGill. She veered abruptly into the driveway across from her building, watched the sedan pass, slammed the car in reverse, and raced backward across the street into her parking lot. The electric gate had no sooner clanged shut than the same sedan passed from the opposite direction. Was she paranoid in thinking an entire world would be after the painting?

After that she drew the blinds night and day. If someone left the back door to her building open too long or didn't close the electric gate, she scolded. At night through a chink in the blinds she watched for suspicious people and suspicious cars. She who always told the truth became adept at telling lies. The biggest lie was to her sister, who called the day after Helena's declaration, "It is!"

"How are you? I haven't heard from you for a while." Sandra asked affectionately.

Justine answered in an unusually subdued tone. "I've been very busy. What about you?"

"Long days. I just finished a 36-hour shift." She sighed audibly.

"I feel as if I've been on another planet: Planet Zaron." Justine involuntarily gasped at the name and Sandra continued, "Can I drop by tonight with Chinese takeout? We could catch up."

Justine panicked. She couldn't involve Sandra. Not until she could get rid of the painting. "I can't." It had an abrupt finality that was unlike her.

Sandra went conspicuously silent on the other end of the line.

"I can't. I can't have you come over now or anytime soon . . . because," she hesitated, inventing on the spot, "because I'm . . . with a male friend." She could hear astonishment in the void on the other end.

"Oh . . . some other time then."

The deflation in Sandra's voice conceded more than disappointment. In one blow, their relationship altered. Justine tried, too late, to soften the bang of the door she had just closed. "Sometime soon, I promise Sandra. Just not right now."

Shocked and defeated by Justine's uncharacteristic retreat, Sandra reflected that the man her sister was seeing should not be *her* concern. Even if it wasn't her business, as older sister and surrogate mother, she felt responsible. She was the admired older sister, the respected healer. But Justine's secrecy about living with a man had brought something to the surface. It was about her, Sandra, despite her best attempts to deny it. Or else why feel so lost? For the hundredth time she asked, "What do I really want?" The question so dominated her thoughts that afternoon that it obscured another question, "What would another—any other—want of me?" A question that one who seeks approval can't risk. She thought of her mother and mourned again her loss. Then she thought of Helena, her second mother. It had been months since she had visited her or sought her advice. But a reticence and pride prevented her calling. Yet later that same evening she found herself almost against her will at Helena's doorstep uninvited.

The door was opened not by her but by Bartram, flute in hand as if he had been practicing. He was as startled as she. "Sandra! This is a surprise. What brings you here? Are you making house calls?"

She ignored the mockery. "Is your mother home?"

"Yes. Is she expecting you?"

"Can I please see her?" she asked with an edge of impatience.

With a smirk and a sweep of his flute, he bowed and waved her inside. Then leaving her standing in the foyer, said, "I'll get her."

Helena had been in the Zen garden ruminating about discreet inquiries she had made within official circles. The word of the painting had not leaked out, but there were still two hitches. First, the lack of a date or inscription. Until she found out why, the painting must stay with Justine hidden in plain sight. And second, how Finny came to be the recipient. He had told Justine that it was a gift from two sisters, former clients. Were they aware of the painting's value? And did they give him a receipt? If not, did it legally belong to them, Finny, Justine, or no one? But if she, the art expert, were to talk to the sisters—she didn't know they were dead—it would attract attention. Soon there would be a line of predators and disaster would follow.

"There's someone here to see you." Her son's voice startled her back from her ruminations. Reluctantly she went in, with Bartram on her heels.

"Mother, I give you the healer of the sick and ambassadress of the infamous surgeon, Dr. Ouruk Zaron."

Helena threw a disapproving glance at her supercilious son and, irritation turning to genuine pleasure, gave her foster daughter a welcoming embrace. "Sandra. It's good to see you."

Sandra donned the professional smile that appeared more like a grimace.

"Let me look at you." Placing both hands on her shoulders, Helena peered into her face. What she saw behind the grin was an anxiety no social disguise could hide. She looked deeper, peering through the present Sandra for the Sandra of the past and future. "You have become a most lovely woman," she exclaimed as she deposited her on a sofa across from Bartram and sat at right angles to Sandra.

From there she continued studying her. Beautiful, certainly. Not even the shadowy rings under the eyes could disguise that. Like Justine, but more rounded, with the polished slimness that a sculptor like Bernini would have loved. She noted the effect on Bartram. His usual patronizing look had been replaced by genuine admiration.

But it wasn't Sandra's beauty or Bartram's admiration that interested her. It was a contradiction in her character. Sandra was so habituated to professional distance that she had isolated herself even from old friends. It was there in a series of false gestures—eyes that avoided contact, the unserious grin followed by laughter, a laugh on the edge of a cry. Dissatisfaction and longing leaked from her. Where was the idealistic young woman who saw good in the world? There still, but weighing on a heart that had once been light.

The three reminisced for a while, until there came, as Helena was sure there would, an awkward silence. Sandra would not say what was on her mind and Bartram exploited it. They were a duo playing against one another as they always had, Sandra's slow adagio against Bartram's witty scherzo, as if there were a general will to countermand the other's mood. So it was up to her, Helena, to guide them to a common tempo.

She was about to speak when Bartram interjected facetiously, "So tell us Sandra, what's Zaron really like? Does he use divine power to cure his patients, or are they healed by his shadow as he passes." Helena's annoyed look matched Sandra's. He noticed yet couldn't resist going further. "Does he expect you to anoint his head with oil and wash his feet with your hair?"

"Bartram, enough!" Helena snapped. Bartram lowered his eyes, and folding his hands as though in prayer, stared off to one side smiling.

Sandra, on the verge, caught herself, hesitated, then said, "I was wondering . . . that is, I talked to Justine today and mentioned stopping by this evening. She said," her voice turned ragged, "she couldn't see me." She hit a dead end. "Not just now but for the foreseeable future because . . . because there's a man there."

Like pennies popping off a dead man's eyes, Bartram's snapped open, "What? Who?"

Helena thought, "The only man Justine would be living with right now is Rothko." The clever girl had probably invented an admirer to keep Sandra away.

"I don't know." Sandra looked from one to the other anxiously. "I thought you might."

Egoism assuring him it was all a mistake, Bartram recovered from his initial surprise. He knew, surely everyone knew that Justine was in love with *him*. "Are you sure you aren't mistaken? Justine probably just has a friend over. Certainly not a lover."

His remark didn't lessen Sandra's concern. But as long as he was in the room, she would have little to confess. "Then," she implored Helena with a wail, "why didn't she name him?"

Helena, amused at this overreaction, took both on at the same time. "She's being discreet. She wants you to judge him, whoever he is, by what you see in *her*. Is she better because of him?" She added mildly, "I think I know who he is and I think she's better for it."

The two gave her a look of surprise. "Out with it, Mother," Bartram growled.

"I'm coming to that if you give me a chance. It's . . . Jonah Hartman," she announced dramatically.

Their astonishment was worth the fabrication. Bartram was so stunned that all the tics of self-consciousness dropped away and Sandra looked defeated, as if the name gave a reality she didn't want to accept.

"You're joking!" Bartram insisted. "Jonah Hartman, the choral director? That can't possibly be."

"The same." Helena answered innocently.

He sprang straight up like an unsnapped lock and began

pacing about the room. "But he's married, and to Victoria Vargas." Then added as though it trumped everything, "She's stunningly beautiful."

Helena grinned at his innocence. "You've never heard of a man with a beautiful wife having an affair?"

"Of course," he muttered, "but not Jonah Hartman. Not possible. He's at least," he exaggerated, "twenty-five years older. He's not Justine's type."

Bartram wasn't the only one in denial. Sandra looked positively shocked. "Justine told me about him," Helena said impishly. "She met him by chance in Piedmont Park. He very much impressed her. And apparently, she, him." The news that Sandra already knew began to sink in like lead. She should have agreed to meet him when Justine invited her to.

Bartram asserted with stiffened pride, "I know Justine. She wouldn't be involved with a married man unless he forced her into it."

Amused, Helena continued the mischief. "But you just argued that Jonah Hartman couldn't possibly be her type and that he wouldn't think of having an affair. Maybe Justine seduced him." That so horrified them both that Helena had to control her smile and her fibs.

This time it was Sandra who disputed her. "Justine would *never* have an affair with a married man. She remembers what *our* father did to our mother!" She reddened at the words.

Helena offered a silent thanks to the unconscious. How the smallest gesture—in this case, blood rushing into the face—gave one away!

What Bartram said next was unconnected to what Sandra said, though intimately connected to him. "Jonah Hartman and Victoria Vargas are world-famous singers. *I* know them both personally. Justine is a lovely, simple girl, and couldn't *possibly* compete with Victoria."

His mother retorted, "Everyone loves Justine and is attracted to her. Jonah Hartman is like that too. Why should it be impossible for two people so loving and so open to fall in love with one another? And what difference does age make?"

Bartram threw back his head, hands on hips, and fiercely denied it. "You don't really believe what you're saying. You analyze everything to tatters until there's nothing left."

"Whatever Justine and Jonah Hartman are doing," she resumed, "it's none of *our* business. Especially none of *your* business, Bartram. At least Sandra has an excuse." Bartram glared back as if it were *indeed* his business. "Now it's time for you to leave us so Sandra and I can talk . . . alone." Sandra looked grateful as Bartram took his flute and his ruffled dignity in hand and retreated upstairs.

"Now Sandra," Helena began. "Your concern is completely overblown. Justine is a grown woman and knows her own mind."

"She's never shut me out of her life, ever. If anyone is at fault, it's me. But she sounded so different on the phone. Not herself."

"Justine is so different from everyone else it's hard to say when she's different from herself. But," Helena paused to consider, "she's made me think of her differently. She's like a pane of glass, so transparent that you forget it's there. She has been in love with you, her mother, youth and springtime. Now she's discovering love has a cost."

The phrase "love has a cost" registered negatively on Sandra's face. She sought in vain for something that she was skirting—as if her will to will the truth had yielded to a will *not* to will it. "You don't understand my concern," she insisted, dismissing what Helena said—by deliberately missing it.

Helena was silent for a while. Then softly, "I've been your friend for years. But I can't help you if you don't tell me the truth."

"The truth?" The effect was explosive. Astonishment, apprehension, horror. "I don't know what you mean," she cried. Had she been lying? To Helena? To herself?

"Yes, you do."

Afraid of betraying herself, Sandra cast about for something, anything. "You think it's Russell?" Then taking a half-step in the direction of candor. "He may not be my dream partner or soul mate—if there is such a thing—but we're well-matched . . . in most ways." She laughed under her breath in contradiction. "We don't pretend we're in love."

"It's not Russell."

"You probably think it's my job. I am overworked and can get a bit isolated." She was pleading now. "But I love what I do and can't imagine doing anything else."

"It's not what you do."

"Then what is it?" She cried, torn between struggle and defeat.

"You're jealous. You want love, but you're not willing to *be* in love. And you feel its absence because Justine may have found it."

Sandra winced. It was not what she wanted to hear and she struggled to maintain control. "I have only Justine's welfare at heart."

"You want her to be happy in love, yes—but with guarantees and by your leave." Helena saw this stung and pressed further. "The practical world is risk-averse. It doesn't want passion. Passion is a suffering that you must be willing to undergo."

Tears welled up in Sandra's eyes that opened wider and wider to accommodate them. When one slipped down her cheek she lacked the courage to wipe it away.

Helena had not missed the alteration. Before she could say anything, she saw another desire surface. The desire not to know. It was apparent when Sandra backed away and looking at her watch, said she really must go.

Sandra left, preoccupied and unhappy. In the car she could no longer hold back the tears. She wept all the way home, and sat for some minutes parked in the garage trying to pull herself together. Every cherished opinion of herself had been on trial. It was one thing to be deceived, quite another to be shown she was deceived. And so, irritable and with thoughts that could find no place to rest, she went inside.

There she found Russell reading in the living room. When he saw the stiff face, he asked what was wrong. She shrugged him off testily. "It's nothing. Just overworked." When he pressed, she lied, "I'm worried about Justine. She's isolated in her new apartment."

When he said that Justine was a grown woman able to take care of herself, she refused to hear. "You're wrong. Justine is alone and unprotected. I'm responsible for her." She knew perfectly well she was being excessive, even wrongheaded. She was using the change in her sister to hide from Helena's words and hide the division in herself.

And when Russell insisted, "Justine's not alone. She has you and Helena and her father and uncle and Bartram," she exploded.

"Bartram? He's nothing to her! He doesn't care about her. He's wrapped up in himself."

"How can he be nothing to her?" He rubbed the razor stubble on his chin in bewilderment. "You've always said she was in love with him."

"She's not in love with him!" she sputtered. "There's someone else. She's *living* with someone." He had listened patiently to what made no sense and growled at her: "You just said she was all alone. Now you're saying a man is with her. So she's not alone." His tolerance on the subject of Justine was spent.

She answered evasively. "I have reason to think he's not good for her."

"Not *good* for her? Who is he?"

Knowing who he was, but caught in her own deceitful web, she hesitated, "I . . ." preparing the lie, "I don't know."

"Well if you don't know, how can you know he's not good for her?" He continued glooming at her, the flesh around his mouth gray with exasperation.

"Let's drop it!" she snapped, and to avoid a truth that imposed choice without guarantee, stormed out of the room.

9

In the beginning, at the intersection of two Creek Indian trails, before there was a city there, or streets to converge, before a place was there, a mile post was driven into the ground and named "Terminus." From a forgotten past, like a ghost arising into presence, Terminus, the ancient Roman god who presides over boundaries and limits was unknowingly invoked to mark the end, and the beginning, of two railroad lines.

The imaginary line, in either direction from nowhere, let a place arise, and a location come into being. A railway station was built at the Zero Mile Post and a tiny settlement named Lumpkinville after the governor. The settlement grew into a village renamed Marthasville for his daughter or, on some accounts, Atalanta, her middle name.

Then history grew there: A war, Jim Crow, segregation, Martin Luther King, Civil Rights, desegregation, the rise of the black middle class. Before urban sprawl and the white flight of the 60s, "Five Points" was a hub, a convergence of five streets fanning out from that original mile post. Russell Baramore grew there. A humble origin at the "Terminus" opened the story of a black boy from nowhere who was fascinated with the idea that you could put a stake in the ground in the middle of no place and make a beginning and an end. It was the power to decide the future. He longed to do the same—without fetters, free from the burden of the past, of what came before.

In 1996 the Summer Olympics came and the inner city brushed

itself off, slicked back its hair, and stood tall. Five Points once again became a terminus, this time a place where differences were celebrated and young boys could dream bigger dreams. Russell's dream was to become a doctor. That dream was a hunger that would turn a nobody into somebody. With passion, he tackled education and wrestled it to the ground. Passion gave him orientation, a homing device that always let him know where he was and where he was going. He attended the University and Medical School on scholarship and, with terminal degree in hand and letters at the end of his name, found a place for himself in a larger world.

His place was Zaron hospital where during his residency he met a fellow internist, Sandra Foxcroft. Whenever he was busy, the question of his identity was off his radar, but his admiration for Sandra's beauty and cultivation made him acutely conscious of their differences. The arts and social graces were not things she had to learn in school. As the daughter of a rich aristocrat and art collector they were in her DNA. She didn't identify herself by them or identify Russell by the labels he had accepted: black man from Terminus, Russell Baramore MD. She saw instead an intelligent, undefinable human being whom she could respect and trust. The two became friends, and later partners, sort of, a relation less of love than convenience. And so, substituting comfort and safety for passion, they moved in together.

Without thinking about it, without the concepts *to* think about it, Russell still lived with the problem of identity. Who was he really? Despite his achievements, he ran aground on sociology. His driver's license identified him. So did his social security card, his passport, and the MD. But he wasn't reducible to a number or a photograph or letters on a piece of paper. They were not who he was. Could the problem be with the notion of identity itself? The question was baffling. When a person was represented by a number, didn't that leave him out or reduce him to the rank of a measurable object? Wasn't that the problem in labeling himself black man or MD?

Or was all this presuming too much and too quickly? Maybe the question wasn't *who* assigned an identity *or how*? If he had been able to think all that through, it might have gone roughly like this: An identity card claims that the bearer of the card is *not* someone other than himself. But the identity attested to by the card, the assurance that he is the same as himself, comes from exterior authority. It validates or invalidates who one is and isn't. Then what about people who don't have a card and can't prove who they are? Doesn't that identify them as *un-identifiable?* As Russell's ancestors were identified as slaves, non-citizens, nobodies? And doesn't that open the way to ethnic cleansing by political ideologues? Then by extension, every racial extermination that rests on the claim to define anyone in this way. But he wasn't able to think all this.

At times when this anxiety about who he was subsided, Russell's sense of himself was of being indefinable, on the way to becoming and never fully arriving, like the nowhere that became an Indian trail, railroad post, station, settlement, village, hub—still on the way.

Whenever he got entangled in all this, Sandra accused him teasingly of falling back into his "Terminus mode." She would say, "You don't have to prove who you are to anybody, including the Zarons of the world—not even to yourself." It became a joke between them.

Then Russell met Justine, the sister, who, after hearing of his humble beginning and about Sandra's calling him "Terminus," quipped: "You mean my sister is with a man whose origin is a terminus?" She had to explain that it was a line from an Oscar Wilde play, *The Importance of Being Earnest*, where snobbish Lady Bracknel objects to her daughter marrying a nameless nobody found in a handbag in a railway station. The remark made Russell see the silliness of trying to define oneself as an object. But that wasn't all. Justine had more to show him. It happened like this:

One afternoon shortly after Sandra had visited Helena and had become "impossible" with Russell, Justine showed up on his doorstep. Sandra had been called in to sub for someone, so Russell was home alone, and consequently, not especially pleased to see her sister.

"Russell, is Sandra home? I need to talk to her." Her tone was anxious.

"She's not at home," he said off-the-cuff like someone about to shut the door.

"Oh!" was all she managed, and turned to go. She blushed at his lack of tact, but excused him. Why should he be tactful about something unknown to him?

Russell had not missed the charged look in her eyes, though he tried and failed to ignore it. "What's the matter?" he asked brusquely. His tone softened. "Something I can do?"

Her face lit up with shy hope. "It's silly." She didn't go on.

"What are you trying to say Justine?" he urged with an edge of annoyance.

She hesitated. Russell had always been distant and taciturn with her. "Someone has been following me," she said at last. She told him about the mysterious sedan and what happened when she tried to elude it. "Today I thought it was following me from work, so I didn't stop at home. I came over here instead." She sagged visibly.

That caused Russell to wonder about the mystery man she was supposed to be living with. Why didn't she tell *him*? Yet if he invited her to come in he'd be involved—again. He settled on the lesser evil of following her home in his sports car. As for her account of the sedan, he only half believed it, not because he thought her judgment unreliable but because it was a bother. But when a dark sedan cut in on him as he was following her and then slowed to a crawl in front of her building—that changed everything. Now he was reluctant to leave her alone and suggested they go somewhere to eat, and off they went together in his car.

It was exhilarating to drive in an open convertible on a spring day, especially with a companion he didn't feel obligated to impress. Rush hour had wound down and the air was permeated with brilliant pastels warmed by an orange sun. By the time they arrived at Babette's on Highland, Justine's charm had won him over. She was not only lively and intelligent but utterly lacking in pretense. With her he didn't have to play a role. She talked naturally and animatedly about art and music and work, described with humility her hopes for the future, and even shared his history and ambitions with enthusiasm. Relieved of the burden of an identity, he thought better of her for thinking so highly of him. The time together was so alive and free that later, glancing at his watch, he was surprised that two hours had melted away in her company.

He had never found her match-stick thinness and over-large eyes pretty. She had none of her sister's glamor. Her face was too large for her long neck and torso—until she smiled and readjusted his standard of beauty. If there had been sexual attraction, it would have compromised the ease between them. With her he sensed possibilities in himself entirely new that awakened a long dormant energy.

Unwilling now to relinquish her company, he proposed they go to the park to hear a reggae band. Enthusiastically she agreed and minutes later they were walking toward the bridge and pavilion on Lake Clara Meer, the mysterious black sedan long forgotten.

The sun was setting and shadows obscured the outline of the urban world, felt now rather than seen. The smell of the wet grass stirred memories in Russell that were usually tamped down by consciousness, and he felt expansive, as if his very humanity was enlarged with each breath.

When they reached the stone bridge it was already packed with people swaying to the joyful syncopations of the band in the gazebo. As a backdrop, tall buildings stood watch like sentinels over the scene with the lake in the foreground and the light from lamps around its perimeter reflecting off its surface. Rather than join the crowd on the bridge and overflowing the path, they made their way down a small incline to a grassy area beside the water where there were fewer people. Here they could see the vast dome of sky and stars above the lake.

Caught up in the infectious mood, Justine began swaying to the rhythm of the music with unaffected grace. It took Russell longer to forget himself as she had, but soon he too was slapping his thigh to the jaunty beat. From time to time he glanced at her with wonder. Why had he never noticed how unassuming and charming she was? Before, he had held her at a distance as a known entity, Sandra's pesky sister. But tonight she answered to no expectation. She was just herself on the basis of herself with her own inner glow. The music continued in a companionable silence until she remarked, "Look Russell." In the water a few yards away, a family of ducks was swimming toward them with gliding movements making gentle ripples in the glassy surface. She and Russell moved to the water's edge to get a better look. As she bent over on her haunches toward the ducks, she lost her balance and tumbled face forward into the lake. Without thinking Russell waded into the ankle-deep, murky water and pulled her out by the arm and shoulder. Her face and hair were covered in mud and water was dripping from her clothes.

"Are you all right?" he asked breathlessly, as a woman offered her a towel from a picnic basket.

Wiping mud from her face, Justine gurgled, "Some-one pushed me."

Several people volunteered that they had seen a man shove her. In the delight of the evening, Russell had forgotten about the black sedan. Remembering now, he glanced helplessly around the grassy knoll and up at the bridge. Whoever had done this would be long lost in the crowd. "Did you see what he looked like?" he asked those nearby. No one had. Then as he helped Justine wipe herself off, saw her shivering and draped his blazer over her shoulders. "Come home with me to clean up," he offered. "It's close by."

They made their way back to the car in silence. Justine had recovered sufficiently from her ordeal but Russell hadn't. His sense of danger and responsibility now was acute. He should have protected her in the park.

As soon as they entered the townhouse he sent her off to use his shower. It didn't occur to her to suggest her sister's shower instead, so strong was the sudden intimacy between them. Twenty minutes later she emerged in his bathrobe. She smiled shyly at him, holding the collar modestly against her neck. Even buried in his capacious robe, she maintained a quiet dignity. It made him choose his words carefully. "Your clothes have just come out of the washer. They should be dry in a half hour." He said it apologetically as if he had been somehow remiss. As she looked around hesitantly, he filled the awkward moment, "Would you like some coffee?"

"Oh yes, please," sitting down demurely on one corner of the sofa, feeling the strangeness of being in Sandra's townhouse with her not there. Their private space—Sandra's and Russell's—made her feel like an intruder.

He returned with the coffees, which she accepted with a winning smile, as he sat down beside her. Each took an embarrassed sip. "Well that was certainly quite an adventure," she laughed. He laughed too and gave her a hug. Still giggling she turned her face toward his, and he felt a sudden urge to kiss her. As her eyes widened in awareness, she drew back, then yielded. Afterwards, shocked and embarrassed, it was he who didn't know what to say. She filled in the gap. "My clothes are probably dry," she declared gently. "I should go now." With a grace that lent dignity to the caprice of the moment, she stood up and smiled serenely. The smile told him that the kiss was a gift given unexpectedly and forgiven, if forgiveness were needed. It let him see that it was not *she* he wanted, but the life-affirming desire for love and friendship without condition. Tonight she had bestowed that grace on him. Then she disappeared into the bathroom with her clothes and reappeared a few minutes later. With the kiss still troubling his thoughts, he drove her home in silence. So ended an evening charged with consequence that neither ever mentioned again.

10

Jonah lay awake in his king-sized bed staring at the side where Victoria usually slept. She was away again for a week of performances. While she was gone he stumbled on a mystery. Justine had given him the photos one day at lunch. At home, he had concealed them on the piano inside the score of *The Passion*. Then they disappeared. The day after Victoria left, he returned to pick up some music he had forgotten and found the photos gone. There being no evidence of a break-in and nothing out of place, he gathered up his music and left.

After class, he drove back to look again. There they were, just where he had left them! A mystery. Only he and Victoria had keys to the condo and she was in Zurich—wasn't she? If she was in Zurich, then who had gained entry? That preoccupied him, especially late at night when he couldn't sleep.

And there was more. He had never doubted his love for his wife but wondered if their passions had now irrevocably diverged. Love wasn't reducible to the feelings of two individuals for each other. To endure, it demanded more. Music had always been that *more*—but no longer.

In recent months Victoria had often come home late from her travels. Flights missed or delayed, last minute changes to an itinerary, extra days for rehearsal—these were the vagaries of performing. Until an accumulation that hinted at something else. What made an abrupt turn in his memory was the look of suspicion on her face the last time she came back, as though mistrusting him because of something in herself.

It took only a minimal amount of digging to find discrepancies in what she claimed to be doing and where. And that made him wonder if these inconsistencies and the disappearance and reappearance of the photos might be connected. Words kept running in his head: *"In perilous plight defend my right, / O Lord, from double faces."*

If two days ago Jonah had been a fly on the wall, he would have seen Victoria kiss him goodbye and twenty minutes later kiss her lover hello. She was indeed on her way to Zurich for two weeks—but by way of two nights with Zaron in Tuxedo Hills. Though the affair still carried an aura of the new and clandestine, the lovers were already easily irritated with one another. Both high strung, ego-centric, and used to having their way, each had little patience for the other's caprices and even less inclination to accommodate them.

Zaron had grown up rootless. His father's back-room deals, mistresses, and lawsuits kept the family moving from place to place, school to school, crisis to crisis, always with the same haphazard indifference and lack of cohesion. As a young boy, Zaron wanted to be many things. One year a race-car driver, the next a painter, the third an engineer, art dealer or bookie. At fourteen he was already a dilettante with an air of privilege that mattered more than achievement. At eighteen he decided to become a physician—not just any kind, but a surgeon. His object was a respected career above the street skills of his father, but in which he could pursue the same goals: money, power, and reputation.

Despite his lust for Victoria and a begrudging acceptance of her demands, he saw their affair in terms of mutual self-interest. So did she, but with a caveat that raised the bar on what he was expected to pay. Not just expensive jewelry, clothes, and other gifts, but adulation, subservience or what she called respect.

It was their second day together after a two-week absence and she immediately assumed the role of *diva*, Italian for goddess, and demanded fresh caviar.

"Look Vicki," he protested, "I don't mind when you call me from Zurich or Verona to tell me about some wonderful thing you just have to have, but I'm not the hired help."

"Whatever do you mean? I'm Latina. I expect a man to treat me as a woman, as if I'm precious, to adore and to worship me. That is how a Latin man treats a woman."

He sniggered. "Is that how your husband treats you?"

She shook her black tresses angrily. "This has nothing to do with him. But yes, he treats me with respect and honor."

"Honor!" He laughed sarcastically. "That's an interesting word."

She glowered at him haughtily and stalked off to her room in the pavilion. Twenty minutes later she reappeared dressed in street clothes. "I left my score for *Traviata* at home. I have to get it."

"What about your husband?"

"He'll be at the University in a class. I'll be back quickly but I need your chauffeur to drive me."

She entered the condo in a rush trying to remember where she had left the score. Searched the living room shelves and the piano bench in haste, paged through the music on the piano stand, and something fell to the floor. It was a folder with a sheaf of glossy photos, front and back views of a large blue painting. Her mind clicked. That lost painting that Bartram had mentioned and Zaron had grilled her about. She smiled and carefully laid the folder aside. Then recalling that the music for *Traviata* was in a suitcase she had decided not to take, retrieved it from the bag and left.

A few minutes later she handed the folder to Zaron.

"What's this?"

"Something that might interest you. You can't keep them. They have to be returned before my husband notices they're gone."

He withdrew the photos. "My God! The Rothko!" He glared at her mistrustfully and demanded sharply. "How did he get these?"

She shrugged. "I haven't the faintest idea." For once he accepted her explanation. Within the hour the photos were copied and the original set returned on the piano inside the score of *The Passion*.

Phineas McGinley was driving his vintage convertible with the top down and his spirits up. He loved the skyscrapers towering above him as though he was driving through a steep canyon open only to the sky. Two buildings were his favorites. One looked like a crazy Mayan temple stair-stepped for giants, and the second like interlocked Legos with two Greek temples above a sort of multiple-domed church. They reminded him of mid-eastern churches in photographs, proving even to skeptics that the spirit of religion was still alive—but translated to secular business.

He passed his Midtown favorite, the Atalanta Bank, with its gilded-topped, open lattice-work pyramid that at night blazed like the richest gold. And then 1100 Peachtree, a wedding cake topped with a pointed octagon. He thought of it still as Bell South even though it was occupied now by its global conglomerate. The names of the tallest buildings had changed over time, Fortune 500 companies replacing other Fortune 500 companies. All part of the wonderful world of Atlanta real estate.

Real estate. To him the words were magic. Real: physically existing blocks, verifiable, tangible, solid, knowable. Estate: landed property of considerable size and wealth. That's what this city was—*Real* estate: commercial, profitable, global. A shame then when they replaced some old-fashioned residences that were taking up space in Midtown and put up the Woodruff Arts Center. It turned the commercial heart of real estate into a so-called center for culture. Art and the Symphony and stuff of that ilk were important, but not necessary to business. Artsy buildings ought to be built someplace where they don't interfere with commerce, like the University. Of course he could never say that, not when his dearly-loved dead sister, detested former brother-in-law, and beloved nieces were culture fanatics. And then there was Helena Gandolfi who, if she heard him say this, would waterboard him with arguments about art until he came up gasping on her side.

Still, through it all, he was a loyal resident who had never left the city even during desegregation and the white flight in the '60s. He was proud of being a true born southern boy—a native. There weren't many of those in Atlanta, not since Sherman burned the place down and Yankee industry built it back up. As kids he and his sister had known a sleepy, laid-back city with a downtown that ran from just north of Davison's department store a mile or so up to Rich's. A whole world was in that space: local banks like Citizen's and Southern, and movie theaters like The Rialto and Lowe's Grande. Public institutions too: the Carnegie Library and the Post Office, and elegant office buildings like the Healey and the Chandler. And the food! The sandwich shop at Davison's where he and his sister ordered toasted chicken salads and chocolate malted milk, or Emile's, where they served French pancakes and the walls were decorated with scenes of Paris cafes. And the big old churches where Sunday really meant a day of rest. And the shiny Gold Capital that was still the symbol of government. All remnants of a time when people and residences huddled around the downtown like chicks around a hen. Back then Midtown was just an area to pass through on the way there. It wasn't its own place yet, except for Mammy's Shanty serving Southern food like fried shrimp and pecan pie. His heart felt a tug of nostalgia when he recalled it all.

But that was the past. After the mighty interstates sliced through Atlanta, cutting off one half of the state from the other half of the state, the city stagnated just long enough to become what it is today: modern and new. Old buildings like the wedge-shaped Flat Iron Building, The Ponce, and The Biltmore still survived, though dwarfed into insignificance by high-rises as tall and solid as mountains. *They* were the future. And as the largest producer for Dorston Alsop Real Estate he, Phineas McGinley, was proud to have contributed to the buying and selling of it all. So why should he let a weird painting that almost no one had seen and that anyone with any common sense and feet on the ground couldn't make sense of—why should he let it bother him still?

He checked his phone. He was on his way to meet Helena at his office, and with an hour to kill before their appointment, he didn't want to waste it on that "thing." What could he do? A strange idea popped into his head: Go for a walk. But where? He never walked anywhere if he could help it. In the suburbs and Buckhead, street life takes place on the roadway, but Midtown was traversable on foot. So he parked on 10th and set off through Piedmont Park. Hampered by muscles long unused, he had to stop every few yards and catch his breath. He paid no attention to the greenery. Trees and grass were stage props for real estate. But he was amazed by what he did see: people everywhere strolling, running, pushing strollers, riding bikes, or simply idling. Sitting on benches, at picnic tables or on the ground talking, laughing, eating, drinking. And not just in the park but in outdoor cafes that lined the nearby streets. How strange! Apparently, you could stroll about Midtown and the park and never feel the emptiness of sidewalks rolled up promptly at five.

But why, he wondered, were they doing nothing on a busy weekday? A walking city, where you inhabit space by strolling through it without aim or purpose was alien to him. Everyone knows that purpose is the essence of modern life, commercial life. Yet in walking through the park his body recalled a memory lost since childhood. It was the flaneur's purposeless strolling that turns its back on the crowd even as he is swept up by it. It was happening to him. He was being dragged backwards into the future toward a city so new it was *old*. He didn't know the word flaneur—stroller, dawdler, idle man about town. But it was what Phineas McGinley for one fleeting hour in early spring became as he discovered an American Paris in his backyard.

A short while later, he waited in his office for Helena with a mounting sense of dread. She arrived as a voice in a whirlwind wanting to know everything about the sisters who had given him the painting. She peppered him with so many questions he could scarce find breath or wit to answer. After rummaging through his files, he dredged up a scrap of paper, handwritten, that said "one large painting in blue 6 x 5 feet to P. McGinley February 2015," signed, "Sophie Sverdlov." He handed it to Helena. She shook her head in dismay. "This is all? No title, artist, or provenance? No other authentication?"

With a longsuffering expression, he looked at her in the good faith of his blankness. "This and the tube to put the dang thing in." He still refused to call it a painting.

She controlled her impatience. "And what about the stretcher and cross bars? Where are they?" His vacant look increased her exasperation. "You know, the wood bars on the back that stretch the canvas and hold it together."

"I don't know what she did with them. She gave it to me rolled up in the metal tube and I gave it that way to Justine."

"Where are the sisters now?"

"Dead."

"Both of them?"

"Yes."

"How long ago?"

"I don't know. Several months."

"Who has their house now?"

He looked it up in his real estate records. "It was sold recently."

"To whom?"

"Doesn't say."

"What do you mean, doesn't say?"

"It's listed to a surrogate." When her severe gaze demanded

that he explain he went on. "It happens. The surrogate, an individual or company purchases it so the real purchaser is kept anonymous."

She groaned almost to herself. "Then it may be too late."

"Too late for what?"

"To find the stretcher bars."

"What for?"

"To look for the artist's signature and a date!" It was all she could do to keep from shouting.

"Who is the artist?" he asked innocently.

Dumbfounded. "You still don't know?"

"No."

"Why, Mark Rothko of course!"

His eyes bugged out of his head. Then it *was* painted by him? The artist of the color blobs? The one he saw at the High? He thought uneasily of a second anonymous email more threatening than the first: "You are at grave risk if you continue to hold a stolen painting. Give it back immediately or suffer the consequences."

She stared hard at him. "Everything I tell you and everything we've discussed must be kept in absolute confidence. Do you understand? Everything! It's not only Justine's safety that depends on it. It's yours as well."

He had never seen Helena so commanding. "The world out there," she pointed outside, "is savage with globalization and domination and will stop at nothing, no price or corrupt act to possess the painting." The nominalizations added a sinister note as if they carried more weight than ordinary nouns. She added more, keeping it up, filling it out, crowding it in, forcing a picture upon him of a world gone amuck, until he felt his goose flesh rise.

She was going to announce the discovery of the painting, she said, but not reveal who owned it. "You must not let anyone know of the receipt from the sisters. The ownership will probably be contested. I'm sure it's a Rothko but without an inscription that too will be open to debate. For now, if the word gets out, the rumor must be that it's *yours*, not Justine's."

Why did he attract such evils? He could take in no more of the horrors she envisioned and resolved to withhold what he knew and hadn't said. Anxiety returned with the throb of a toothache. He might have to tell Helena about the sister's cottage after all.

11

Atlanta's Fourth Ward late Sunday night. It's a lively area near downtown reclaimed from urban blight, where tonight the streets are quiet, almost sepulchral. Phineas McGinley drives slowly and deliberately on his nightly route. Turns right off Freedom Parkway into an area rescued from old factories and warehouses by lofts and condos and slows to a crawl past Justine's apartment. Finding nothing amiss, he slowly wends his way back to Midtown. Though it's unlikely anyone would attempt something criminal in a building so well-protected, the nightly cruise assuages his conscience. What had started out as a sop to guilt has become an obligation to protect Justine from evil.

As he turns onto Ponce something makes him waver. As a superstitious man, he gives undue credit to what he calls "instinct," a kind of hunch or sixth sense that has served him well in real estate. The belief is so strong, that the times his hunches have been wrong are forgotten. Relying on his intuition now, he turns around and heads back for one last survey.

All seems well at Justine's building . . . until . . . Wait! A light in her living room window? No. There again, light . . . in motion. Doubting the instinct he uncritically trusts, he parks and looks again. It's late. If he calls it might frighten her—if she's even home. He counts the seconds to thirty and is about to leave when . . . There! Light—moving in circles behind the blinds! Getting out of the car, he runs across the street where his way is blocked by an electric gate.

How to get inside? Not a particularly agile man, overweight and under exercised, he faces the insurmountable barrier with its vertical points at the top. Grasping two of the uprights, he lifts a leg to a foothold and tries to hoist himself up. He slips and misses. The iron clangs loudly. Panting, he tries again. Clang! Misses again. The third time he makes it halfway. One foot swings over as an ankle scrapes sharply against the metal and rips a pants leg. He strains to get the other leg over and an iron post jabs him in the buttocks. "Ouch!" he mutters, lifting himself off the point. He teeters, hands behind on two uprights for support, and jumps. As he lands, his knees give way and he collapses face down on the ground. Tentatively he lifts his head off the pebbles and tries to get up. First one hand and knee, then the other, finally succeeds. Shaking, puffing, aching all over, he hobbles stumbling to the back entrance where he finds the door unlocked and a piece of duct tape over the latch. He limps down the hall to Justine's unit.

All the while, Justine, having gone to bed early after a long and anxious day, lies awake in bed staring at the ceiling. She has not slept well since Helena asked her to keep the painting a while longer. Love of the world is being tested and with it her trust. Reality has forced her to think skeptically about what she once loved with abandon.

She hears a sound, she thinks, reaches for the phone under her pillow, listens, again hears nothing, and begins to doze. Startled awake, she sits up in her men's pajama top, the phone still clutched in her hand. Listens. Nothing. Waits. About to drop back into her pillow, she hears a tiny scratching sound like an animal. She strains, and it comes again. Her entire body is an ear as she slides out of the covers, pulls on a t-shirt and shorts over pajama top, and creeps cautiously into the dark living room. Again, the tiny scraping sound. Perhaps at the door. Heart in her throat, the hair rises on her arms as she watches the knob turn slowly. Someone trying to get in! She creeps back into the bedroom and commands her shaking hands to press a number on the phone. The ringing pounds in her ear. "Hello" an alert voice says.

"Someone's trying to break in," she whispers nervously.

"Call 911!" Jonah insists.

"I can't. They're after the painting! Police will ask questions."

"Then get out of there! I'm coming."

She might escape by breaking the window in her bedroom. But she can't move. They'll find the painting before Jonah gets here. She must prevent them. Awkwardly, with hands still shaking, she reaches under the bed and pulls out the metal tube. Lifting one end above her head, she stands trembling behind the bedroom door. A flash of light through the crack. Her thumping heart deafens her. Another click and the knob on the front door slowly turns. The door opens, and a flashlight searches the dark space. One . . . two dark shapes. Then a circle of light on the living room wall and a voice. "Is that it?" Another voice, "Must be." Falling back on a forgotten habit, she begins to pray.

Finny bursts through the front door. Flickering lights reveal in the darkness two figures all in black, faces and heads covered. One tall and slender, the other short and squat. The short one holds a knife over the portrait of Kate on the wall. The other holds the light. "Stop!" Finny loudly croaks. The stocky man drops the knife.

Finny is unable to move, his face contorted in fear. The tall man holds up his hands in a sign of peace. "We won't hurt you," he whispers. Finny tries to say something but the saliva has dried in his throat. The tall man shines the flashlight on his face and adds through the mask, "It's all right."

A sudden flash and the overhead lights go on. Justine springs from the bedroom. The tall slender man whirls about and faces her wielding a long metal pipe. Frozen in time she and he stare wildly into each other's eyes.

Later Justine will recall it in wonder, as she will recall the gold color of the eyes and the dark abyss of the pupils behind the mask. But this is reacting, not thinking. He tries to fend her off, "I won't hurt you. It's all right!" But it's too late. She slams the metal tube like a bat sideways across the man's face, hitting him squarely under the nose. Blood gushes down his mask.

The squat man, seizing the moment, runs over Finny in the door, causing him to fall backwards and smack his head on the tile floor. Justine drops the metal tube, races to his side and wails, "Uncle Finny!" The tall man, seeing his chance, leaps nimbly over Finny's body as Jonah appears in the doorway. He instinctively makes a fist that lands on the man's jaw. As he reels backwards, Jonah grabs him by the shirt but he wrenches free and escapes.

Justine, kneeling beside a prone body with a knife clutched in her hands cries, "Uncle Finny, Uncle Finny, speak to me!" The eyes are closed, the face blue, and blood pools on the floor beneath his head. She bends over to check his breath, lets the blade slip and it slices open her palm.

Retrieving a dish towel from the kitchen, Jonah wraps it round her wound. "Who is he?" he asks breathlessly.

"My Uncle Finny," she cries, tears streaming down her face. "Is he . . . ?"

"He's breathing. I called 911. Are you all right running girl?" Then spotting the metal tube, "Did they get it?"

"I'm fine," she answers numbly. "They didn't get it."

"But the tube?"

"It isn't in there. It's . . ." She looks up on hearing the sound of a policeman, now framed in the doorway, pistol at the ready.

Jonah points to the back entrance. "Two burglars in masks out that way! We need an ambulance! This man and woman are injured."

◆

Sandra is having an easy night at the hospital. There is an uncanny quiet at 2 a.m. During the day she deals with multiple tasks at once: new patients, staff meetings, consultations with other physicians. But late at night, freed from human interference, the hospital takes on an eerie calm.

Here, over a cup of bad coffee, Sandra has time to think about personal things pushed aside by expedience. She and Russell don't love each other. They've never loved each other. It's been a relationship of exchange at a reasonable price. "We each wanted our due," she thought, "only then would we agree to love in return. But *that* isn't love."

She peers at the dregs in the bottom of her cup, yearning for something cast aside. Her reverie is interrupted by a shout. "Sandra!" She is surprised to see Justine in shorts and t-shirt with a pajama top underneath and a bloody towel wrapped around her hand. Justine throws herself into Sandra's arms sobbing, "It's Uncle Finny. Downstairs in emergency. Unconscious."

"Uncle Finny?"

"Someone tried to rob me. Finny came. I don't know how. The robber . . . robbers . . . he, one of them, knocked him down. He's bleeding. Bled."

Passing over the incoherence, Sandra asks, "Finny is bleeding?"

"From the back of the head. Oh hurry!" Together they run down the hall, catching their breaths in the elevator where Sandra asks, "What happened to your hand?"

"I cut it. Stupid. It's all right."

She directs Sandra to the cubicle where Finny is lying on a gurney attended by a medic. Beside him is a tall man with a lion's mane of dark curls and an unreadable expression. Sandra stops lifeless. Lights flash before her eyes. It's the man from the park! *Jonah Hartman*, his dark eyes, even here radiating intelligence. Dizzy, she struggles to command herself. "How is he?" she asks the medic.

"I ordered an MRI," he answers. "He'll be fine."

Under the gaze of the man who has preoccupied Sandra for weeks, her world takes on a different tonality. She is divided between awareness of him, of feeling herself feeling his presence, and demands that eliminate everything not reducible to a medical object. The body on the gurney needs her skill, yet he is flesh of her flesh, a beloved Uncle. A shocked bystander is a beloved sister who needs her reassurance. Setting aside the human, she recurs to the processes of medicine. With practiced hands, she examines Finny. "And the bleeding?" she asks the medic mechanically.

"A surface wound."

"He appears to have only a mild concussion," she says to Justine with a reassuring nod, and gives an order to the attendant. "Send him up to me overnight just to be sure."

He leaves. In the space opened by his absence everything shifts.

Jonah is following Sandra's every move, attending to everything she says. Not shallow curiosity but thinking. Under his scrutiny, she feels objects stand out from the indistinct background. The harsh florescent lights, humming machines, the smell of disinfectant, the cold room. She shivers, feeling graceless and dull in her white coat and scrubs. Lifting her eyes to Jonah, the two stare at one another without speaking. Riven by the intensity, she turns away and pretends to check Finny's vital signs.

"You're a doctor?" Jonah asks.

"Yes. Dr. Foxcroft. I'm a hospitalist here." She reddens like a school girl.

"Dr. *Foxcroft*?" He asks puzzled.

Justine, whom they have forgotten, pipes up. "Jonah, this is my sister Sandra. Sandra, this is Jonah Hartman." A perfunctory nod, as if they hadn't met already.

"You're the sister of the running girl!" He looks at Justine then at her as if tracing the family resemblance. Sandra tries to smile but her facial muscles refuse to oblige.

"She's my *big* sister," Justine answers proudly, and turning in her direction, "Jonah is a hero. He rescued me." She looks up at him with wonder. "I shall always love him for that." Sandra receives the words as a blow. Pieces of a world unthought have tumbled in a torrent on her tonight. Everything else, everything left out, has broken in.

Justine meanwhile continues her narrative: "If Jonah hadn't come, I don't know what would have happened to Uncle Finny and me. The burglars tried to steal the portrait of mother. Jonah was marvelously brave," she warbles, the emphasis on *marvel*. "He struck one of them in the face." He frowns uncomfortably as she beams at him.

Animatedly she describes their ordeal, as Sandra listens in a state of paralysis. Justine looks adorable, with hair tousled in wisps around her face and her eyes batting a blessing on everyone. Sandra's thoughts run something like this: "Can anyone resist her charm? Resist falling in love with her? He came when she called, rescued her. Isn't that proof?" He is listening intently to everything Justine says with the warmest expression—though occasionally his eyes move from Justine to her with a question. It's all Sandra can do to hold back tears of disappointment.

She wonders if he really is married. His arms are folded so she can't tell until he lifts his left hand to scratch the stubble on his chin and reveals a wedding band. Married! And having an affair with her sister! She winces as Justine smiles at Jonah and he smiles back.

"Will Uncle Finny be all right, Sandra? In the ambulance when I was holding his hand, I thought for a moment he squeezed my hand."

Sandra's pager interrupts. She ignores it and answers the question in detail—with Jonah listening intently, as Russell walks in.

"Sandra, answer your pager," Russell chides. "You're needed upstairs." Still she delays, gives Justine a hug, and holds out a hand to Jonah which he clasps tightly, and holds on a moment longer than necessary.

"Nice to meet you," she says lamely.

His face is awash with questions, but all he can say is, "And you." Then, as if walking from a lighted place into a dark tunnel, she goes, leaving her heart behind.

12

"I heard on my floor about an assault and burglary. Were *you* involved?" Russell asks, looking curiously from Justine to Jonah. It's only an idle wish to know something at no cost to himself. Justine obliges with a brief account interrupted by two police officers who need a statement. Then another interruption when two medical attendants show up to take Finny to a room on Sandra's floor.

As Justine and Jonah leave and Russell is about to return to his own floor, a young man walks in through the emergency entrance, his face bleeding and his clothes smeared with blood. Olas Lindgard, the man who works for Sir Reginald! The Apollo who had caught everyone's attention on Russell's floor a few weeks earlier. Apollo stares for a second at the retreating figures of a young woman and a tall, dark-haired man and through swollen lips and a cloth pressed to his nose says, "I had an accident with my bike. I think I might have broken my nose and cracked my chin."

Russell motions him into the cubicle just vacated by Justine and Jonah and draws the curtain. He isn't assigned to the ER and knows perfectly well he should be on his own floor, not examining *their* patient. "Let me see," he says, as he inspects the young man's wounds.

Despite being bruised and swollen-faced, Olas Lindgard is fair beyond the measure of men. His fairness is not physical beauty only. It evokes an atmosphere, an aura of mystery. It summons a faraway mood of fjords, deep inlets and a distant elusiveness. Every gesture, every shift in his features speaks to an indefinability that prevents Russell from reducing him to a distinct object.

Russell gently examines the cuts on Olas' face. Their eyes meet in an awareness that no gaze can sustain, and something passes between them better left untouched. Yet Russell desperately wants to see *more*, not just the visible. Shaken, he turns away to fetch gauze and swabs. "Your nose isn't broken but it will hurt like hell for a while. How did this happen?" Moments ago, he had responded with indifference to Justine's account of the burglary. But this is not curiosity, not the idle desire to know something just for the sake of knowing. It's deeper. Intent on Olas, what he most desires is not given to knowledge.

Olas replies perfunctorily about the bike trail at night and changes the subject. "Who was that leaving with the police when I came in? The girl and the man with the dark curly hair?"

It's an odd question and Russell hesitates. "It was the sister of a colleague and the man who rescued her. Apparently from an attempted burglary." Having seen Olas come from Zaron's office just weeks ago, Russell is reluctant to say more. The question he does *not* ask is, "Why don't you know the daughter of Sir Reginald Foxcroft?"

"The man who rescued her I suppose was a neighbor or relative?" Olas' tone is strangely incongruous with one suffering from his injuries.

Russell is staring again and Olas feels him staring. He can't keep his eyes off Olas, whose hair and face glow like that of an ancient Roman sprinkled with gold dust. "I don't know who he was. I didn't get a chance to ask." Unasked is why Olas has been on the beltline at two in the morning when it closes at 11. Though Russell is needed back on his floor, he delays with an excuse: "You're in shock and could probably use a cup of coffee. I'll take you there."

Olas consents and Russell leads the way through a long empty hall to the hospital snack bar. He dispenses coffee from one of the machines and they sit down together. At this hour no one else is in the room and the emptiness fairly shouts their nearness.

After a long, awkward silence, Russell attempts conversation. "I know you work for Sir Reginald . . ." He leaves the sentence dangling. "Is that all you do?"

"I'm an artist." Olas offers.

The answer is unexpected, and Russell smiles as worry shifts from mistrust to caution. "What kind of artist?" It's too little to ask for the too much he wants to hear.

"A painter. I'm studying at the University."

"The University," he echoes. "What kind of painter?" The question awakens ideas he's never thought about.

Olas smiles as if the question is not limited to a category. "The short answer is a painter who paints the void. I'm also studying mathematics."

Russell is hungry for more, even if in his dazed state he doesn't understand. "Mathematics and painting?" His brow wrinkles in puzzlement.

Spurred by his interest, Olas explains. "Yes, strange as it sounds. Set theory is the mathematics based on zero or the void." Then in an about face, he interrupts himself by asking, "Do you like Rothko?"

Russell answers eagerly. "I do. I'd like to own one." Anything to keep Olas there a while longer.

It's all Olas needs for continuing a favorite subject. "Then you know how Rothko presents sets of two, or sometimes three or more rectangles, multiples within multiples? But he does it without counting or unifying his rectangles into a totality. It's like set theory." He attributes Russell's absorption to the wrong thing and, encouraged, goes on. "The blurred and smudged rectangles have a deliberate unfinished quality, so they can't be separated into objects." His words are mesmerizing. "When we look at a Rothko we see a complete incompleteness." Olas looks off into space, gazing at the painting in his mind.

All this makes little sense to Russell, but it brings something else to mind for the man whose origin is a terminus. Isn't *he* too an incompleteness—blurred, smudged, unfinished? "Well," he says, a little warily, "I don't know what to say." Then he changes the subject. "I saw you in the hospital the other day. You seemed to be coming from Dr. Zaron's office." He doesn't ask why Olas would be working for Sir Reginald and fraternizing with his enemy.

Olas grins and answers boldly, "A man has to eat." When Russell looks uncomfortable, Olas does not miss the change. "I guess I'd better be going. Thanks for the coffee and the face lift."

He gets up and leaves, but Russell remains seated.

The night has been filled with strange new impressions. The talk about art reminds him of a painting by Turner he had viewed with Sandra at an exhibition. It was of an angel standing in the sun. At the time he didn't think much of a scene without form and color. Like trying to see a whiteness so bright it obliterates its object. But tonight, with Olas he has felt what the painting attempts to show. He sighs deeply, then like an automaton seeing nothing, retraces his footsteps down the long hall, and takes the elevator to his floor.

◆

The same night that Jonah and Justine couldn't sleep in their respective beds and Finny made his nightly round past her apartment and Sandra and Russell worked their shifts at the hospital and Olas Lindgard had an accident on the beltline—that same night Helena and Bartram went to Druid Hills. The former went with a plan, the latter grumbling. What prompted this late-night outing was something Finny had tried and failed to conceal from Helena when they met at his office. Noting the evasive look on his face, she had said impatiently, "For God's sake Finny, I am not a conjurer out to trick you! What haven't you told me?" Sheep-faced, he answered that the cottage belonging to the two sisters who had given him the painting was being demolished.

She had rebuked him for holding this news back. "We need to find those stretcher bars even if there's no name on them. Otherwise the authorities will conclude there's something fishy about the sisters giving *you* the painting and *your* giving it to Justine. You could be accused of being a secret art dealer or, since you're related, a surrogate for Regie. Maybe even a fence of stolen art." As though that weren't sufficient to turn Finny abject with worry, she had piled on more, "I know a lawyer who specializes in tracking art and he works for Ouruk Zaron! If Zaron bought the sisters' house, he may have already discovered the bars. Then you and Justine *are* in his sights." Exasperation conquered tolerance. "You are a fool Finny not to have told me!" In response Finny's pudgy face had curdled with pain.

Immediately after learning this news, Helena had driven past the house in Druid Hills, a hilly wooded section of town near the University, where she discovered that demolition was indeed underway. A large dumpster heaped with debris was parked in the driveway. To enlist Bartram's help, she would have to tell things that had been kept from him: the discovery of the painting, Finny and Justine's part in it, the missing pieces of wood, and her plan. When she explained, he vigorously objected, and she blithely overruled him. "I can't ask Finny. He wouldn't be able to tell the difference between a wood bar and a 2-by-4."

So here they were at 1:30 in the morning dressed in old clothes and armed with flashlights, about to raid a dumpster full of trash. The cottage belonging to the sisters was set back from the street up an incline and nearly hidden under a forest of old trees. It was a typical Craftsman bungalow with a peaked roof and deep front porch running its width. The front door was boarded up and plywood had been laid over the steps to facilitate removal. It was an odd way to demolish a house—odd, unless there was something valuable inside.

Helena instructed Bartram what they were looking for. "Heavy duty stretcher bars should have traces of M. Rothko or M. R. in printed letters on it, and a date. Be sure to wear your gloves. We don't want *your* fingerprints on them." He knew enough to justify resisting the instructions with a superior look. And when he saw the jumble of lumber and plaster chunks and shards of glass and rusted metal, he rolled his eyes and grimaced. "We'll end up killing ourselves."

"What we'll do is examine the contents systematically. Push aside anything large, or drop it out of the dumpster," she instructed matter-of-factly. "Look for the keys or shims." She put her hands on the metal edge of the dumpster, stretched one leg over the side, straddled the top, lifted the other leg over and carefully lowered herself inside.

He climbed in after. "Whoa," he yelped, as he slipped on the shifting debris and lost his footing.

"Not so loud," she whispered. "You take one end and I'll take the other." They made their way carefully in opposite directions, stumbling across the shifting contents, trying to avoid sharp edges.

"How do you expect to find anything in this mess in the dark," he carped, tossing aside pieces of lumber indiscriminately. A steady stream of complaints echoed in the night air as he dug. These were accompanied by mutters, groans, snorts, and quips about "wild goose chases" and "snipe hunts." But after a while, resigned to his fate, he followed his mother's lead and systematically examined every odd piece of lumber before discarding it. In no time, there was a significant pile beside the dumpster that would have to be put back once their quest was over.

The more hopeless this search for a needle in a rubbish heap, the more vigorously Helena exerted herself. A picture came to mind from Dickens of the poor nineteenth-century souls who sifted the dust mounds, as the trash hills around the periphery of London were called. After an hour finding nothing, bruised, bent and sore, she turned her flashlight on Bartram, sitting on the edge of the dumpster making glum comments. "What would happen to my reputation," he grumbled, "If I were found illegally rummaging in a dumpster in the middle of the night on private property! You did notify the press, didn't you?"

Helena ignored him. But in another half hour, even she was ready to give up when she heard a loud "Ouch!" followed by another expletive. Bartram had slid on a piece of stone and got himself wedged between two large pieces of plaster.

"Are you all right?" she asked.

"Of course, I'm not all right! A gigantic sliver has gone through my glove and under my nail!"

Helena stumbled awkwardly toward him. "Let me see your hand," she commanded. With a groan he bared his wound like St. Sebastian with many arrows. The point of a sliver several inches long had wedged beneath the nail of his middle finger.

"I'll probably never play the flute again," he moaned, and snatched his hand from her grasp. The movement caused his footing to shift again and bang his knee hard against something. "Shit!" he yelled. He bent down to rub his knee with the bad hand and it brushed against a cardboard box protruding beneath some pieces of metal. Pulling on it with his good hand, the box spread open. Inside were several wedge-shaped pieces of wood. He shone a light on them. Thin pieces joined in the middle. He looked more closely. Cross bars! "Mother," he cried. Helena turned her light in his direction. Forgetting the pain in his finger, he cried gleefully. "I found it, Mother. I found it. M. Rothko, 1970." Yes, there it was on an angled piece in faded letters, an open double loop of the letter M, a fat period, the large cursive Rothko, and a date—1970! She sat down abruptly on a chunk of plaster, turned her face to the sky, and stared. Is this the stuff dreams are made on?

"That's it. You found it, Bartram. I can't believe it."

"Neither can I." Their elation did not last long. It was interrupted by the sound and lights of a car slowly moving up the driveway.

"Quick, grab all the pieces you can reach," she commanded, "and give them to me." He handed her as many as he could retrieve from the box. "Now get out of there!" Offering him her free hand, she helped pull him up from the debris and they scrambled out of the dumpster in a panic.

"What about the stuff we discarded?" he asked of the large mound heaped next to the dumpster.

"Leave it, you fool! Run!" They rushed into the woods behind the house just as the car reached the top of the drive. They never looked back, just ran like frightened deer down a hill and through several back yards to their car and raced away.

13

The adventure in the dumpster—the pain and jubilation—was tempered by news of the burglary. Helena received a call from Jonah early the next morning.

"What if the burglars had succeeded?" she speculated. "The painting would now be at the mercy of people who might sell it, hide it, even deface or destroy it." She fell silent for a moment. "Do you remember when Immendorf Castle burned at the end of World War II? They destroyed Klimts and Schieles—so called degenerate art—that had been stored there for safekeeping. The loss is immeasurable, like losing part of our humanity." She clarified, more for herself than for Jonah. "Can anyone but a lover understand? Discovering a missing Rothko has nothing to do with possession, value, or notoriety."

Jonah, sighing thoughtfully, added a simple, "Indeed." Then, when she told him about finding the stretcher bars, he said, "We're fortunate then that the burglary didn't succeed."

"This time!" she exclaimed and fell silent. Neither had the heart to explore the subject further.

After they hung up she examined the bars again with a magnifying glass. Some of the sticks, she discovered, were marked with red letters. She checked her photos of the painting. The letters matched similar red marks on the canvas edges for reattaching the sticks. Proof absolute that the signed bars from the dumpster belonged to the missing painting!

Disappointment succeeded elation. She should have taken the

painting when Justine first offered it. Justine would have yielded without a second thought. Yet that was precisely why she *didn't* take it. But her concern had been misguided. It belonged to the practical world of means and ends. She felt responsible not just to persons—Justine, Finny, Rothko—or objects—the material canvas, the university, the art establishment—but for a city and world that relegates art to the dumpster.

Relief came from an unlikely place: Bartram. Propped on the sofa, the bandaged finger resting on a pillow, he whined, "My flute playing may be ruined forever." But when she told him about the burglary and Justine's rescue by Jonah, preoccupation with his injury—the sliver and the tetanus shot—was superseded by a new wound: jealousy. "Justine called *Jonah Hartman* to rescue her in the middle of the break in?" The idea staggered him.

"She wouldn't have gotten much help from the inside of a dumpster," Helena countered, jabbing at his vanity. "It's understandable that she would call the man she's in love with."

"In love with?" he challenged. "How do you know she's in love with him? This is something you've concocted."

"Well say then, her hero. He's certainly that after saving their lives."

"*Hero?*" The question was dismissive.

"Yes, hero. He responded instantly in the middle of the night to intruders in her apartment. Wouldn't you, wouldn't I, have called 911 before rushing off into danger?"

"But he *did* call 911," he replied, injured that she'd think he would do less than Jonah Hartman. "You said so."

"Yes, but the difference is that *he* never thought for a second of himself or his danger. He only thought of *her*."

This blow upon a bruise raised another strident objection. "You imply that I would think only of myself. You have no faith in me!"

"Of course I have faith in you, Bartram dear. But I also know you. After your complaints about raiding a dumpster you can't blame me for thinking you might have hesitated—only for a moment mind you—at taking on two brawny burglars." She smiled, recalling his droll figure in the dumpster.

His hurt look made her back off a little. "You're right though. Finny is the true hero. He risked himself to save Justine and has a blow on the head to prove it. Did you know that he had been driving past her apartment every night for weeks to make sure she and the painting were safe? He didn't simply talk about what he might do, he did something."

With that Bartram's high ground dissolved under his feet. Jarred from his narcissism, he abruptly sat up, upsetting the pillow and a glass of poppy-seed tea for soothing his pain. "I've got to see Justine and make sure she's all right."

Finding the stretcher bars, redefined his relation to the painting. It was no longer an item identifiable in a catalogue, but indisputably real. So while Helena cleaned up the spilled tea, he ran up the stairs two at a time, changed clothes in a lather, and ran back down.

As he flew out the front door, Helena called after him, "But what if Jonah is there?"

"To hell with Jonah Hartman," he shouted back, "he doesn't own her!"

◆

Ouruk Zaron, MD, was doing his surgical rounds when he heard an interesting piece of gossip. Sandra Foxcroft's sister and another relative had ended up in the emergency room as her patients. Though he wanted to know more, the patient had been dismissed and Sandra was gone for the day. However, there was one person who might enlighten him, Russell Baramore.

After Victoria had given Zaron the photos he had not been idle. His mercenaries had been searching for the painting, and with that in view, however low he might have to stoop, he would build his temple to art, a temple to himself.

Telling Little, Telling All

All smoothness and charm, he cornered Russell in the hospital cafeteria. The same cafeteria, now crowded, noisy, and prosaic, where Russell and Olas had been alone the night before. Then the space had trembled with incalculable possibilities; now it belonged to the commonplace. "I've heard about Dr. Foxcroft's sister and the attempted burglary. The gossip is that she has a valuable painting from an unscrupulous relative who acquired it illegally. And *he* was aided by an accomplice, Helena Gandolfi, who wants it for her former lover, Reginald Foxcroft."

Some of this was news to Russell and of real concern, but the topic was disquieting. It brought up like a serpent from its hole a secret he was hiding from himself. Not ready to think, let alone accept an attraction to someone of the same sex, he recoiled from the temptation that had nearly overthrown him the night before. In the sober light of day, he consigned it causes—curiosity, the late hour, and an empty cafeteria.

"I say illegally," Zaron droned on, "because the painting is stolen." When Russell's brown eyes took on a yellow cast of surprise, he expanded the point. "The painting they claim is theirs is rightfully *mine*. I acquired it when I bought the estate of two Russian spinsters. They had a second-rate collection except for one modern canvas, supposedly the Rothko everyone is talking about." He sneered loftily, "Personally, I know it has to be a fake. Why would *they* have had such a valuable work? I only bought their collection for sentimental reasons. My father you know was Russian." His lead-colored eyes acquired a drop or two of dampness. With a mawkish smile he added, "Did you know that he and the sisters were from the same village?" The line between Russell's eyes deepened at this ludicrous appeal to family feeling.

With an infallible predator's instinct, Zaron responded to what he saw on Russell's face. "You may not believe me when I say I want what's best for art." His tone became confidential. "I'm going to open a new museum for my collection. The capstone would be the lost Rothko—if it's ever really found. I plan to make Atlanta a world center for art." All he intended by these extravagant words was to loosen Russell's tongue. It wasn't the robbery he wanted to know about, it was information about the missing painting.

Divided between loyalty to Sandra and preoccupation with Olas Lindgard, Russell made no reply. He felt justified in having warned Foxcroft of a threat to Justine, but he didn't trust his and Olas' employer even when he was flattered by his attention. "I know nothing about the painting belonging to Sandra's sister," he said loftily. "But I can't imagine that she would knowingly harbor a stolen canvas. The robbers apparently didn't get it, whoever the painter is. And as for Sandra's uncle, I've never met him."

Zaron listened to this explanation weighing its truth. An edge of craftiness crept into his voice as he threw his loaded dice: "I have a young man working for me I'd like you to meet. His name is Olas Lindgard." Zaron saw Russell struggling to maintain his composure and added, "He knows a great deal about art and wants the painting—if it is a Rothko—to be in a place where everyone can see it. Not squirreled away at the top of that high-rise penthouse in Buckhead."

Whether or not Zaron knew about the meeting between Olas and Russell, he had an uncanny ability to detect the self-interest of others. "Since you're a collector yourself, you and he, I think, would enjoy knowing one another." Russell looked ill at ease at the association. Beneath the utilitarian white coat designed not to reveal, the tension in his shoulders was visible. "Maybe the two of you can convince that naïve little Foxcroft girl to stop harboring stolen goods for her sleazy real estate agent of an uncle." He clucked in mock-sympathy, "I'd hate to see Dr. Foxcroft implicated in this if it ever gets out. The publicity could be rather ugly for the hospital."

Russell showed alarm, not because of his relationship with Sandra as Zaron may have thought. As her partner, he cared about her role in all this, but it was the mention of Olas that aroused things he didn't want to go near. So he went home that day out of sorts and more ignorant of his desire than ever.

People in turmoil. Going in circles. Desire and anguish, promise and abandonment, pleasure and suspension confounding their hearts. An event has revealed to each a new reality as life occasionally does—unexpectedly. Frustrated and divided, they want to know with certainty what isn't certain. Certainty is fine in its way for entities that subsist in the world. But are people entities? Or do they pass through time and change, becoming other than themselves? Open to possibility. And that precludes certainty.

Between the time Justine thought someone was breaking into her apartment and her return from the hospital, the entire world changed. As if she had entered a worm hole to another universe and returned to discover she had been gone for an eternity. As her eyes moved mechanically over the rooms, everything was the same yet different. The book she was reading was still beside the sofa, the lilies fresh in their vase on the coffee table, the bed unmade and the covers on the floor. Until last night, she had seen the threat to the painting in the narrow terms of people and objects—burglars and dark sedans. Now it was as though she had hit the shift key and the small letters had all become capitals. What should she do? Here was the question that concerned her alone and foretold a different future.

As she sat in her living room staring blindly at the portrait of her mother considering this question, it was as though the two of them were weighing the matter together. Almost as though in the shifting pixels and geometric shapes she could hear her mother's voice urging her to distinguish between what really matters and what doesn't. That was the question.

Then the outside buzzer interrupted. "Justine, it's me. Bartram. Can I come in?"

"Bartram!" She exclaimed, surprised. "Yes of course." She pressed the button and let him in.

He entered unshaven and with uncombed hair sticking straight up in places. Glancing around the living room he asked, "Is Jonah Hartman here?"

"Why no," she answered. "He did call earlier."

He stared at her like a stranger, uncomprehending. "I heard about the burglary. I had to see that you were all right."

She smiled softly, touched by his concern but from a distance. "I'm fine. Finny's fine." He was reassured by her answer, and yet she was different somehow. Their relation had altered. She appeared older, not in age but in demeanor. The girlish charm had been displaced by sober awareness. Before, she had always acquiesced to his superior judgment. He was a world-renowned professional, older, cultivated, traveled, while she was a simple young woman he had known since girlhood. Now she was looking at him with the intense, searching eyes of an equal.

He was different too. A mysterious third had been admitted into their circle and come between them. He had lost his favored position in her affections and the mask of confidence slipped.

"What happened?" she pointed to the bandaged finger, "Your hand."

He looked at her blankly. "Oh this?" he held it up. "Oh, that's nothing. Tell me what happened Saturday night." He listened not as in the past with a weary cynicism of one who had seen and heard it all but with an air of irresolution. When she finished, he seemed carried away in thought. It was so unlike him. But then *she* was so unlike *her*.

"Bartram, what's the matter?"

He started, shaken out of his trance. "Sorry. What you went through, the danger, it made me forget what I came to tell you." He paused, reluctant to go on.

"What is it, Bartram?" she prodded.

And so he told her of the adventure in the dumpster and of

finding the wood bars—this time without painting himself the hero. Her danger during the burglary left no space for bragging.

"You and Helena found Rothko's inscription! How marvelous! I'm so glad she told you about the painting."

He had never really cared about "a pile of formless matter." But the events of last night had changed that too. A painting was not just a piece of canvas covered with paint. It was never that. Now it had acquired the heightened reality that comes from being engaged. "Mother told me about the people who are trying to get their hands on it. You should have called *me*, Justine, when you needed help. What will you do if they try again?" His brown eyes lighted with concern.

She stared beyond him into space. The dark obligation before her demanded she respond to its measure. "I will do what has to be done," she said slowly, enigmatically.

The day after the night in the hospital that changed everything, Sandra is pedaling furiously on a stationary bike going nowhere. A tenor voice sings in her ears: *"Ah! If my love / Thy stay could be . . . How gladly would I watch with thee."* How many times has she played this aria without recognizing who was singing? It was even written on the jewel case, "*St Matthew Passion* with Jonah Hartman, tenor." Headlines along the way had fairly shouted it: "Jonah Hartman triumphs as Don Carlo in Zurich;" "Tenor Jonah Hartman marries soprano Victoria Vargas;" "Hartman abandons flourishing career to teach voice;" "Atlanta welcomes the new director of the ASO Chorus: international opera star, Jonah Hartman."

She had rummaged through her CD's and found his name on three of them. Last fall he had been introduced at Symphony Hall, yet she hadn't connected him with the man in the park. A name in the headlines is not the same as a real person one can love. All her preconceptions of what she can know have been only the assumption of one who remains persistently in place. So, going round and round, she ends up again where she began.

Afterwards, she drives to his building in Ansley Park, stops, and stares at it through the car window. Another coincidence! It's not far from her townhouse. How has she missed him on her neighborhood walks, in the grocery store, at the filling station? The stately building where he lives with "The tempestuous Latina beauty, soprano Victoria Vargas" gives concreteness to a world he inhabits with someone else. And if he would suddenly walk out the door and see her? Thirty-three years old and acting like a teenager with a crush. Denial: It doesn't matter!

Yet it matters enough to determine the rest of the day: shopping for clothes, having her hair trimmed, nails done, body massaged. She lies on the table pummeled in spirit. Madness for a man with whom she has exchanged only a few sentences. She must keep this from Justine. It's as if she has borne a bastard child that has to be hidden away.

This dull round is interrupted when the masseuse comes back into the room: "You're finished Dr. Foxcroft. You can go."

"Yes," Sandra asks herself, "but go where?"

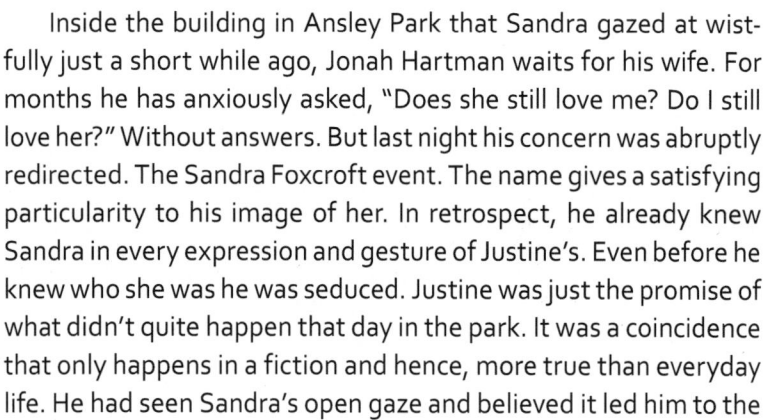

Inside the building in Ansley Park that Sandra gazed at wistfully just a short while ago, Jonah Hartman waits for his wife. For months he has anxiously asked, "Does she still love me? Do I still love her?" Without answers. But last night his concern was abruptly redirected. The Sandra Foxcroft event. The name gives a satisfying particularity to his image of her. In retrospect, he already knew Sandra in every expression and gesture of Justine's. Even before he knew who she was he was seduced. Justine was just the promise of what didn't quite happen that day in the park. It was a coincidence that only happens in a fiction and hence, more true than everyday life. He had seen Sandra's open gaze and believed it led him to the real person. Even when she turned away, he still believed. Not in an object or goal—those call for ownership, a possession of some person or thing. He simply had hope—nothing but hope. It broke a cycle of despair.

The burglary last night also shed new light on the lengths people will go to prostitute art. And so he wonders: "What has Victoria done, and to what extent, for Zaron and his people?" The missing photos and shortly thereafter the attempted burglary suggested a connection. If that were so, then the betrayal of Rothko was worse than her betrayal of him. It was the ultimate betrayal of art and of them as artists.

Sometime after these musings Victoria arrived. Seated now, sullen and unresponsive across from him, they are like players engaged in a game of chess. He looks straight at her while she stares away from him into space. Once upon a time, she had looked at him with an undefended face. Now she offers nothing more than a façade that forbids her to be seen.

Only after being told of her triumph in Zurich does he quietly ask the question from which there will be no going back. "Who did you give the photos to?" Not really an inquiry into who, what, or why. To those questions he knows the answer. It is a test of her willingness to lie in the face of truth.

She looks at him haughtily, debating the question, and with a stiff frown answers. "I haven't the faintest idea what you're talking about." It is indifference of the falsest kind.

Though his heart falls at her answer, he remains outwardly at least unmoved, his eyes locked on her. "Yes, you do. The photos were missing just after you supposedly left for Zurich, and they returned the same day. You didn't arrive in Zurich until three days later." He doesn't twitch a muscle as the words drop like lead.

She shifts restlessly in her chair, throws her head back and glares at a spot above his head as if he has insulted her. Nothing would induce her to admit what might compromise a good opinion of herself. "What are you accusing me of?" she throws the words sharply at him.

Advice from the *Passion* comes to mind—"*Forbear / Though deceiving tongues may sting me!*"—and he doesn't answer.

Then still refusing to engage his eyes, she picks up a copy of *Opera News* from the coffee table, glances at it, throws it down in disgust, and begins pacing the room. She can't, she won't confess, a thousand times NO!

There is a moment when, as she turns away, he wishes to spare her. It comes to him, knowing the truth. What stirs him above all is her audacity. She sings from a libretto so preposterous, so full of deceptions, self-justifications, and incriminations, that its very splendor is admirable. She struts and declaims, attacks and denounces everything he might say. She is Brunhilde, in a higher and higher flight, flaming aloft. Then, with a defiant toss of the head, she finally meets his eyes.

"I know about the affair," he says calmly, still posed in the chair. "He is a dangerous man who will not hesitate to ruin you." She looks perplexed as if she remembered something, then tries to forget it. When she opens her mouth once more in protest, he gets up, slowly walks out of the living room into the study and shuts the door. A half hour later she enters in a sexy nightgown. The rest is the bitter stuff of bedroom farce.

They had made love. A silly term, for he had no more *made* love to her than she had made *love* to him, as if it were a product. Afterward, she had fallen asleep or pretended to, her dark hair spread like a fan across the pillow. It let him see her as a person he no longer knew.

The next day he went silently about his routine. Studied scores, prepared for classes, read, biding his time, waiting to see what she would do next. Would she continue to pretend that something had been settled between them?

After several days drowning in a silence that saturated the domestic space, she had had enough. At the end of a dinner in which the scratch of cutlery across plates and the noise of glasses lifted and set down had become deafening, she said in a low flat voice, "I want you to leave." He had the sense then that nothing he had ever done would hereafter be the same or count so much. It brought to a close the moment in his life when he had the least to say. Without explanation, he packed his bags, gathered up his music, and left.

14

In the interest of his reputation as a philanthropist, Zaron's father once gave the Atalanta Bank a minor collection of paintings from the seventeenth, eighteenth, and nineteenth centuries. In the late 90s, the bank renovated a glass-enclosed atrium to house the collection. The idea was to appeal to broad public taste and enhance the reputation of the bank while avoiding controversy. The works on display—representational landscapes, portraits, genre paintings—could be enjoyed without demanding much from the viewer. The idea worked. In exhibiting works of the same period from other local collectors, and avoiding an assault on conventional tastes with anything difficult or avant-garde, the gallery became extremely popular and earned a reputation for supporting the arts in the city.

One day the bank's Chairman of Art Acquisitions received a call from Justine Foxcroft. The bank was about to feature an exhibition of portraits, so she offered him the Chuck Close rendering of her mother. The Chairman, who always had to cajole Sir Reginald into lending them anything, eagerly pounced on her idea. Accepting a work from the daughter might get them works from the prickly and difficult father.

Justine had her own motive of course. After consulting with Helena, they had agreed that this would be a way to get *both* paintings away and safe. If she lent the Close to a major art museum, its secret would be discovered. But if she lent it to the bank and had a clear say in how it was displayed, *both* would be secure.

However, there were obstacles. First, she had to persuade the art board that the contemporary work was appropriate for the gallery, but the second was a more formidable obstacle: Dr. Zaron was on the board. As he never attended the meetings—the collection was beneath him—and had his creature, Felicity Hardcastle represent him instead, Justine was willing to risk the Close and its secret inside the camp of the enemy.

On the day of the presentation she carefully applied makeup, put on her best suit and pumps, checked her hose for snags, combed her hair in a smooth curve and donned her most winning smile. Then, after rehearsing what to say for the twentieth time, she gathered her wits and set off for the soaring bank building in Midtown. Along the way, she went through a mental list of the faces and names of the board members.

Among the city's beautiful churches and temples to ancient religions, the bank asserted its place as a cathedral to the not-so-new religion of money. The gleaming landmark of tawny-colored granite rose to a pyramidal tower capped in gold that soared majestically above a plaza of lawn so green, so evenly trimmed, so free from weeds that it seemed artificial. It was as if a modern replica of the highest mountain in Arcadia had been created above the well-watered glen where Atalanta dwelled.

When Justine emerged from the parking garage, she found herself at the far end of the plaza. To reach the entrance, she either had to walk around the plaza or take a shortcut across it. She took the shortcut. Halfway across, the sprinkler system came on and sent torrents of water in all directions. Though she ran as swiftly as a fleet-footed goddess, she was soaked by the time she reached the other side. In the nearest restroom, she dried off her clothes and shoes as best she could and peered at herself in the mirror. Her short hair was plastered flat and streaks of mascara made black scars down her face. She washed her face, slicked back her hair, and took the elevator to the top floor.

As she entered the glass-ceilinged room, she had the sense of floating inside a mountain with all the city below. The steel-ribbed, open pyramid was so soaring, the glass room beneath it so translucent they helped clear her head. In the middle of the room, like a stage before the play, a group of people stood posed around a glass conference table. Among the tailored suits and made-to-measure faces, two were surprises and unnervingly familiar. One was her father, who acknowledged her with a disapproving glance, and Dr. Ouruk Zaron the other, whose flinty eyes glinted at her like mica shards. With fixed stare and pose of a Greek statue, he appeared wrapped in an invisible garland of superiority.

The Chairman of Acquisitions, Geraldo Tomosso, greeted her warmly and generously overlooked her appearance. The art board, he explained, was made up of local citizens and several VP's from the bank. But today they were honored with two special guests. He gestured down the table, "Your father, you know of course, and the man at the end is Dr. Zaron, whom I'm sure you've heard of." It was obvious why Zaron was there but why her father? He no longer owned the portrait and wasn't on the board so why would he object to seeing it on display? Was it possible that he and Zaron, confirmed enemies, had conspired together to oppose her?

The Chairman called the meeting to order and introduced her. There were curious and half-embarrassed glances at her soggy appearance. "Hello everyone," she began in a sprightly voice. "Thank you for inviting me here today to show you Chuck Close's portrait of my mother, Kate Foxcroft." Eighteen pairs of eyes, several hostile, focused on her. "You may think from my well-watered appearance that my presentation is washed up before I even begin," she giggled in her pleasant, not-quite-British accent. "I took a short cut across the beautifully landscaped plaza downstairs at the exact time the sprinklers came on. I ran as fast as I could, but I wasn't fast enough. So rather than delay you and appear in my skivvies, I decided, at the risk of seeming wet behind the ears, to come as I am." An outburst of laughter broke the corporate ice—except for her father and Zaron, who took turns glaring frostily at her and at one another.

The Chairman responded jovially, "I don't think this lively

explanation will dampen our enthusiasm for Ms. Foxcroft's presentation."

No one appreciated more than she this lightening of the spirit of the room. Except for her father and Zaron, it was in no one's interest for her to fail, and in realizing that, she breathed more easily. She opened her laptop and a portrait of Rembrandt came up on the screen. "Let me begin," she offered, "by showing you works by one of the most innovative portrait painters since Rembrandt." After presenting a dozen or so examples, she showed them photos of her mother's portrait taken from distances and different angles.

Then she described the artist's technique: Typically, he took photos of the sitter, drew a grid of it to create tiny squares with dots, and with dabs of pigment and paper created an abstract mosaic that, viewed from a distance, assembled into a face. "Think of the portrait as an unexpected image that arrives in fits and starts. It makes us wait for it to show itself." The very exuberance of this challenge added authority to her slender figure. "The result is a dazzling illusion that flickers and shifts like bits of glass in a kaleidoscope."

Except for her father's stoicism and Zaron's scorn, the faces around the table expressed interest, and questions followed. "What response from the public do you expect to this portrait?" This one came from Felicity Hardcastle in a hysteria-tinged voice with a nervous glance at Zaron.

"I can't speak for anyone but myself," Justine came back playfully, "but I can say that I look at and talk to the portrait of my mother as if she were still with me. It has something to say every time I look at it. No photograph or representation of her can do that." It was not what the frowning Felicity expected, but the answer raised the interest of the audience.

At this point her father glowered at her accusingly and interjected in a voice of doom. "I'm here to object formally to the public display of the portrait of my late wife. It is a deeply personal memento of my grief and was never meant for exhibition." He continued to glare at her haughtily. This interruption of familial resentment embarrassed the room.

Justine lowered her large eyes, and smiling still, gazed wistfully at her folded hands. "Father, should we rehearse a family disagreement in public? You know perfectly well that Mother gave the portrait to me before she died because you didn't like it." If her father had thought he could intimidate her into submission, he had clearly miscalculated. And the faces round the table suggested, with one exception, that the room was with her.

All the while, Zaron maintained the stillness of a viper about to sting. Now, with a superior look he rose from his chair and loomed over everyone. Walking slowly and deliberately around the table, every stride, every motion of his body called attention to his being utterly confident and knowing perfectly what he was about. He stopped in front of Justine. All eyes were riveted on him as he looked down at her with a sneer.

"I don't pretend to be an expert on Mr. Close. He is not an artist that *I* own, nor whose work *I* would consider worthy to be included with the masterpieces in *my* collection." His stare grew harsher, "As for the public, were I to offer my portrait of Rembrandt for display here, it would attract more viewers than an artist they've never heard of whose 'portrait,'" he used the word with contempt, "is more a lesson in geometry than a representation of a real person." Mention of the Rembrandt provoked murmurs, but Zaron swiftly quashed them. He had no intention of lending the bank his masterpiece. "However, my chief objection to this thing is that it doesn't reflect the traditional taste or style of the works we exhibit here. People won't like it." The *we* made it sound as if he who never attended a meeting and the board were in harmony.

That was enough to cloud the atmosphere. As if some greyish mist had filled the open pyramid over their heads. To restore a more favorable climate Justine smiled sweetly and said, "Personal taste, liking or not liking, is not a criterion for a work of art. The individual is neither the judge nor the jury. Works of art shake up how we conceive things to be. That's why they sometimes offend and outrage." Some heads nodded in agreement and some turned to Zaron questioningly but without effect as he tried to stare people into submission. Justine continued, "The argument for the painting should be debated, don't you think? Not with exclamation marks that close the conversation, but with dashes of an ongoing debate?"

Zaron hadn't moved from his predatory position in front of her. Now he swayed slightly, as if toying with his prey, and countered with a different complaint. "I object to the painting on other grounds." He was in his element now. "We have to consider the artist's predictable record of offending people."

Before he could go further, Justine shook her head as if he were not really serious. "Is predictability a criterion for judging a work?" she asked with authority. "Doesn't predictability predictably recognize only *inferior* works? What everyone can foresee and feel comfortable with?"

Then Zaron, who was not about to yield, played his trump card. "I have taken the opportunity to bring along a consultant, an expert on the subject who is also an artist at the University. Let him speak before we decide. He turned to one side saying, "May I introduce to you Mr. Olas Lindgard?"

On cue, a side door opened and a young man glided in, dressed in creamy gold like the angel of the annunciation. Gleaming from head to toe, he gestured with a raised hand as if in blessing. It was a startling, indeed spellbinding image rich in connotations, as if he had descended the heavenly pyramid to greet the mortals. Zaron grinned at him wolfishly, while Justine stared in shock. Something about the man was familiar. The graceful way he moved. His confident manner. The unusual bronze hue of his eyes. He caught her glance and did something extraordinary. He winked as if they shared a secret. And she was reminded of the robbery.

All eyes were riveted on him as he began to speak. "I have been asked to explain Chuck Close's achievement. The work belongs to the avant-garde. It is the kind of unconventional work that generates controversy and debate." He paused and shook his head as though bemused at the thought. Then continued, "His portraits break down the human face into technological fragments by creating tiny geometric shapes and associative colors. They create the effect of character without reproducing the appearance of the person. It's an example of what in mathematics is called category theory. It uses arrows and points to intimate dynamic movements and relations."

He let them digest this mouthful a moment and then went confidently on. "This highly cerebral art is not the kind the average person who visits this gallery identifies with. It has the potential to arouse strongly negative reactions and by its proximity raise antipathy against this bank." He shook a graceful, reproving finger at the listeners. "No one likes to be assaulted by something they can't understand." There was just a glimmer of irony in his expression, as if he knew he had demonstrated the very thing he was expected to criticize.

He effectively put the board in a dilemma. If they agreed with him, they would align themselves with the average viewer; or if they disagreed, they would appear highbrow and elitist. In Sir Reginald's case the impasse was acute. Disagreement would undercut his own objections to displaying the work in public, but agreement would line him with the enemy. As for Zaron, whose face teemed with pride and temper, he acted as if a decision in his favor was secured by this testimony.

Aware that he had raised an embarrassing quandary between quality and accessibility, Olas lowered his eyes demurely. "Though the public supports and applauds corporations like this one that promote art and artists in general, it is also fickle in its appreciation of art in the particular." He sighed audibly as if troubled by the thought. "Despite what they might say, people feel most comfortable with works that are representations of what they already know. That's what has made this gallery so popular." A few heads nodded at the common sense of this, while other heads shook.

Radiating unconcern, he went on. "Avant-garde, controversial art might be fine for a city like New York, but for a traditional, though forward-looking city like Atlanta?" The question hung in the air as he looked up into the pyramid searching for an answer. "If the Atalanta Bank wants people to feel good, if it wants to assure customers that they are banking with a secure family-oriented business"—he paused to let the sense of security settle in, then his face became earnest. "If it cares about the community and the values of ordinary citizens . . ." What was coming next they wondered? He leaned forward, as though taking them into his confidence and lowered his voice to a stage whisper. "It cannot promote a work by a *disabled* artist who has to paint abstract wedges because he no longer has the use of his limbs."

There were nervous asides, whispers, angry stares at the young man, disapproving glances at Zaron. The look of shock and consternation on the face of Zaron almost made Justine laugh out loud. "Disabled?" He hadn't intended his expert to go this far and had assumed that most on the board would not have heard of it. The board members, who saw themselves so tolerant and liberal-minded, would never reject an artist because he was disabled. So dismissing the objections out of hand, they quickly agreed, some with vigor, to accept the loan and display the Chuck Close in the gallery.

Afterward, a relieved Justine made her way down to the atrium where to her surprise she found Olas Lindgard waiting for her. He was about to say something through his broad grin, when her father approached in a cloud of disgust.

Without a glance at his daughter he snarled at Olas, "I must commend you on your loyalty. A viper working for Zaron when you work for me. How could you? Didn't you see it as a conflict of interest?"

Olas answered, angelically unflustered. "Dr. Zaron hired me because he objected to hanging the Close in the bank. Where's the conflict when *you* objected to it too?"

"Don't use your chop logic on me, sir. You know why. He is my enemy. What you do for him works against *me*. Why didn't you tell me you were coming here? Why did you never tell me you were an artist?"

He shrugged indifferently as the heavenly light fell from the atrium on his face. "You didn't ask."

Sir Reginald nearly choked at the bland response. "I don't believe for one minute that Zaron objected to the painting for the reasons you said. So what is he up to?"

Olas glanced at Justine, cast about, and offered as raw beef to a salivating dog, "He thinks your daughter has a stolen painting that belongs to him." Justine's huge eyes widened into brown globes.

"Stolen painting? What stolen painting?" Sir Reginald snapped.

"A Rothko."

A mortal blow this. "Then why should he object to the portrait?"

Olas lowered his eyes and smiled faintly as if the answer were obvious. "Because he wants to discredit your daughter and through her discredit you." For a second time he looked at Justine with the ambiguous wink that made her wonder what he, hired by both her father and Zaron, was doing aligning himself with her?

Sir Reginald's mouth contorted in a grimace. "Well thanks to you, he didn't succeed." Olas smiled beatifically as if in agreement. "You know of course that you can no longer work for me," Foxcroft growled, while Justine looked on helplessly. He acted as if she wasn't there. Was she so insignificant?

"I suspected that might be the case."

"He pays you that well, does he?"

"Well enough."

Justine interrupted this exchange that was so unsatisfactory to her father. "I hope you're not terribly unhappy at the outcome. Mother would not be." Olas looked from her to Sir Reginald, his face alive with interest.

The proud British knight, impeccably displayed, point device, answered in brittle tones. "I have nothing to say about the merits of the artist whose renown is considerable. But if your mother were alive today, I'm certain she would *not* approve." Then in an even higher flight of mettle, "As *I* was the one who commissioned and paid for the portrait, *my* concerns in this matter should have been considered, Justine!" He looked at her balefully. "You have tainted the Foxcroft name by associating it with Ouruk Zaron."

She maintained her composure. "Let me remind you again Father, that Mother willed the portrait to *me. You* no longer own it. Your concern is beside the point."

When he sniffed, and waved a hand dismissively, she let it pass with a wistful look and turned to Olas. "Mr. Lindgard, what you said about the mathematics of the artist was marvelous. I don't know anything about category theory, but I do see what you mean about the use of geometric wedges and color. If I understand you correctly, Close uses geometry to subtract representation of a person and convey the character.

The corners of Olas' mouth rose in a broad grin. "Yes, that's right."

"So what you said goes directly against Dr. Zaron's idea of a representation."

"Right again."

Sir Reginald, standing between the two, looked at the smiling young man and his equally smiling daughter, mystified.

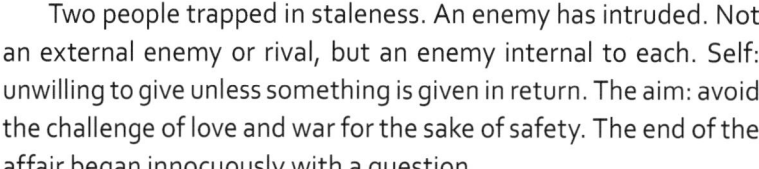

Two people trapped in staleness. An enemy has intruded. Not an external enemy or rival, but an enemy internal to each. Self: unwilling to give unless something is given in return. The aim: avoid the challenge of love and war for the sake of safety. The end of the affair began innocuously with a question.

"Russell, I wonder if we should ask Justine to move in with us for a while." Sandra was pretending to make a question crafted ahead of time sound spontaneous. "She's not safe in her apartment. What happened at the bank with Zaron . . . he's trying to intimidate her. I wouldn't be surprised if he had something to do with the burglary." She missed, or chose not to see, Russell's angry frown. He had been thoroughly unpleasant ever since Justine showed up at the hospital the night of the robbery. Disregarding the consequences, she deliberately forged ahead. "Did you know that Zaron has hired the young man we once saw coming from his office as his art expert? He showed up unexpectedly at the bank to argue against the portrait of my mother."

Russell stared at her woodenly from a chair in the living room while she made a sandwich in the kitchen. "What young man do you mean?" The last thing he wanted was to get close to the topic of Olas Lindgard, and even less to discuss Justine.

"You know, the young Apollo in the biking outfit who stunned everyone at the hospital."

If she didn't really know about Russell's interest in Olas, she had intuited something and chose now to exploit it. He winced at her reference to the god of light. It raised a nameless anxiety. He had been resisting, despite the evidence, a longing for someone, something. He still resisted with the stiff-necked energy of a counter-will thwarting itself. He struggled to maintain a calm façade before replying in a cross voice, "Are you being your sister's keeper? Did she ask you if she could stay here?"

"No, she wouldn't," she paused before the open refrigerator, a carton of milk in hand. "She'd be afraid of intruding. Russell, she's not safe alone in that apartment." Her emphasis was not misplaced, though there was an alternative motive. If Justine stayed with them, Jonah Hartman would know that *she*, Sandra, was living with someone. In essence, it would will Justine to him. What was she doing then when she pushed Russell? Forcing a crisis? She knew, but chose not to see that far.

"Then she didn't ask." Russell made a point—and staring, insisted on it with a frown. "Stop meddling!" He sat up straight in his chair looking churlish, opened an art magazine, and pretended to read. It was his evening off and he didn't want it interrupted by a discussion of Justine. As he stared blindly at the open page, another image intruded against his will: Olas Lindgard alone with him in the hospital snack bar. He tried to regain the stoicism that protected him from panic.

Sandra read resistance in the tensed shoulders and stiff expression and persisted. "What am I missing here? Why are you so resentful?" That set off an explosion.

"I'm not resentful," he shouted in an aggrieved tone. "I'm frustrated at the way you've chosen to live with your thoughts elsewhere. You've packed them up and hauled them away and only pretend to be here still." Anger provided justification for what Russell secretly desired but could not admit—that his relation to her hindered what Olas had set in motion. A desire toward which Russell, with pervasive uneasiness, was tending.

What he said was near the truth, but unwilling still to admit that her heart lived elsewhere, she evaded. "I'm preoccupied with my job, but so are you. We agreed that our careers would always take precedence. Now you want something more." From the beginning, they had consented to a stagnant relationship, a quid pro quo that only tolerates its own emptiness. But tolerance cannot withstand the difficulties of living with difference, and tolerance was no substitute for a desire that had nothing whatsoever to with expediency and everything to do with love. Only love would have the strength, the will to see beyond the present impasse.

In the quarrel that followed, the hollowness of their relation was laid bare. Several hours later when it was all over and the passion had drained away, they agreed that they should separate after Sandra's birthday party. How quickly it all happened. It was the fulfillment of a possibility latent for months, an excuse for what all along they both wanted. As if a mysterious, half-formed thought had been shadowing them, but every time they turned around it disappeared. Then suddenly there it was in the flesh. Russell could not afford to see it in that light. Whereas Sandra had help—a sledgehammer from Helena, who made her see what a self-deceiving, contradictory force desire is. Now in the light of what just happened, her heart had had its way. In Russell's departure, her sacrifice of Jonah to Justine was annulled. As for the topic that triggered their argument to begin with—Justine staying with them—that wasn't mentioned again.

15

The date arrives. The table is set. The guests assemble. Justine is giving a birthday party for her sister. Invited are Helena and Bartram, "dear" Uncle Finny, Sandra's partner Russell, Jonah (who has pleaded another engagement), and two special guests. One is her father, who hasn't been in the same domestic space with his daughters since their mother died a decade ago. His invitation, in the spirit of reconciliation after the bank, will surprise everyone. As for a secret guest, his presence will provoke astonishment.

Helena arrives and immediately picks up the mood of the room as more subdued than celebratory. Sandra, though especially lovely tonight in a red sheath and new hairdo, is preoccupied and distant, while her father exudes an air of detached ennui. Finny is seated glumly off in a corner, Russell stands about frowning, and Bartram poses casually on the sofa smiling at the absence and presumed vanquish of his rival, Jonah.

The mood may have something to do, perhaps more than something, with *two* absent paintings. The room feels bereft. As if the air has been displaced by undetectable dark matter weighing on those present. Justine tries to dispel it with glasses of champagne and bright comments about the occasion. Nonetheless, the mood lingers. The robbery, the episode at the bank, the upending of Sandra and Russell's practical arrangement, all have contributed to an indefinable unease.

Sandra looks mournfully at the empty wall, a sign of her empty life. Justine notices and says sympathetically, "The apartment seems lifeless without mother here."

Sir Reginald too stares at the wall and remarks pettishly, "The Close must have overwhelmed this space." He glances around the tiny apartment with distaste. "And it faced due West. The sun would have ruined it."

Justine, bristling with awareness, answers her father. "You're right. The portrait did overwhelm the space. But isn't that what we want a work of art to do? Overwhelm?"

"Overwhelm?" Sir Reginald looks sharply at Justine, taking in her appearance for the first time. Like her sister, she conveys glamor in her simple black dress and pearls, as if a creature of substance had been hiding beneath her slight presence all along. No longer the clueless girl, but a poised young woman with grace and intelligence in every look. For a moment, something grips at the wizened organ of his heart. He glances about the room appraisingly and back at her. She's not a fool like McGinley, or a supercilious ass like Bartram Gandolfi, or an overweening climber like Baramore, but like—with a gasp of surprise—a worthy adversary, like Helena herself.

While he observes his younger daughter, Helena is observing him. She sees what he sees: a change in the sisters. Sandra is tight and stiff while Justine is as serene as a Buddha. "Your daughters have blossomed into mature young women," she says. "And in Justine's case the transformation is breathtaking." Foxcroft merely harrumphs in reply.

"À *table*," Justine cheerfully announces and directs everyone to the table set with her mother's best china and crystal retrieved from Sandra, who has no time or desire to entertain. She places her sister, the laconic guest of honor, at the head and herself at the other end. On her right is her father and, on her left, across from him, Uncle Finny. Bartram is beside Sir Reginald with Russell to the left and Helena to the right of Sandra. That leaves room next to Finny for the mystery guest.

They unfold their napkins and are about to dip their spoons into the soup when the buzzer rings. Justine gets up and opens the door to a young man dressed—singularly dressed—all in white with tight-fitting pants, tight jacket with Nehru collar and long waist. The looks of surprise and wonder on her guests are precious.

"Everyone, this is Olas Lindgard. Olas, whom some of you already know, is a student at the University and an artist who knows a great deal about our favorite painters, Rothko," she grins mischievously, "and Chuck Close."

Sir Reginald, feathers ruffled at meeting his "disloyal" former employee, appears divided between protesting and preening. Sandra is puzzled. Wasn't Olas hired by Zaron? Bartram is distantly curious, Helena intrigued at the change in the room. And Russell? Russell is thunderstruck. As for uncomplicated Uncle Finny, he brims with unexpected consciousness. He has seen the young man somewhere before and that reminds him of something else he has seen. It's that painting. No matter how hard he tries, he can't shake it off like a dog shakes off water.

The new guest seats himself gracefully between Helena and Finny, and without ceremony addresses the latter. "I heard that you rescued Justine while she was being burglarized." The two are players on a stage with the others as attentive audience.

Finny shrugs modestly, "It's what any uncle would do for a favorite niece." A pause, then expectant silence.

Russell, now as visibly prickly as a hedgehog, inquires in a sulky voice, "I assume you recovered from the bike accident and your nose is intact?" Before Olas can respond, he adds shrilly, "Olas appeared in the hospital with a bloody nose and chin the same night Justine was robbed."

The remark causes surprise and visible tension, but does not jar Olas, who responds with aplomb: "My minor accident that night was nothing compared to what happened to Justine and her uncle. But I'm indebted to you, Dr. Baramore, for soothing me with coffee afterwards." Sandra's brown eyes shift between Russell and Olas, increasing the former's awkwardness. He's acting like a criminal.

Justine responds in an ameliorating tone, "One of the burglars was going to cut the portrait from its frame but Uncle Finny stopped him."

The news appalls her father. "Cutting a painting from a frame is barbaric. The burglar must have been a fool," he rumbles dismissively. "Not to mention the fact that he would reduce its value."

Olas appears amused at this response. He glances significantly at Justine. "Is it anymore barbaric to cut a painting from its frame than to buy and sell it as though it was a hind-quarter of pork?" Regie stiffens and looks as if he wants to slap him for this impertinence, while the others grow silent again and for a while the only sound is soup spoons scaping against bowls.

Helena is analyzing every downcast eye and scrape of cutlery as though it were a painting in which tiny details reveal a secret narrative. Despite Justine's attempt to provoke community, everyone is on edge, or off kilter.

The main course is served to an atmosphere as stale as yesterday's bread. Since no one has taken up Olas' question, Helena says with delicious provocation, "Regie dear, are you still interested in acquiring the Rothko?" Regie dear nearly spits out a mouthful of salmon. "Have you thought what a disservice the collector does to a work of art?" The question sends a collective jolt around the table.

Regie puts on his most pained, forbearing expression. "Whatever can you mean, Helena? A disservice? I have rescued hundreds of masterpieces from obscurity and neglect. How is that a disservice to art?"

She glows at him with her sterling face. "Because a work is not a product like a piece of furniture. If it's put in a museum, people make pilgrimages to see it. You collectors imprison a work and make *yourselves* the center instead of *it*." This speech disrupts the bland social politeness that kills thought.

Taking umbrage at the word imprison, he responds tersely.

"Collectors preserve and protect works of art that may otherwise never see the interior of a museum." He declares his justification: "All the museums in the world wouldn't be able to afford or even have room to hold all the works owned by the *great* collectors."

His self-defense causes more than one smile and encourages Helena to press on. "Why should a collector deprive others of a work just because he can afford it? A work of art belongs to the world, not the market."

"And how, pray, can it avoid the market?" He sniffs, irritated that she would attack him so openly.

"It can't, but it shouldn't be subservient."

"I presume, then, that your condemnation of collectors also includes popes and kings."

"Not quite all. They were public, not private figures. Their works were on display in courts, palaces, and churches. The collector tries to be master over the work by possessing it. But the work of art is not a thing one can possess."

Sandra has been detached and distant all evening, especially with her father. But having felt the sharpness of Helena's scalpel herself not long ago, she comes to his defense. "The finest collections eventually end up in museums, so the public *can* see them."

A scoffing Bartram intrudes: "Museums stuff so much in a building you *can't* really see it. And most of what they collect is squirreled away in a vault where *no one* can see it."

Habitually annoyed by anything he says, Sandra snaps. "Would you get rid of museums then? Besides, you missed Helena's point, that the market shouldn't be the judge of art."

"But he has a point too," Justine pipes up defensively. "Museums do keep most of their works in a vault."

"You've illustrated an unresolvable problem," Helena concurs. "The work of art ought not be a consumer product in the market, nor hidden away. Besides, art makes the marketplace possible, not the other way around."

"How so?" Regie asks, still miffed.

"It transforms the way the world is viewed. The market and economy only replicate, they don't create."

"I agree with Dr. Gandolfi," Olas says, entering the discussion. Russell, who has been following every word like a limp Adam awaiting the divine spark, looks to Olas for some—for any recognition and receiving none drops his eyes in dismay. Olas continues. "Art is the radical exception that doesn't fit our expectations. It's always new, like the invention of imaginary numbers or the square root of negative 1."

Justine takes up the thread encouragingly, "Olas is a mathematician as well as an artist. He sees mathematics behind the work of art."

Nobody is prepared to follow up on that, so Helena, noting the currents of desire around the table, changes the topic. "Art directs us away from a desire for things or knowledge, toward desire itself. It's not ever satisfied with objects that fade away or entertain. Each experience of a work of art is different. It makes us want to keep coming back. It keeps us desiring."

Regie rolls his eyes, and his entire body seems to roll with them. The room goes quiet again. Sandra's dark eyes are charged at Helena's mention of desire. It makes her more sympathetic toward her father, who is plunged in gloom. "Maybe the point isn't to condemn the collector," she offers gently, "but to question the attitude of possession itself. That applies to a museum, museum viewer, even an entire culture."

Bartram rushes to add, "Musical art is movement and anticipation in sound. No copyright can ever wholly possess it."

"Good for you Sandra, Bartram," Helena responds to both. "The issue of possession is a threat to all the arts." A pleased Bartram, seldom his mother's object of praise, catches Justine's eye as though to say, "See, *she* appreciates me."

Finny has been enduring this discussion with concealed yawns, but the topic has touched on something close that he's never thought before. "My job is selling houses. It's *all* about ownership and possession. But often the buyer ends up complaining, 'I don't own my house. It owns me.'"

Helena responds. "You have just described the way art captures the viewer. It exceeds the condition of an object that the gazer would try to possess." This is not quite the meaning Finny sees in what he said.

During this discussion, Russell has been gagged. Finally, with a gust of air this bursts out: "You all act as if art will save the world. Look, I love art too, but I'm not blind to the fact that art is elitist."

That causes an embarrassed silence. Moody to the point of despair, Russell adds almost as a cry of anguish, "Here we are, two physicians, an art professor, a British aristocrat, an art student, a realtor and a company manager. You're all talking like white folks who haven't a clue about how the people I come from live. They're just trying to survive. They don't have time for art."

The atmosphere, pregnant with the forbidden, almost succumbs to social politeness—until Helena responds sternly, giving Russell one of her sharp, silvery looks. "Art's truth is universal. It excludes *nobody*. It's elitist for *everyone*." Her look is regal as a monarch's. "Haven't we just been advocating that?" She lets the question drop then picks it up again with a declaration. "There's a vast difference between art and the world where it's found. The more raw the city is and more awry the world is, the more it needs art!" Defeated, Russell slumps down into his chair.

During this discussion, Finny, who has been sighing heavily in the manner of the long suffering, is inspired to speak. "You all talk as if a painting is some sort of weak little will-o-the-wisp that needs us to save it from destruction. But what little I've seen of *one* painting, it doesn't need *us* to protect it. *We* need protection from *it*."

"Bravo, Finny," Helena claps her hands. "Spoken like a man who just received a blow on the head from Chuck Close." Finny shakes his head, not thinking of Chuck Close at all but of the terrifying thing he once saw spread on the floor of this very apartment.

Helena continues. "When art is viewed according to what

is expected, our preconceptions, we're pleased aesthetically. Whereas when it exceeds expectation, it opens us to wonder... or to terror." Finny may not follow all that but he understands enough not to pursue the matter.

"And that said, dearest Helena," Justine chimes in, "we'll have dessert, which is a work of art that will exceed your preconceptions." With that she bounds into the galley kitchen and fetches a birthday cake from a Midtown bakery that does indeed exceed expectation.

At one time Ouruk Zaron thought of turning the mansion in Tuxedo Hills into a museum for his collection, but now he had bigger ideas than Atlanta. He dreamt of a palace of art, a museum of museums that would crown his own achievement and redeem his father's sins. Then a series of setbacks: the meeting arranged at the High to force Gandolfi to his side had gone badly. Not only had he learned nothing about the painting, but adding injury to insult, Gandolfi had stood up to his threats with counter threats of her own. Then the debacle at the bank. The attempt to discredit the Foxcroft girl had failed and he had to find another way to force her to reveal the painting. Worse, someone had searched the debris from the house in Druid Hills, though nothing appeared to have been taken. He cursed the stupidity of the people he hired for not having found anything that would support his own claim. In their imbecility, they may have left valuable clues for his enemies.

And he had another vexing problem: Victoria. By pilfering the photos, she had foolishly let her husband discover their affair, and then, after throwing him out, had established herself more or less permanently as queen in *his* mansion. Though she assured him her husband would make no trouble, even half-convinced him that her fame would enhance his own, he didn't want the affair known while he was touting his museum and securing his reputation as a philanthropist. Now she was threatening to make their affair public unless he married her. But until the painting was safely in his hands, he couldn't risk a confrontation with Jonah Hartman over the affair and the photos.

About all this, however, Victoria had ideas of her own. "You should let *me* promote the painting," she insisted. "My fans care about art. I have only to mention it on Facebook or Twitter and thousands will respond." He regarded her skeptically as she continued, "When my poster was placed outside Covent Garden, they had to assign guards to keep people from blocking the entrance." In the *Tosca* poster her amazing bosom nearly escaped her gown. Reluctantly he was persuaded by her notoriety that she might promote his plans after all.

Then, a stroke of luck. He heard of Russell and Sandra's amicable breakup and saw in it the chance to learn more. But there was another motive. In Russell he recognized the familiar desire for admiration that might help overcome his loyalty to Sandra, even her sister and her friend, that Gandolfi woman. With that in mind, Zaron invited Russell to his luxurious and very private 10,000 square foot cottage on Lake Lanier, a man-made reservoir northeast of the city.

They were seated at the pool beneath an enamel sky. A warm stillness radiated off the water. Beyond the pool a perfectly tended lawn led to a wooded promontory and a splendid view of the reservoir. It was a scene of cultivated leisure—though not conducive to recreation. "So you and Dr. Foxcroft are no longer together," Zaron repeated for the pleasure of saying it.

"We're still good friends," Russell replied politely. Despite the sunny afternoon and the lush surroundings, he appeared less confident than usual. There were umber shadows beneath his eyes, and his usually upright body was hunched and brooding.

"You've heard about my new museum?" Zaron asked.

"Yes," Russell answered eagerly, his eyes brightening.

"I will of course be its director."

"How will you find the time as Chief of Surgery?"

Zaron looked at him as if he were naïve. "It's important that a famous name be listed on the credits of the museum. Besides, if I hired a director from a major art museum, I'd have to pay through the teeth and share control. There are lesser-known, equally qualified art advisors, experts, and consultants who would be happy to share in my enterprise. As they say, why bother to *be* an expert, when you can buy one."

He paused and searched Russell's eyes. "You for instance. You aspire to be a collector. That's why I invited you here today. I want you to help me run my museum." He watched Russell straighten and lean forward into the idea. "You'll lend distinction to it. An MD gets more esteem than some esoteric expert with a PhD."

"What would you want me to do?"

Zaron kept the answer vague. "I need someone to stand in for me socially when I can't be there." Before Russell could respond he added congenially, "Let me pour you another drink while you think about it." They sipped their drinks looking out over the lake in the distance, as Zaron continued to disparage experts. The peaceful sunny afternoon encouraged Russell to rationalize Zaron's manner of speaking. "So you *are* going to help me," Zaron said with a grin. Russell nodded. "Good." Zaron mused for a moment, or seemed to. "Then you'll also help me with my claim?" He didn't miss the flash of conflict on Russell's face. "Maybe you can tell me where my painting is now?"

"I don't know," Russell answered with a wrinkled brow. "It was in Sandra's sister's apartment at one time and may have been removed." His answer, though vague, conveyed guilt.

"How could it have been in her apartment?" Zaron pretended ignorance. "You said it was a very tiny space."

"It must have been in the tube she used to beat . . ." Russell thought for some reason of Olas, "one of the people who tried to . . . find it." The sudden rumble of a fast-moving speedboat caused Russell to squirm down in his chair and miss a change on

Zaron's face. The crafty expression had momentarily dropped away as if to say, "Aha, so it was there after all." The gears and instruments of measurement in his mind saw everything and everyone as a manipulatable object. Now he mapped Russell's mind—its obstacles, hesitations and resistances—though the map may have borne little resemblance to Russell the human being.

They parted later after several hours, each thinking he had understood the other. Zaron guessed that Russell's misplaced loyalty to Sandra and her friends might return unless something better took its place. In the form perhaps of the beautiful Victoria Vargas? Russell, still haunted by the problem of identity and seduced by a vision of glory, believed the boss to be misguided but in need of his help. So he made a vow to himself, conveniently forgetting an idea of Helena's rejected at Justine's party. He would help by making sure Zaron's collection was not elitist and excluded no one.

◆

"Zaron has shown his hand in trying to prevent the Close from being displayed at the bank." This from Helena to Jonah as she looked up and found him observing her from an open office door. He had been following the movement of her thought—puzzled, pensive, ironic—as she studied something on her desk. He was still not used to her mercurial changes in mood. Changeable, but not quixotic or impulsive. Quicksilver was a better term than mercurial. A silvery element that flows like liquid, moving and shimmering as if alive. Her thought was like that: a living thing responding to every shift and quiver in her surroundings.

If she was absorbed in something outside her academic duties, then their moods matched. He too was preoccupied waking and dreaming of Sandra. But that's not what he came to talk about. "Why do you think Zaron did it? What did he hope to gain in preventing the Close from being displayed?"

"It was a preemptive strike," she replied. "And it tells us he will stop at nothing to get the Rothko. To him the affairs of men are only about power. He'd rob his grandmother to get what he wants. Rules, ethics, mores, are to him the pastime of fools. The future and spirit of the city are at stake. But if art is taken over by money, humanity loses." Though neither spoke as they pondered this gloomy reality, her face revealed an extreme disquiet. "You know the story of Atalanta and her foot race, don't you?" The leap to the idea changed a tarnished tone to brightness.

"The race she lost to her suitor?"

"Yes. Atalanta, who had vowed chastity to Diana, never lost a race. She was proud of her feats and reputation and didn't want to change her status as a virgin. But Aphrodite wanted her to marry. It's the story of Eros, the spirit and force that drives everything. So she tempted Atalanta with three golden apples. During the race Atalanta was sidetracked by the glittering balls, and lost."

Helena pulled a book off a shelf and opened it to a reproduction. "Here's a painting of it by the Baroque artist Guido Reni." Jonah came around the desk and looked over her shoulder. It showed the figures of Atalanta and her suitor Hippomenes partially dressed in flowing scarves and running in opposite directions. Atalanta, distracted by an apple, was running away from the finish line, while Hippomenes was running toward it. "See how their scarves indicate the tension between opposing movements? They highlight the moment when Atalanta succumbs to the temptation that will determine her fate. Her story is our story."

Helena closed the book with a snap. "We're in a race right now. What we do next may in a subtle way determine the direction of our city." She returned the book to the shelf troubled by what she said. "Will we succumb to the proud, commercial model that exploits the world, or will we rediscover the human spirit? That's the race we can't afford to lose. Atalanta didn't want to yield to the demands life makes." She mused on the notion for a few moments. "We have to be ready for whatever is thrown at us for good or ill. I think Zaron will try to force the painting into the open. But he doesn't know that we found the stretcher bars." She extended her thought. "Perhaps it's our turn for a preemptive strike."

"How?" Jonah asked, his smoky eyes searching the room as though for an answer.

"I have an idea, but I won't say." When he looked taken aback she clarified. "The fewer people who know the better. It will keep Zaron away from *you*."

When Jonah acquiesced readily, Helena guessed there was another topic on his mind. As he retreated again to the door, she studied his brooding figure, the tall frame, broad shoulders, and sensual features burdened with thought. Behind the smoldering eyes were traces of a pent-up passion, not wild or tempestuous, but a disciplining force. "There's something you're hesitating to tell me."

It was encouragement enough to open the topic of Victoria's affair with Zaron and the stolen photos. Without dwelling on details, he recounted his betrayal with a detachment that invited no sympathy.

"So that's how Zaron knows so much," she mused. "It explains how he had a copy of the photos at the meeting in the High." She continued to speak bluntly, inventing as she went. "A man like that inevitably overreaches himself." This led to another thought. "If we force him to show his hand, then war may be upon us."

"What do you want me to do?" They were university colleagues and practitioners of the arts. But the painting had changed the tenor of their acquaintance. Now they were compatriots in a cause and he would do whatever she asked.

Her playful mood had reemerged. The grey eyes sparkled as she smiled mischievously. "Do what you already do. Be a friend to Justine. . . . And me." He was unprepared for her answer after so starkly stating the consequences if they didn't act.

She noted his disappointment. "Be patient. There may yet be something you can do."

She was staring at her clasped hands as he stood above her. She lifted her eyes to his. "We need to work together. I think it's time you met Justine's sister Sandra."

His eyes opened wide in astonishment as if she had read his mind. What did she mean? Did she know that he had already met Sandra—three times? If so, what was she telling him—or not telling him?

Helena had not missed the shift in his countenance from heavy to light-filled. Whatever worries he had or burden he was carrying, the fires of passion had not been extinguished. "We do nothing yet let nothing go undone," she murmured, repeating the *Tao Te Ching*. His eyes glowed showing he understood.

That same evening at the Woodruff Center Jonah ran into Justine and Bartram on his way to a chorus rehearsal.

"Hello Justine, Bartram," he said warmly, thinking again of her sister.

"Jonah!" she greeted him engagingly.

Bartram growled a brusque "Hello."

"I promised to meet a client down the street," she said, "and Bartram insisted on accompanying me. He thinks I need protection." Bartram glared at Jonah as if *he* were the one from whom she needed protecting. She searched in her purse for something. "My keys, I think I dropped them. Where could they be?" She looked around distractedly. "Oh, now I remember. Bartram would you mind looking by the car," she pointed down the block. "I'll keep looking here." Bartram grudgingly obeyed.

With a look at Jonah that could pry secrets from the darkest souls, Justine pulled the keys out of her purse. "I've been thinking of you. A lot. Would you stop by the Atalanta Bank the day after tomorrow? I couldn't ask you in front of Bartram. He's jealous over your rescuing me during the burglary. I thought you might want to be at the installation of the Chuck Close."

He hesitated. The peremptory invitation must be about more than the installation. He wasn't needed for that. There was more than a casual suggestion in her voice and he guessed it had something to do with the Rothko. Helena's exhortation from the Tao, prompted an emphatic answer. "Yes, I'll come."

"I'm so glad," she warbled, blessing him with expressive eyes. "You and my sister Sandra are the only ones I've invited." Waving the car keys, she called out gaily, "Yoo hoo! Bartram! We found them." And a glum Bartram returned like a defeated hero.

After they parted, Jonah wondered what Justine meant by inviting only him and Sandra to the bank. And in the light of the invitation, what had Helena *really* meant when she said it was time for him to meet Justine's sister?

16

"Come to the bank for the installation," Justine said to her sister on the phone. It will cheer you up." Justine was solicitous for Sandra who seemed dispirited after breaking up with Russell. "Jonah Hartman is coming. He's the only other person I've asked."

"Oh," was all Sandra could manage with a catch in her throat.

"He's broken up with his wife and may also need cheering up."

Sandra's heart soared—then plummeted. Only for a moment could this news dispel the dark nights spent imagining the worst. For weeks she had been burdened with the thought that Jonah was in love with Justine. It pressed on her heart like a coffin of lead and she could no longer conceal her misery: "Then the two of you are free to love one another."

There was a quizzical pause at the other end. "What *can* you mean Sandra? I'm not in love with Jonah. He's a dear friend, that's all."

"I assumed you were seeing him when you told me not to come over or call."

Justine laughed. "I just made that up to keep you away." This was followed by a chuckle. "How could you think I was in love with Jonah? You know I've always been in love with Bartram."

"Bartram?" Sandra echoed, incredulous.

"I know you don't think much of him. I've been waiting for him to grow up since I was six." Justine's comment, if Sandra cared to reflect on it, said she was not misled about him.

However, Sandra's skepticism required a more substantial

answer than Bartram. "But you called Jonah for help the night of the burglary. At the hospital you said to him, 'I will always love you for that.' I heard you!"

"Well I *will* always love him for coming to my rescue. Really Sandra, there is more than one way of loving, it's not all romance."

Sandra's head was reeling. She dared not hope what she most hoped. "I supposed . . ." she hesitated, "I *assumed* that Jonah Hartman couldn't resist you. You're just too lovable."

An idea sprang ful-blown into Justine's mind. Sandra was interested in Jonah. The idea took on a rightness as she considered the possibility. With that in mind she said pointedly, "We're just friends. Nothing else. After all, he is more *your* age than mine, Sandra."

So it was with bright anticipation and differing expectations that the sisters arrived early at the bank the next day. Even as they looked at the portrait, majestic in the open space of the atrium, Sandra's mind was elsewhere. Preoccupation with an imaginary Jonah was now, after months of thinking about him, to confront reality. How to respond, too late and no longer impartially, with coherence and avoid absurdity. The twists of fate that had opened her up and delivered her over to him had happened outside her will. Something impossible had become actual without her, almost in place of her. As if she hadn't been, couldn't be, would never be herself again.

These thoughts were chasing through her mind while she listened for him as if her entire body were an ear. Sounds. Voices and echoes. Then, the tap of footsteps. Coming nearer. Nearer. She waited, breathlessly waited, until they stopped behind her and, slowly, she turned around.

Justine was welcoming him with a warm hug. "I'm so glad you could come." He was smiling at Justine, but his eyes were on her. "Jonah, you remember my sister Sandra?"

He held out a hand that she received like a life line to the drowning. She saw nothing but him. For a moment when he let go her hand, she wondered if she'd survive. It had nothing to do with happiness. It was as though her being were wrapped in some dark, heavy liquid squeezing the breath out of her chest. In the distance Justine was saying something she couldn't hear over the sound of her heart pounding like waves on a rocky coast.

Jonah obediently focused on the portrait, though his eyes kept straying to her. She attempted to look at it too, but saw only him. How long they stood there, dumbly, not hearing, not seeing she didn't know—until a voice broke in.

"Ms. Foxcroft," the voice addressed Justine. "Would you like to come with me? The president of the bank would like to meet you."

Justine addressed the two liltingly, "Is it all right if I leave you two for a while?" They stared distractedly as she walked off. Alone now, they looked searchingly at one another, knowing without knowing that they felt the same.

He was the first to speak and he spoke away from what they were feeling. "I see a resemblance to you and Justine in the portrait. The same eyes and mouth. But it goes beyond resemblance. There's her beauty of character, her liveliness of spirit and intelligence, her wit."

With a stab of delight, she accepted the compliment and deflected it to the art. "It captures movement, change even. My mother appears ageless and alive. Not frozen in time."

It was an excuse for him to look at her again. "Yes, she's here in you." He slowly traced the facets of light in her face. It was as if he had touched her flesh. "You two are alive in the same way."

Dazzled still, she flushed and looked away. It took courage to look at him again. His eyes were waiting and this time she did not look away. How was it that *these* eyes full of smoke as of a slow-burning fire answered to all her longing?

"It's strange how we got here," he mused.

"Stranger than strange." She was thinking of the times they met. Each time a gift. Each time given—even for the possibility of refusing. "Yet here we are," she said gaily.

"I was hoping for a chance to say something real to you."

He qualified. "I've rehearsed it a hundred times these past few months." They lapsed into a joyful silence.

Justine had returned and stared at them in surprise as though their earth had shifted on its axis. Surprise yielded to wonder and wonder to amusement. The look on their faces was so unguarded she was tempted to say, "I've heard of love at first sight, but never this." Instead she laced her arms through theirs and fondly drew them near: "Now I will tell you why you're here. Look at the portrait of mother. Really look. What do you see?"

They looked closely. Primed to see yet seeing nothing unexpected. After a few pregnant moments, Justine could keep quiet no longer. She lowered her voice. "Chuck Close and mother are hiding a mystery." She thought, then corrected herself. "No, they're protecting something, someone. Guess who?"

Sandra and Jonah looked at each other, then at Justine and said in unison. "The Rothko!"

Their response delighted her. "He's hidden in mother's 'head.' Isn't she immensely clever? He's been filling her head ever since Finny gave it to me. You could say she and Chuck Close have been thinking all this time about him. I lent the portrait to the bank as the only way safely to hide the Rothko. It's almost the same size. You two and Helena are the only ones who know mother's secret. I don't dare tell anyone else for fear it might leak to *him.*" She declined to mention Zaron by name. Clutching them tightly she whispered, "I charge you two with helping me keep the painting from all harm. When the exhibition is over we have to find another place for it."

They looked at her, then at one another and solemnly nodded. When they left the bank, they emerged like time-travelers into another place. It was the first day of year one in a brave new world.

◆

The following articles appeared in the local paper in rapid succession:

Joanne Cutting-Gray

Lost Masterpiece Discovered in Atlanta

A great mystery of the art world may be solved. A painting by abstract expressionist Mark Rothko, missing for forty-five years, has been found in Atlanta. University Art Historian Helena Gandolfi, a Rothko expert, recently examined a large blue and silver painting. It is considered the last work of the artist, who died in 1970.

"The painting has to undergo more tests," Dr. Gandolfi stated, "but I have no doubt of its authenticity." The work, now worth hundreds of millions, was long rumored to be in the city. Apparently, the artist gave the painting to relatives, reclusive sisters Sophie and Raisa Sverdlov. They amassed a valuable art collection in their tiny cottage in Druid Hills. This spring one of the sisters died and willed the painting to a local resident, who wants to remain anonymous. Then recently, the second sister died. Dr. Gandolfi, who represents the work's new owner, expressed confidence that "the public will finally get a chance to view this masterpiece by one of the twentieth-century's greatest artists."

Art Discovery Called into Question

Dr. Ouruk Zaron, well-known surgeon, philanthropist, and art collector, contends that a painting recently discovered in Atlanta is not, as has been asserted, the last, lost work by abstract expressionist Mark Rothko. "The painting is absolutely not genuine," Dr. Zaron declared in an interview. "It does not bear any of the hallmarks of Rothko's late dark paintings and cannot be ascribed to him. Most important, the inscription of the artist apparently is absent and any evidence that he painted it is ephemeral. As for the so-called expert who claims authenticity, this is clearly a case of wishful thinking."

Atlanta Surgeon Claims Ownership of Rothko Masterpiece

Dr. Ouruk Zaron, Atlanta surgeon and art collector, now claims that a recently discovered twentieth-century masterpiece, purportedly painted by abstract expressionist Mark Rothko, belongs to him. "The work is part of the collection I purchased on the death of my relatives, Sophie and Raisa Sverdlov, and I have a signed receipt to prove it." When asked why he didn't come forward sooner with proof of ownership, Dr. Zaron explained: "The receipt that Mr. Phineas McGinley claims was given to him is patently false." Asked how Mr. McGinley, who is unrelated to the sisters, came to possess the painting, Dr. Zaron insisted, "It's not for me to explain how it ended up with Mr. McGinley in such a highly suspicious manner. It's up to Mr. McGinley."

After this news was shouted in the media, Helena knew that the danger to the painting was increasing. Now that the Close was on loan to the bank, Zaron might stumble on its secret. Another secure place for both paintings would have to be found. A major museum was the obvious choice. Indeed, Helena knew of no museum beyond the reach of Zaron's tentacles. He was already planning the new museum with the Rothko as its centerpiece. There was only one other person in Atlanta who had both the space and means to keep both paintings secure—though it would take Helena's silvery tongue to persuade him.

Meanwhile, she had to wade into the muck of public opinion, since only an expert would be able to understand what "authenticity" meant. She had bargained on the fact that as soon as the discovery was announced, Zaron would try to discredit her. She was right. Her announcement had been bait to draw out his poison. Alas, poor Phineas! He suffered the viper's sting deeply. It also stung someone else who was about to react with too much venom of his own.

Sir Reginald Foxcroft entered a Midtown restaurant in dark sunglasses, that, as they hide one identity, announce another to the world. He didn't remove them until he reached Helena's table. "I suppose this place is one of your jokes," he said, looking around with distaste at the down-home diner famous for its southern cooking. He was wearing his haughtiness beautifully, his tall torso and long legs in light camel slacks and shirt, a sweater carefully draped round his shoulders. "What in god's name did you think you were doing, Helena?" he said condescendingly. "How could you broadcast the news of the painting before it was authenticated?" The fierceness in his manner was tinged with impatience.

"'*God's name,*'" she grinned, "has nothing to do with it, Regie. Unless you're referring to Rothko's painting the divine absence?"

Ignoring what he considered to be her intellectual arrogance he sniffed, "You practically invited Zaron to shoot you down."

"I didn't *practically* invite him to shoot, I *did* invite him. This is war. And now we know his battle strategy."

He dismissed this with a wave. "And what of the inscription? Why isn't it signed?"

"Did I say it wasn't signed?" she asked disingenuously.

He looked away, retreating. Then, as if something had been overlooked, he demanded, "Did Zaron specify what was on the receipt he found?"

"In the first place, I haven't asked him and, in the second, his word wouldn't count."

"You think his receipt is a fake?" He inquired severely, not caring who heard. The ordinary mortals in this pretense of a restaurant surely wouldn't know a receipt from a recipe.

"Worse than a fake. It's an outright forgery. He learned it from his father, who forged receipts of sales ownership marks and exhibition labels. There's nothing he's not capable of." She paused to consider how to manage his response. "Don't worry Regie. All the evidence is there for any *true* scholar to see."

He sniffed. "The true scholar is not necessarily a *connoisseur*."

"That's why I agreed to meet you here today. I need the connoisseur's help."

"How can I possibly help you?"

The answer came with an interesting history:

Several days earlier in the Art Department at the University,

Helena had asked Olas Lindgard, "How quickly can you copy this?" She pointed to the blue and silver-grey painting in the Catalogue Raisonné. Olas was known for his copies of famous paintings.

He looked closely at the glossy reproduction. "The colors aren't true enough."

"Then how about these?" She handed him a sheaf of photos.

He sifted through them. "Better, but we need higher resolution."

"I also have this," she gave him a computer disc.

They pulled up the images. "Helpful, but the real thing is best."

"Excellent! Now I know how good your eye is. That's why you're such a good copyist. I can show you the real thing—if all goes right." He had stared at the news. "Of course, you are pledged to secrecy, now that you've admitted what you did and declared yourself on our side."

And that cryptic remark, implicitly understood, had an equally interesting history that bore directly on what Helena was about to ask of Regie:

It seems that when Justine first saw Olas at the bank, she wondered where she had seen him before. Afterwards, talking with him, she knew. They had taken each other's measure in her apartment eye to eye through his ski mask before she beaned him with the metal tube! She had considered at the bank whether to let him know she knew. Instead, she surprised him in his studio one day, the same studio where Helena and Olas met to discuss the painting.

Justine caught him up as soon as she walked in the door. "I thought it was you."

"I guessed at the bank you knew it was me. I was hoping we'd meet again, so I could explain and you might understand."

"I'm glad to see your nose is all right." She had pointed to the delicately shaped feature. "It would have been terrible if Jonah or I had broken it. It's the perfect nose for your face." He was impeccably handsome despite the paint dabs on his cheeks, hands, and t-shirt.

"I deserved it." His eyes danced, matching the sparkle in hers, their delight increasing by the minute.

An idea was gathering force. "I think I can guess why you did it."

"Can you?"

He had worked for her father in Buckhead, where he received the first intimation that the painting might have been found. He had decided to go to Zaron, in part because he needed the money, but on the whole because he loved Rothko and didn't want to see the painting prostituted. He had thought the best way to advance into a den of thieves was to pretend to be one. As a result, Zaron hired him to track the painting. Then, when he learned that Zaron was going to hire some thugs to steal whatever work they could find in Justine's apartment, he had volunteered to be one of them.

"It was a way to protect it. I became a burglar for hire and was rewarded with a blow on the chin and a bloody nose." He beamed at her. "Those blows earned Zaron's trust. Ergo, the presentation at the bank."

She turned it over. "So you intended your presentation to be rejected?"

"Yes. Didn't you enjoy the look on Zaron's face and your father's afterwards?"

"Oh, indeed!" Her large brown eyes turned velvety with approval. "And now that you've confessed, what are you going to do?"

"Do what I wanted to do all along."

"Which is?"

"Help you!"

And *that's* how Olas Lindgard joined the guardians of the painting and became the surprise guest at Justine's birthday party for her sister.

And *that's also* how it happened that Helena visited Olas in his studio, showed him the photos, and conceived her bold idea. But it would need the help of the man Helena mischievously now confronted in the restaurant.

And *that* was because of something *else* that happened at Olas' studio: After perusing several of Olas' canvases, Helena had observed critically, "You are a magnificent copyist." At the time, she had been gazing at his copy of a Vermeer. More than a copy, almost the work itself.

Olas paused on the word *copyist*. "I try to understand other artists' thinking by following their work, stroke by stroke."

"You're happy being a copyist rather than an artist in your own right?"

"I rather like it. There's nothing wrong with copying a painting if the copy's good enough. Hang it in a museum and it will do what the original does."

"As in the artists in the Renaissance. They copied Greek and Roman art and workshops faithfully executed copies for the master they trained under. Raphael copied Perugino, only better, and created something entirely new." The glint in Olas' tawny eyes had signaled enthusiasm. "And how would you feel about copying Rothko?"

She had asked the question warily. As a test. Just a hint that it would be easy, and she would know better. Her radical plan for saving the Rothko required a copy—the world would say a fake—but she didn't want it to be false exactly, a cheap fraud. It needed be so close to the original as to be mistaken for it. Of two minds about the integrity of her scheme, she had awaited Olas' response.

His eyes glowed with burnished fire. "Feel about it? Honored! I know I can't reproduce the original. You can only be inspired by it. I'd make it a bit smaller of course to respect the original. An exact copy is just a fake." It was the answer she hoped for. And it had given her the nerve to arrange the meeting with Regie.

And *that* is why she was now at the restaurant about to ask Regie something that would shock him—just as Olas Lingard sauntered up to their table as if he had stepped off a designer's runway. Regie had to decide whether to be affronted or aloof. Before he could register either of these, Helena said, "I asked Olas to meet us here."

Olas held out a hand, "Sir Reginald, I'm happy to see you."

Regie hesitated, then reluctantly accepted the outstretched hand. Feigning innocence, Olas smiled sweetly. "You may glare at me if you like over a glass of wine."

Regie put his glare on hold while a waiter took their orders. Then Helena opened her agenda: "As soon as the exhibition of the Chuck Close has ended at the bank, we need to take it, Regie, to your condo, if you are willing."

"Excuse me? I seem to be missing something. Why should I want the portrait of my ex-wife in *my* condo when my daughter has proclaimed to the world that it's hers?"

"Because he is, you might say, the surrogate for Rothko."

"I fail to understand," he intoned indignantly at being put upon by the lower orders. But even as he said it he caught a glimpse of her idea. "You mean . . . ?"

"Yes!" She lowered her voice. "Rothko is behind the Close. They're about the same size. It was your daughter's ingenious idea."

"And you want me to keep it at my place so . . ." Again, he considered, and again an idea dawned on him.

"So Olas can copy it."

This was enough to stir even his aristocratic aloofness. "You're going to try to pass it off as . . ." He couldn't bring himself to utter the word.

She answered with sterling assurance. "Certainly we are." The pronouncement included the smiling Olas. "If you're willing to help Justine by keeping the painting in your place and letting Olas copy it there, we can insure that Zaron doesn't get too close. It will keep both paintings safe. But don't worry" —she touched Regie's sleeve reassuringly— "your part will be innocent and altruistic. And you can help us judge whether Olas' Rothko can safely pass for the real one."

"It may be altruistic," he countered, "but it surely won't be innocent." He knew, even as he lamented the fact, that resistance was futile. He felt like a reluctant Matthew in Caravaggio's *The*

Calling, when Jesus with a finger silently calls him and he responds astonished by pointing at himself as if to say, "You mean me?" Helena would have her way. And he, Sir Reginald Foxcroft, scion of a family that traced its noble ancestry back 600 years, would be a probable accessory to a crime.

17

Side by side, knees and hands touching, two lovers gazing at one another, amazed beyond measure. Searching his face for a clue to her joy—the unruly curls, the powerful nose, the sensual mouth—her disobedient eyes stray to his, waiting for hers. Nothing between the two save this look of infinite trust. To look openly into the eyes of another is dangerous. More intimate than sex and more powerful. It risks defeating the self you think is yours. Is that why people avoid one another's eyes?

Even if she tries, Sandra cannot not love Jonah. She *has* loved before—with a false and miserable pleasure—and is no longer willing to love half-way and self-protectively. Just one look gives her over to his safekeeping.

It is the third day after the event at the bank. That day had been cut short by work, his at the University, hers at the hospital. That evening they rehearsed their lives into the dim hours of the morning. Less a rehearsal, hearing the past, than an initiation of a lifetime together. Now on day three of the new creation, overwhelmed by all that has happened, they sit side by side silenced by joy, until he murmurs quietly: "*And if the world is too small for thee / Ah, then for me alone shalt thou / Be more than world and heaven.*" Silence, again. They don't notice that with the shades not lowered, sunlight is pouring into Sandra's living room window and the air conditioning is working harder, or that they had left the coffee pot on in the nearby kitchen and their cups of coffee have gone cold.

"Are we going to stare at one another all day?" he asks.

"Ah," she answers gaily, "that's a question without an easy answer."

"I love you," he says. These words absorb the "I" and the "you." They are undefinable, not a question, and yet they ask for a reply: Do you love me?

"I love you," she says in response. Had she answered with anything more— "I love you, too," "a lot," "very much," it would have quantified the immeasurable and negated the words. He bends over to kiss her tenderly on the cheek, and she meets his lips instead. Another long silence.

Yet some things, even for lovers, are too pressing to be laid aside. Jonah's brow knits and the rugged features take on a stormy aspect. "I hate to bring up an unpleasant topic, but I must."

She nods, sobered by what is coming. "Zaron."

He shows her the photos that she hasn't seen before. Even in facsimile, the work exceeds expectation. The deep blue is almost blinding as though security was slipping away. It's what she feels with him, a shattering of individuality, even at times coherence. "I can only imagine what it must be like full-size, in the flesh."

"It's revolutionary. It tells us that we are revolutionaries."

"Revolutionaries?" she repeats, amused at the idea.

"The new is always revolutionary. *We're new*," he looks at her with significance, "ergo . . . ." And he restates the issue: "We may have to blackmail Zaron to keep him away from your sister and the painting."

She takes him up with pleasure. "What do you have in mind?"

"Diversion in the camp of the enemy. A ruse. What if I threaten to make trouble over the photos? Expose his part—Victoria's part—in stealing them? It's a flimsy threat and would never hold up in court, but might frighten her enough to persuade Zaron to drop his claim." That, they agree, might give Helena time to finish her authentication and chart her next move.

"I have an idea too," she counters, "though it's not new. Zaron is an intelligent and competent surgeon, but as chief of surgery and benefactor of the Zaron wing, he thinks he has carte blanche. I was afraid to challenge him before, but now all that's changed." The determination in her voice reveals a new dimension of her character. No hesitation, no concern for a career. That has fallen into a past that no longer is. "I've been keeping a record of his lapses in medical protocol. I might threaten to take them up before the hospital board."

Shaking his head, he answers, "I don't think threats alone work with a man like him. We have to overstep the rules and take a risk."

"Yes!" she answers, her eyes brightening at an idea rejected just days ago. Their love is no longer seen from the perspective of one, or even two. The painting, a third, has imposed a logic of its own.

After exploring everything that might be done, they fall back into staring at one another. "Here I am beside you," she thinks. "I knew your voice long before I knew *you*. It seduced me with its beauty. You sang and cured my deafness. You touched my heart and I burned."

"What are you thinking?" he asks, puzzled by the peculiar glimmer in her eyes.

"I've been thinking of the beyondness of your voice."

"Then I hope it's singing what *I'm* thinking."

◆

Entombed in his office, Phineas McGinley obsesses on his unhappiness. "Why am I thinking about this?" he asks himself perversely. He exhorts himself to think of something else. But when he tries to think of something else—the million-dollar condo he just sold, the realtor's convention coming up, his favorite Irish pub—his disobedient mind strays back three days when *this* was declared to the world: "*The receipt that Mr. Phineas McGinley claims he was given is fake. It's not for me to explain how it ended up with Mr. McGinley. It's up to Mr. McGinley.*"

He keeps thinking about this no matter how hard he tries to

think of something else. "So why think the worst? Isn't that an illusion?" he asks aloud. He understands now why people avoid thinking. To stare into one's thought is dangerous. If he persisted in thinking about the thinking, he might lose the self he thinks he is. So he takes care not to take thinking to extremes.

As a child in school he had been dealt with firmly for this tendency to think, even warned that such persons are dreamers and troublemakers. Never think! Stick to the facts and the real world. His hands touch his knees convulsively as he wonders, "How much more must I endure because of that painting?"

Three days ago Zaron had accused him—Phineas McGinley, ABR, CRS, GRI, respectable Associate Broker and Realtor Consultant at the exclusive agency of Dorston Alsop—of being a liar and a thief! Mercifully, *that* catastrophic day had been taken up with his job. But the same evening he met Helena and they rehearsed his disaster into the wee hours of the morning. There was a great deal of unpleasantness before Phineas McGinley, ABR, CRS, GRI, could accept that his reputation was to be sacrificed for a piece of canvas he never wanted, intensely disliked, and heartily wished at the devil. It was like falling off the edge of the known flat world into warped space. Throughout this ordeal his only consolation had been that Justine "wouldn't have to hang on the cross in his stead."

Misery took root during what Helena called their "little chat." Chat. Disturbing little clicking word. As usual, Helena had been able to persuade him to do things entirely against his will, his reason, and even against his character. In the white, clean space of her living room he had no place to hide as she invented a map of his future. He had listened, conscious of what he was opening himself to, as she compared Justine's "heroism" to the city of Atlanta.

"Justine is fighting for the spirit of the city. Is it to be the descendant of Lumpkinville, another center for commerce and the bottom line, or a place for the human spirit?" He must have looked confused. She immediately added, "Lumpkinville was the name of the original railroad crossing. One name for the settlement."

When he still looked baffled, she prepared him for heroism. "Let me tell you a story. The fleet-footed huntress Atalanta and a man named Meleager took part in a hunt for a monstrous wild boar savaging their city. Meleager killed it, but Atalanta struck the first blow." She sought some sign of understanding on Finny's vacant face and finding none continued. "The myth explains our, that is *your*, situation. The boar—that's *b-o-o-r*—savaging *our* city is Zaron, who represents the profane spirit of a commercial culture. Justine, like brave Atalanta, inflicted the first wound on his bristly hide, and in a chivalrous act Meleager—that's you, Phineas—" she said with a silvery luster in her voice, "Meleager killed the boar and presented the head to Atalanta in homage." A pure white flame was in her eyes making her unavoidably present to him.

She added ironically, "I won't *bore* you with the details. It's all there in a marvelous painting by Rubens." She went to a shelf, pulled down a book, and showed him the work in which Atalanta, with the heavy head of the boar in her lap, turns in gratitude to Meleager. "Justine is a modern incarnation of the hunter-goddess."

"She doesn't look like her." His literal mind could find no resemblance between skinny, waif-like Justine and the fleshy, half-naked Rubenesque goddess.

"She will." Helena insisted enigmatically. "See how the boar's tusks seem to extend beyond the picture plane into our space as Meleager offers her the hairy pelt?"

He looked dutifully. The ferocious head of the boar—tongue hanging out, beady eyes staring out at him—was not an image to inspire courage. "Nothing surely could be more noble," she offered as a salve, "than to fight for the spirit of a city. You'll have to take the brunt of whatever Zaron throws at us—lies, accusations, suits, counter-suits." Lifting her glowing face to him in blessing, "But a noble deed can still find a place in our world."

"What happened to that chap, Meleager," he asked glumly, not relishing the danger implied in "a noble deed."

Her grey eyes flickered darkly, "There was a battle contesting the right of Atalanta to the trophy, and Meleager . . . perished."

"Perished?" His eyes bugged in horror. Helena saw. Snapping the book shut, she replaced it on the shelf, and offered him a whiskey.

Now three days later entombed in his office, with the words "Meleager perished" still ringing in his ears. Three days and no resurrection. A Meleager battling the mob. He groaned, "I wish the painting had never come to me. I wish it had never been painted!" That made him recall something else Helena had said, "The sun isn't missing, the blind man just doesn't see it." When that thought didn't please him either, he consoled himself: "Thank you, but I prefer blindness."

He winced, as compulsively he repeated words he didn't want to hear. "Lies, accusations, suits, counter suits." A silent voice accused him. For distraction he checked his phone. Fifteen messages he didn't have the heart to read. The drone of the office intruded: the insect clatter of the printer, the buzz of the fluorescent lights, the whine of the air conditioning—all the rumble of a faceless, indifferent void.

◆

"Imagine, Bartram," Justine said on a burnished summer evening in the park, "Sandra thought I was in love with Jonah!" Her grin suggested happy incredulity.

"How could she think that?" concealing his previous anxiety on the subject. "He's more than twenty-five years your senior." It was a deliberate exaggeration. "He's going gray."

"That's what I told her. Well, not the part about the going gray."

"She should have known you better."

Her large eyes glowed mischievously. "There's more," she teased, playfulness restored. "I'll tell you after the concert."

Justine and Bartram were taking in a jazz festival on the oval of Piedmont Park. The evening, neither too hot nor too humid, brushed everything with pleasure. And yet, as they sat on the grass and listened to joyful sounds in tune with the setting, she was unaccountably restless. In an abrupt change of disposition, she suggested they forego the concert and walk to the Botanical Garden. The current exhibit was called an "Evening with Nightshade" featuring plants that release their scent at night.

She set off with a rapid pace for the gardens, leaving Bartram in the dust. The source of her agitation was the painting. For twenty-three years she had sailed on a smooth open sea and suddenly slammed into a submerged rock—the Rothko.

Catching up to her out of breath, he asked, "Are you in a race?"

Preoccupied, she had completely forgotten him. "Sorry."

"You took off so quickly, you didn't hear my question. What happened to Sandra to change her mind? About you and Jonah."

The question dissolved her pensive mood, and she responded with amusement and even greater conviction, "They came to the bank to see the portrait and instead saw each other. It was love at first sight."

Bartram stopped dead on the pathway. Sandra and Jonah? Not possible! If Justine hadn't told him this herself, he would never have believed it. An idea that encroached on his vanity had to be wrong.

Justine turned to where he stood dazed by this news and looked at him curiously. "Why did you stop?"

"No reason." He shook his head and fell silent. They continued along the sweeping path arched by a tunnel of trees. Shaken from preoccupation with Sandra and Jonah, he now took account of the setting. The two-story glass building with a garden visible on the roof greeted them at the end of the wide walkway. They entered a soaring atrium with a swirling Chihuly glass sculpture as colorful and alive as any specimen. As they emerged into the garden, the exotic fragrances of jasmine, orchid, and ginger, the sweetness of alyssum, four o'clocks and lily enveloped them. Seduced by the delight of the evening and Justine's companionship, his mood became relaxed and happy.

The lure of the garden had turned their walk into more than a path between two points. Every few yards they stopped to take in the fragrant displays. The cool air, living sculptures, blooming plants, and twinkling lights made everything magical. They climbed the canopy walk high in the trees where floral scents floated in the air and the warble of birds and the thrum of cicadas. The walk wandered through a wood and gradually wound to a cascade garden where a living earth goddess, her face and hair made of thousands of tiny plants, meditated beside a waterfall whose threads flowed through her open hand.

Justine pointed to the tranquil expression on her face, "She's the goddess of serenity."

Instead of looking at the goddess, Bartram stole a look at Justine. Her entire body was engaged in the act of seeing. They made their way in companionable silence to a rectangular courtyard planted with the tall trumpet-like Datura whose pendant blossoms in white, pink, and apricot were strung like lights on the drooping branches. Justine leaned over to inhale the perfume. "Hmm," she murmured, as impulsively she pulled a tall weed sticking out of the bed for the pleasure of feeling it yield. Crumbs of soil still clung to its roots and gave off an earthy scent that delighted her.

Bartram stood transfixed. "Why have I not noticed this about her before?" She had only to raise a weed to her nose and smell the singularity of common things. Her flesh, smoothed to perfection, lent her a natural grace as delicate as the pendant flower. Justine still, but a self-possessed woman with the childish wonder for which one mourns the loss. Her presence was unsettling to his robust sense of himself. He had once taken as an axiom that Justine should love and appreciate him. It was what he deserved. But tonight, in the atmosphere of the garden, he no longer thought love was something that could be deserved.

―◆―

In Tuxedo Hills Zaron sits beside his pool crafting his next move in love and ambition. His current Proserpina is in her pavilion pouting and he has time alone to think. The setting sun is still hot. He moves into the shadows and the first hint of an evening breeze. He fantasizes on another beautiful Proserpina—other, that is, than the two, painting and mistress, he keeps at home—imagining her, too, at the beck and call of his lust. Sandra Foxcroft has made an unusual appointment to see him at the hospital on her day off. It's a sign. So far, she has eluded him. But with Baramore wholly out of her picture, she may be ready to be added to his collection. Any woman, he presumes, especially one in his sphere of influence, will not be able to resist him forever.

There is an old question here that needs to be asked again: How can a man like Zaron, intelligent, handsome, charismatic, rich; a skilled surgeon running a hospital, manipulating public opinion, amassing an art collection, attracting beautiful women—how can such a man be utterly blind to himself? He can be credited with all these, yet he's trapped in the double-entry bookkeeping of blindness and desire. And these are dangers. Anything not reducible to a fixed object, anything doubtful or beyond his control, threatens his idea of himself. In presuming to be all powerful, he blinds himself, lives a lie, and makes himself weak.

The next day he sits in his office eagerly awaiting the beautiful internist. Arriving at the hospital smartly dressed in suit and heels, her dark hair artfully coiled atop her head, she causes more than one head to turn in the hallway and more than one eyebrow to lift. It isn't only a change in clothes that creates ripples of curiosity, or the fact that she's here at all. It's that unusual radiance.

For the first time since becoming an internist Sandra Foxcroft is really free. Just weeks ago, all her actions were cautious: "Weigh all options and consider all risks." It had been her mantra. If cowardice is the name for what makes a courageous act unthinkable, then she has been a coward. If the true act is free from external necessity and internal compulsion, then her radiance may owe something to this first true act. Her purpose, so close, so clear, gives her the courage she needs to confront the chief of surgery.

"He's expecting me," she declares firmly to the receptionist. Without waiting for an answer, she knocks sharply on the office door.

It's immediately opened by the chief himself. "Dr. Foxcroft, a pleasure," he hails her obsequiously. "Please come in." His eyes travel over her figure-hugging suit and shapely legs. What fuels his appetite is not just her appearance and the fact that she requested the meeting, but something that happened yesterday at his mansion.

At ten in the morning, Jonah Hartman had driven up, parked, and rung at the front door. It was opened not by a servant, but by Jonah's estranged wife, Victoria. She stared with open mouth, shocked to "meet the enemy at the gate." "Jonah, what are *you* doing here?" she scolded, disconcerted. She quickly recovered, insolence in the dark eyes and tilted head as the glittering jet on her caftan trembled in indignation. With haughty stare, outthrust bosom, and arm dramatically barring his way, she was Carmen . . . Donna Elvira . . . Lady Macbeth.

"Are you going to invite me in?" he demanded brusquely. "I don't have time to waste on theatrics. I came to see you and Zaron."

Her stage expression slipped a little and was replaced by genuine surprise. "He's not here. What do you want with him?" she asked haughtily, with an edge of suspicion. When he didn't answer, she hesitated as if deciding what to do. Then checking to see that no one was watching, she gestured him inside and carefully shut the door. "This way," she announced majestically, and glided down the hall expecting him to follow. The jet beads on her caftan clicked lightly as she passed in turn the grand living room, the dining room, and moving smoothly into a smaller but equally elegant sitting room, motioned him to a chair. With a click of beads and sweep of caftan she arranged herself across from him on a loveseat and stared. In the short passage down the hall she had settled on a stance: defiance.

Without preamble Jonah laid out his course of action. He was going to publicly press charges against her and Zaron for stealing the photos and using the information to make a false claim for the painting. He watched to see how she took this.

While he was speaking, the color rose in her exquisite face, until, temper aroused, she attacked angrily. "You have no proof! You're doing it for revenge against me."

He frowned—with her it was always the personal. "Don't waste my time. *You* stole those photos and gave them to your lover. You're responsible."

She refused his gesture. The fragile shell of the self couldn't allow it. The beads on her caftan shook uncontrollably. She was loving and pure and persecuted. One large, perfect tear slid slowly down her cheek. Then, like a scene in slow motion, the lips curled, the eyes shot black sparks, the raven head tossed accusingly as though to say, "How could you be so cruel? How could you do this to the woman you once swore you loved."

What she screamed instead was, "You're jealous and a failure! You couldn't bear that I was more famous than you, so you gave up your career. You're jealous because I left you for someone ten times the man you are." She hurled spitballs of invective. "You want to get back at me and ruin my career. But I won't let you!" Rising like a vampire, jet beads shaking, she threw herself at him. Calmly he grabbed both wrists and shoved her down hard on her knees. For a second she lay like Tosca crumpled in a heap before Scarpia. When he made no move to assist her, she glared up at him and, gathering the folds of her caftan, slowly got up without help.

He turned away in silence and headed for the door. When she

saw he was leaving, she grabbed the back of his shirt to detain him, but he twisted away and walked slowly down the hall. She followed behind calling him names, the beads clicking like insects. She still was screaming imprecations after he had let himself out and shut the door.

That evening there were two quite different accounts of this event. Jonah gave Sandra a brief, dispassionate account. Without dwelling on the dramatic excesses, he described the charged mood. "Victoria was shocked and resentful as you might expect. The threat about the photos frightened her enough, I think, to pass the blame onto Zaron."

A theatrically embellished version of this event was what Zaron heard from his overwrought diva. Jonah's "violently cruel behavior," and "menacing threats," related between bouts of tears and protestations of innocence, told Zaron more about what really happened than if he had been there. He had listened impatiently to a hysterical tirade that blamed him for everything. She would be accused as a thief and her reputation ruined because *he* had forced *her* to take the photos. He dismissed Jonah's threat outright as inconsequential, and to spare himself more histrionics, reassured her. As he placated and soothed her like an actor reciting lines by rote, he thought instead of the appointment the next day with the bewitching, ever so-much-more-rational Sandra. Finally, patience exhausted, he bit back waspishly, "Cut the histrionics, Vicki. You're not on stage. Go powder your face, and we'll have some champagne beside the pool."

With a haughty snap of her head, she stalked off to sulk in her pavilion, leaving him alone with the pleasure of plotting his next move with Sandra. She would undoubtedly bring up the painting and he was eager to argue the topic point by point. Confident he was the quintessential man of sufficient reason and wielded a calculative power that could out-maneuver any argument. Yet argument is only foreplay to what he really wanted: a woman. Not just any woman, but one that challenged him, matching him wit to wit until she succumbed to his power.

This then, is the background when Zaron with gleeful emphasis shuts the door to his office behind a dignified Sandra. "Please sit down," he offers gallantly to his unsmiling colleague, and points to a chair in front of his desk. There is something inherently false about his tone, as if he has practiced it ahead of time. "I seldom see you in street clothes. Hospital scrubs disguise a woman's beauty." The words make no impression, so he tries again. "You wouldn't be here on your day off unless you had something important to say. I hope I can help."

When this attempt at pleasantry is received with silent disdain, he opts for the personal. "I'm sorry to hear about you and Dr. Baramore. You made a fine couple."

The mawkish expression of concern causes a look of contempt to pass across Sandra's face. "We're still good friends," she replies sarcastically.

He puts on a false smile as if her answer pleases him. She stares the smile down. "Let's forgo the small talk, shall we? I'm here for one reason only. I demand that you publicly withdraw your claim to the Rothko."

Her peremptory request startles him. She has brought up the subject he's been fishing for, but not in the petitionary manner he expected. He leans back in his chair, touches his fingers together tip to tip, and studies her face cagily, preparing to sidestep the demand. "Now why would I want to do that?" A cold stare makes him dodge again. "The painting is clearly *not* a Rothko!"

Still she says nothing. Plays him like a fish on a hook.

He can't resist another jerk on the line. "The picture is rightfully mine, you know." She stares at a point above his head as if she hasn't heard him.

He grows visibly uncomfortable in her resolute silence until this bursts out: "I never give in without a fight. You ought to know me better." He bares his teeth in a menacing grin.

"I would not presume." The words crackle with irony. "The picture, whatever it is, belongs to my uncle and my sister."

He clucks disapprovingly, "Now Dr. Foxcroft, Sandra, we both know what this is all about and who you represent. I'm hearing someone else speaking, not you." He gives her a sympathetic look that says he's on her side. "You wouldn't make such a pointless demand otherwise." Even if he's callous, he's unnerved. He wants her so he's both engaged and annoyed. But he's attracted and she's not. The object of his desire is refusing to act like an object.

"And I'm hearing nothing but evasion." She speaks coldly as if he were a chattering squirrel guarding a nut.

By now he's provoked to the point of threats. He gives up the role of seducer for that of tyrant. "You seem to forget who *you* are and who *I* am. We're colleagues, yes, but I'm also your superior. Your position as an internist in this hospital depends on me." When she remains indifferent to this too, he begins to squirm.

If the fear he tries to arouse in her isn't working, it's because the discomfort she arouses in him is. She is forcing him to regard her not as an object of conquest, but as a mystery. That a human being might not be a mathematical equation or an organism under a microscope or a player in a winnable board game—these are ideas incongruent with everything he loves. For he does love. There's no question of not loving. It's just that what he loves has already been decided: He loves hating the truth.

And yet she is silent. And so it presses him to defend himself. "Why should I give up what's in my self-interest?" In the contest of gazes, his is the first to yield. He looks away for a moment. What he says next takes on the gesture of a shrug. "Everyone acts from their particular interest. Even the people you represent."

She refuses to give an answer to this repellant man who assumes that "self" and "interest" are givens. If he thinks she will be provoked to explain herself—a ruse to lustfully admire and tear her down—he is mistaken. She rises majestically from her chair. "If that's your answer, then it's in your *self-interest* to know what *I'm* going to do. I'm charging you before the Hospital Board for lapses in medical protocol that stretch back several years." And then with contemptuous irony she says, "Thank you for seeing me." She grins her social smile but does not offer her hand. For a brief second, he is stunned.

"I'll show myself out."

He had just been subjected to one of those infamous short sessions in psychoanalysis. The sudden shutting of the door that produces a shock and the questioning effect that undercuts certainty. It's like removing a chair from under a person in the act of sitting. If he had known anything about himself or about psychoanalysis, he might have understood some of that. She had come to demand he give up his claim to the painting and he had rejected it as a bluff. This imperious breaking-off and walking-out however is entirely unexpected and comes like a voice in a whirlwind. It leaves him speechless. Not given to *not* having the last word, he calls after her as she walks out the door, "Then you and I are at war. And *I* never lose." The only answer is her figure retreating down the hall.

18

"You played beautifully," Helena said to Bartram as they were leaving Symphony Hall. He had performed the tender flute solo in Brahms's First Symphony that evening for an enthusiastic audience. He accepted her compliment with a princely smile. They lingered on in Woodruff Plaza enjoying the magic of the city lights. The evening had the serene aura of late summer yielding to a milder fall, as if the harmonious sounds of the orchestra had spread over the city and dulled the noise. Here in the green enclosure of the plaza, the city hadn't given in to the showy glamor and alien jumble of neon, glass, and steel. "This is the heart of Atlanta," Helena said almost to herself. "Midtown, middle earth."

Bartram caught her thought, "And complemented by the canopy of trees."

She looked at him sharply, surprised that they shared the same thought, and answered emphatically, "Oh, indeed!"

They crossed Peachtree and slowly wound their way home through Ansley Park—a village within the city—admiring what they knew so well they didn't have to see—the rolling landscape of cultivated yards, parks, and perfectly maintained Craftsman-era homes. "Want a nightcap?" she asked as she opened the door and turned off the house security system.

"Yes," he answered, "lemonade. I'll be right down." He headed upstairs to stow his flute. Helena was in the kitchen when she heard the shout, "Mother! Mother, come quickly!"

She hurried upstairs and stopped in the doorway, thunderstruck.

The contents of his bedroom and study were strewn across the floor, drawers emptied, clothes, music, papers, scattered everywhere. "We've been robbed!" He said mournfully as he picked up a valuable piccolo that had been discarded on the floor.

Impossible! The security system had been on while they were gone. "Call 911," was all she could manage. He called, nodded, and grabbing her tightly by the arm began dragging her toward the stairs.

"What . . . ?" she questioned loudly.

"Shssh," he whispered, and pulled her down the stairs, out the door and down the driveway. "The police said to leave the house immediately. Someone could still be inside."

She shivered despite the warm night air. "But how could it happen? The security system . . ."

"My bathroom window was broken. That's how they got in."

"How?" she asked dumbly. "It's on the second floor."

"I don't know. Let the police tell us."

Within minutes a patrol car arrived. Two officers stepped out and instructed them to remain outside while they searched the house and grounds. Fifteen minutes later one returned to explain. "They used a ladder to get in and exited the same way to avoid the security alarm downstairs."

"What does that mean?"

"That it was probably an inside job. Whoever it was watched the house and broke in when you both left."

The words, "inside job" left Helena reeling as Bartram asked, "But where did they get such a tall ladder?"

"From somewhere in the neighborhood probably," the policeman conjectured. "It's still leaning against the house, so someone will claim it." Bartram was taken back upstairs to see what was missing. He looked at the mess on the floor. "They didn't take anything valuable as far as I can tell," he said, and pointed to the music case on a table. "I had my gold flute with me this evening."

After the police and forensics left, Helena and Bartram,

exhausted from the shock and upheaval—it was now one in the morning—sat disconsolately in the kitchen. As Bartram drank lemonade and Helena sipped bourbon, they discussed what had happened.

"If nothing was taken I can only come to one conclusion," she opined. "Zaron! He meant to intimidate us." Bartram agreed and for once had no smug reply. She had never come so close to futility. Wasn't it inevitable that the tentacles of money and power would reach far enough to trap or strangle her? When they had rehashed the event sufficiently, they wandered off to bed. The next morning Helena received an urgent phone call.

"Helena, it's Jonah. I'm at school. You'd better come down here quickly. I'll explain when you get here."

Jonah met her as she walked up to the Fine Arts Building. "I'm afraid your office has been broken into," he explained gently. Her face, heavy and slack-jawed, already the image of dismay. They found several security guards stationed in the office doorway. Inside was a macabre repetition of the night before, only worse. Books were thrown off the shelves, the desk emptied, file cabinets opened, papers scattered helter-skelter across the room. A life's work in total disarray! She was usually a model of self-control, but now she wanted nothing so much as to collapse on the floor and wail.

Jonah picked up a chair that had been tossed into a corner, righted it and had her sit down. "I arrived early and found your door open and the room ransacked. Ever since Justine was burglarized I check on your office when I go to mine."

She could barely take it in. Brought low by two break-ins in less than twenty-four hours. He was saying something about the police being called in to investigate, but if she heard, it came as a distant inarticulate babble. Thoughts fluttered like fireflies in her head lighting up in one place and then another in a dizzy blur.

Jonah prodded her gently. "Helena, we should see if anything important is missing."

She got up stiffly from the chair and began half-heartedly sifting through the rubble. Unable to think straight, see clearly, feel coherently—she didn't have the heart to try. For the moment chaos overwhelmed her reference points.

Jonah saw her condition and gently set her back in her chair and began putting things in general piles. He went about his task, neither asking questions nor disturbing her in any way. Gradually, his calm, steady presence roused her sufficiently to want to help, and they continued the disheartening job, she directing, he sorting. As he returned books to the shelves according to her directions, they discovered what the intruders had been after: a book on Rothko with a number of pages roughly torn out and thrown aside.

"They were looking for my authentication notes on Finny's Rothko," she said softly. Jonah looked at her in alarm. "They didn't find them. As a precaution I've kept everything related to the painting at home in a safe and I take my laptop with me when I leave, even to go to lunch."

"So you were expecting something like this," he declared in quiet admiration.

And that's when she told him what had happened the night before.

"Whoever did this," Jonah offered, "was either ignorant of what he was looking for," he pointed to the torn book, "or diabolical enough to want to demoralize you."

"Or both," she said in a tone of futility.

He nodded in agreement, "What will they try next? I think the sooner you bring the painting into the open the better."

"I'm going to have to go straight into *la bocca del lupo*," she lamented, "and tell Zaron what he wants to hear. Let him have the painting for his new museum. At least it would be available to the public rather than locked away in a collector's vault." But then she thought of Rothko's preference not to have his works exhibited at all rather than in a way that was destructive of their meaning. He had had a deep sense of responsibility for the posthumous life of his pictures in the world. Could she have less? Should she allow her feelings to prevent her doing him justice?

"And what will be in 'the mouth of the wolf'?" Jonah asked, worried that in her present mood she might do something imprudent.

"'Vanity of vanities, all is vanity,'" she quoted bleakly. "Did you know Hebrew has no word for *all*? Things are *struck* with vanity? The word actually means to fly off and dissipate like smoke. I've been asking myself the same question." She raised her eyes from the floor, still piled with papers, "I've let myself be defeated. But I won't make that mistake again." Then continued without self-pity, "I don't know what I'll do." With the toe of one shoe she shuffled through a pile of debris. Spotting something on the floor, she reached down and fished it from under a folder. It was a print of *Wrecks* by Alex Katz minus its glass and frame. She laughed out loud.

Jonah who had been putting files in order looked up. "What is it?"

"*Wrecks*, Katz's dog. They took the frame and left the print, which is worth several thousands."

"It's a sign," he said.

"Of what?"

"That we're not *wrecks*, from this. That whatever you decide to do, don't let a *frame*"—he underscored the word— "constrict your action."

She laughed, then quoted one her favorite obscure writers. "You mean, let an act emerge 'from the luminous darkness where thought gives itself to be thought'?"

He stared, "Indeed."

She had overcome her darkness.

◆

Russell was shocked. More than shocked. He had stopped at the door of a patient to read the chart: trauma, mild concussion, cuts and bruises, no internal injuries. Then he read the name, blinked, and read it again. It was not a mistake. What to do? Send in another physician? That would raise questions.

In becoming entangled with Zaron, Russell had swept his recent past aside like so much chaff. Introduced to the world of fame and money, he let everything else fade. His ideal as a healer betrayed by expedience, his loyalty to Sandra, to Justine, to Helena conveniently laid aside. Even Olas, once the most luminous star on his horizon, diminished. No matter that Zaron expected him to play Dogsberry in everything from architecture to art collecting—the most menial tasks were carried out with inflated pride. He even escorted Victoria Vargas to social functions when Zaron couldn't. It was all immensely flattering to one who secretly modeled himself on the surgeon-art collector. Until he read the name of a patient on the chart outside his room.

How does truth burst into a world of illusion? In a flood of sensations. As he froze at the door, his hand grasping the handle, joy and fear seized him. He took a deep breath, prepared his professional face, and firmly strode inside.

The bandaged face in the bed was barely recognizable. A swollen upper lip may have inhibited Olas Lingard's speech but not his vehemence. "How could you? How could you sell yourself to such a man!" The young man in the hospital bed sputtered. "Have you no shame? Where's your pride? You sold your soul to that panderer, that seller of indulgences, that . . . that Lothario of Art!" Olas winced in pain as he shook his head in disappointment, then he turned into the pillow unseeing.

The gesture destroyed what was left of Russell's restraint. Abandoning the professional demeanor, he sat down at the bedside and reached to stroke the bruised forehead. When Olas tried to push his hand away, Russell caught him by the wrist and drew his hand to his breast. Olas did not resist as tears rose in his eyes.

"Tell me what happened, Olas," Russell begged, still clutching his hand tightly.

Haltingly he told of riding his bike to Zaron's mansion and finding the door unlocked. "I snuck inside to search for the fake receipt of the Rothko. I got no further than the picture gallery when a couple of security guards found me. They pounced on me," he said in a broken voice. "Beat me. Then they threw me out the door laughing. I dragged myself off and rode here."

Incredible! Russell thought. In this state, Olas had ridden nearly seven miles *here* when other hospitals were closer. Why? To find him on duty? "Did they recognize you?" he asked, worried. "If Zaron found out that *you* were the intruder he might do much worse than have you beaten." He raced through excuses that could keep Olas from being arrested. "Do you know if they filed a report with the police?"

"I don't think so. I had on a bandana to disguise my hair. The guards probably thought I was just a snatch-and-grab hoodlum."

Russell's shook his head. "It was a dumb thing to do."

"No dumber than your joining forces with Zaron," he retorted, snatching his hand away from Russell's clasp. "Anyone who gets close to Zaron is tainted. Lying, cheating, bribing mean nothing to him. He thinks everyone does what he does and judges by his own dishonesty." He was weeping now in distress and it was all Russell could do to keep from cradling him in his arms.

"Please don't Olas," he pleaded, as bereft as a barren tract under a dark cloud. "I'll cut my ties to Zaron."

"How?" Olas snapped between sobs.

Russell fished for an answer and found none. "I'll find a way." He resumed his doctor's manner. "Now let me check your injuries." Finding nothing serious, he concluded, "You'll be able to go home tomorrow. Pain killers will get you through the next few days."

Olas had calmed down and regarded him thoughtfully. "Do you really mean it, about giving up on Zaron?"

When Russell saw the earnest, imploring look on his face, his heart took flight again. "Yes, of course. I've been wrong, really wrong. I lost my way," he confessed remorsefully.

"Good, then you can begin tonight by helping me break into Zaron's office."

Russell registered incredulity. "You're crazy. I can't break into his office."

Olas looked at him cockeyed shaking his head. "There's nothing to it. You take pictures with your phone of anything you find. I'll be your lookout and pretend to be lost if someone comes along."

"What if I'm discovered?" The consequences horrified him.

"Say you found it unlocked so you checked to make sure everything was okay. They might suspect *me*, but they'd never suspect *you*, one of their own physicians, of trying to break in. Besides, you're not really *taking* anything," he gave a lopsided grin.

In vain hope, Russell asked, "How would I break in? It's locked. I have no access to a key."

"A door like that is nothing to get into," Olas asserted confidently. "I could use a scissors if I had to. But I don't have to. Most doors are secured by tumblers and a few metal pins and springs to keep them from turning. A key pushes the pins into position so the cylinder rotates. Instead of a key you use two metal picks."

Face to face with what he most desired and too long denied, Russell gave up his objections. If it were between losing his job or losing Olas, the job would have to go. Extricating himself from Zaron and his museum would be difficult enough, but extricating himself from Olas was now impossible. Every inclination argued against it. Still he clung to the hope that Olas would change his mind. But Olas was an artist with an artist's passion indifferent to convention or the law. If he, Russell, didn't do what Olas wanted, it would be done without him. Though Russell had rounds to finish, he lingered. By the time the door to Olas' room closed behind him, Russell was planning how efficiently to examine the contents of Zaron's office.

◆

That night the hospital floor was inhabited by a ghostly silence. While the staff on duty enjoyed the quiet hours before dawn, the attending internist nervously crept toward the darkened end of a corridor that contained the staff offices. He was followed by a barefoot hobbling young man in a hospital gown. With shaking hands, Russell held a flashlight while Olas inserted two picks into the lock of the door. Seconds took on the weight of eternity, as anxious and sweating, he watched Olas deftly work on the keyhole.

"Damn!" Olas cursed under his breath when for the fifth time his pick slipped against the cylinders without tumbling them.

Russell would have given up, but not Olas. Another minute passed. And another. Silence, then rhythmic footsteps sounding down the hall. Closer. Closer. They stopped as, breathless, waiting, Russell standing, Olas crouched at the door. Russell was ready to drag Olas away by force when he heard a tiny click and an elated "Yes!" The door opened. As Olas got up, he pushed Russell inside. Then the steps faded. "Don't worry. I'll remain on guard in the hall," he whispered and shut the door.

Moving over the contents, Russell's shaking hands barely kept his penlight steady. First he tried the desk. Locked. Then the file cabinet. Not locked. Straining against the slightest sound, he searched. Top drawers: medical records. Second drawer: more records. Third drawer: the same, until the letter Z. Opening the drawer wider, he pulled out a file labeled Zaron Foundation. Laying it on the desk, he shuffled through until he came across the words Art Acquisitions. He photographed the entries, returned the file to Z, and shut the drawer. Listened again. Nothing. Emboldened, he drew a metal probe from his pocket and tried to tease open the desk drawer lock. After a few seconds and much to his surprise, it clicked open.

Fishing in the back of the drawer behind the usual desk paraphernalia: pens, paper clips, post-it notes, rubber bands, he felt something soft and leathery. It turned out to be a small, crumpled pocket diary from 2012-2013. He thumbed through entries. There were no names or times, just dates and figures. He was arbitrarily photographing the entries when he heard Olas talking to someone. Hastily he turned off the penlight, returned the diary to the back of the drawer, and listened.

"Where is Dr. Baramore, nurse? I need to see him," he heard Olas ask. He couldn't hear the answer. "Where is Dr. Baramore?" Olas repeated in a feigned panic. "I won't go to my room until I find him!"

Was it a signal? Reassuring sounds were followed by more cries for "Dr. Baramore." What should he do? Stay put? Hide behind the desk? He waited as the cries and soothing murmurs gradually faded. Gingerly he opened the door. No one about. He shut it softly, and scurried down the back stairs to the resident's quarters with the buzz of the pager assaulting his ears.

19

The stalwart, honest healer of the sick is driving his accomplice, the man who tried to burgle Zaron's mansion and Justine's apartment—driving him in broad daylight on busy Peachtree toward Zaron's neighborhood! There are reasons why Russell feels not himself: breaking into Zaron's office the night before, getting little sleep afterward, and absconding from the hospital with Olas in the passenger seat. And yet he feels strangely free. He steals a cautious look at Olas, who, scrolling through photos on Russell's phone, gives him a lopsided grin. The lips are swollen but they don't conceal a delicately modeled refinement suggesting tenderness. The smile raises a smile on Russell. They arrive at their Buckhead destination, park, take the elevator to the fiftieth floor, and ring at the penthouse door.

Of all people Helena opens it. Behind her are Sir Reginald and another surprise, Phineas McGinley. In the background hanging like a portent on the wall is a huge blue and silver painting next to an almost equally huge, unfinished copy.

"What have we here?" Helena asks wryly when she recognizes who Olas is with. Regie stares censoriously, Finny, curiously, at the battered young artist and his companion, enemy and former friend.

Pointing accusingly at Olas, Regie finds voice enough to ask, "What happened to you? And what is *he* doing here?"

Helena ignores Regie and grabs Olas' right hand roughly to examine it. "Good. At least you haven't injured your painting hand."

"We broke into Zaron's office in the hospital," Olas declares gleefully through his pain. A response to this depends less on what the others know, then how far they can see. Helena, wondering what new hazards this portends, raises an eyebrow questioningly. Finny's face alternates between blankness and curiosity. Regie is all suspicion. His whole body seems to back away from what he'd prefer not to know.

Russell meanwhile stares at the finished painting unsure what he's seeing. "That isn't . . .?"

Finny looks mournfully up at it then back at him. "Yup, that's it. Him."

Before Helena can explain Regie breaks in: "Explain yourself young man." Whereupon Olas describes to a captivated audience how he got beaten at Zaron's mansion, and with more enthusiasm how he and Russell broke into Zaron's office. It is apparent from the look on Regie's face that in spite of this account, he mistrusts the internist. "See here, Olas, what makes you think Baramore there," he points accusingly at Russell, "won't turn coat again and report us all to Zaron? How do you know he won't tell him about *this*?" An arm sweeps majestically across the room at the paintings.

Russell looks meekly at each person in turn and asks, "What *are* you doing?"

Helena is impudently brazen. "What does it look like? Olas is making a copy." Regie bristles at this disclosure. If his concern is that Olas has brought a viper into their midst, Helena doesn't seem to care.

Russell looks questioningly from one person to the next. Olas hasn't informed him *what* he's been doing here, only *that* he is living there again.

"I'm making a copy of the painting," Olas volunteers almost reverently, "under the supervision of Dr. Gandolfi and Sir Reginald." His admiration of Helena and her alliance with Sir Reginald has restored a respect for his former boss.

"But why copy it?" Russell asks, confused. His blinders about

Zaron may have been removed, but he can't see how Olas would agree to a copy. In Russell's mind, a fake.

Helena interrupts, "First, tell us what Zaron is up to." She has no time to waste on explanations.

Then Olas interrupts. "First, you need to look at what's on this." He hands her Russell's phone.

Helena takes the phone and leaves the room. She's gone for an hour, but when she returns the mood has changed. A nearly empty whiskey bottle and three empty glasses attest to some conviviality. Phineas, who is usually gloomy around his former brother-in-law, is regaling them with a comic version of the burglary to peals of laughter. Olas is lying in his chair with one leg draped over the arm, while Russell wears a dazed but happy look, and Regie, who seldom drops his stiff façade, may have drunk himself into a relaxed American mood.

"I hate to interrupt this pleasant tete-a-tete," Helena comments wryly, "but I have news." The suddenly sobered faces look immediately at her. "I've been going over the pages in Zaron's diary and I've found something extraordinary." She pauses dramatically and nods at Russell with approval.

"The prices Zaron paid for his paintings?" Phineas pipes in.

"No."

"Kickbacks paid to his cronies?" Regie interjects.

"No."

"Paid for his *misht*reshes?" Olas mumbles from some degree of consciousness.

"No!" She looks at Russell expecting him to guess. He only shakes his shoulders and looks blank. "Taxes."

"Taxes?" they chorus.

"Almost. Taxes unpaid. Or taxes avoided. For two years, he has claimed enormous deductions for art donations he didn't make. I checked it all out. The dates match his foundation acquisitions. Inferior art at ridiculously high valuations. He needed more funds for his museum."

Even Phineas is excited by Helena's discovery. He reads in it a promised retribution for injustices suffered. "You are going to tell the IRS, I hope, Helena?" His simple, empirical mind can't be sure she will do what he's certain everyone would do in her place.

"I will to do no such thing." Her answer rings with finality.

He resumes a habitual look of gloom. In his cause and effect world, to know with certainty is to know by evidence. But what he does not know is that certainty leaves everything else out. All the intuitions he over credits, everything that happens to him every day without a cause or reason.

Helena assumes the far gazing eye of a seer. "We save this information for whenever we need it." Then she turns an eagle eye on Russell like a bird of prey fixed on her quarry. "I presume *you* will keep mum about this? Otherwise, you may find yourself defending your life of crime in court."

The warning does not pass unheeded. The unspoken concern is Olas' copy. Now, looking at it again, Russell's eyes grow as large as an owl's. "Won't Zaron be able to tell the difference between a copy and the real thing?"

"Zaron will never be able really to see a painting, any painting, because he doesn't want to. There is none so blind as one who does not want to see. He would never allow a mere painting to bedazzle and humble him. But if he can keep a work of art under his command, there is little to receive. He only gets himself back as in a mirror."

Russell has never heard art spoken of like this, except perhaps from Olas. He looks again at the original and the copy beginning to see. Caught up in the mood cast by Helena's words, the others gaze at the paintings. Then everyone begins talking at once. When Russell tells them forthrightly what he has been doing for Zaron, he unconsciously straightens in his chair. Confession has released him from a burden he didn't know he carried.

With the aid of strong coffee they begin discussing their next course of action. Olas is silent, which they attribute to the mixture of alcohol and pain killers. Suddenly he declares: "If Zaron has reported me to the police it could jeopardize what we're doing here. Especially what *I'm* doing," and he points to the unfinished copy. "There's only one thing to do. I'll turn myself in. I'll say that I burglarized Justine's apartment on Zaron's orders."

Accounting for Olas' condition, Helena interjects dryly: "It's admirable that you would sacrifice yourself, Olas, admirable but unnecessary. Zaron won't press charges against you. It would reveal what he did. He will deny he ordered the break-in and prevent being implicated." She becomes stern: "What you need to do is give up crime and harebrained schemes like breaking into houses and offices. Concentrate on painting. Stop trying to fix the world. Learn a lesson from Rothko: Art is *not* self-expression. Keep self out of what you're doing as he did in his work. Then *your* Rothko may catch the spirit of the *real* Rothko."

A somber expression and moist eyes show that Olas has taken the message to heart. He climbs unsteadily to his feet and announces that he is going to bed.

The others linger in Regie's living room. The presence of the painting has stripped away their individual interests. Without expecting to get anything, Russell is discovering the place where his desire has led him. Regie too seems different, still a bit officious and stiff, but charged with a shared commission, as if loneliness has abandoned him. Even Finny, who can still barely look at what he calls "those color splotches" without wincing, is moved. Better said, he is pushed—as a weight pushes by its own momentum—to let the painting, "have its way with him."

Helena knows there will be disagreements, clashes of will, possibly even betrayal before their charge is accomplished. Yet she feels the painting guiding them.

Jonah and Sandra are talking in the living room of her town

house. He says, "I have new insight into the *Passion* because of all this talk about art. Bach's work is not some museum piece of the past. It speaks to us now as a witness." Since he moved in with piano, scores, and a few bits from his condo, Sandra had become a participant in his way of thinking aloud about music. Sometimes he asks her a question just to see what she will say. Their intimacy grows in this kind of conversation, where questions are discovered in neglected corners of thought and where answers are not the point.

He continues thinking aloud. "In the same way that Rothko embeds color in his rectangles, Bach embeds color in the choral lines. He reworks a single tune in the *Passion* in different keys and textures that bring new layers, new colors to the drama."

She nodded slowly as she took it in. She wasn't a musician but one event in her life had prepared her for Jonah. It was a print of Raoul Dufy's *Red Orchestra* that first hung in her room as a child, then in her dorm at college and her apartment at medical school. Her mother had given it to her to "chase away the blues." She had adored the intensity of sound that rose in a fiery red mist and blur of quick brush strokes over the orchestra. It was as if Jonah had always been waiting in some back corner of her mind.

They are still deep in conversation about the concert performance when the front bell rings. Sandra opens the door to Justine. "I bring news and gifts." Retrieving a large package from the steps, she hands it ceremoniously to Sandra. "A housewarming present."

Sandra answers dryly, "A little late, don't you think? I've been living here for two years."

"I beg to differ," Justine winks at Jonah and corrects her facetiously. "You've *occupied* this house for two years, only now are you beginning to *live* in it." She looks around the once pedestrian living room that has acquired a new liveliness. The piano is the focal point of the entire first floor and gathers into harmony the eclectic pieces that Sandra acquired as a newly-minted MD. The sofa and chairs have been rearranged close enough together for conversation rather than spread randomly around the room to fill empty space. The posh, trophy kitchen, with more pretense than cuisine, is now filled with the happy clutter of utensils, shiny cookware, fresh vegetables, flowers and pleasant cooking smells. A world shines forth reconstituted by the couple and their new life.

Smiling in anticipation, Sandra opens the box, which contains four packages. She hands two to Jonah and they unwrap them. The packages hold framed copies of the four Rothkos in the Phillips Collection. "I once owned a real one," Justine cries gaily as Sandra gives her a hug, "but you'll have to live with copies."

After admiring the pictures, came the question where to hang them. Sandra is for hanging them in the living room, but Jonah proposes a line ascending the staircase. Instantly all three agree it's right. Only then does Sandra remember and ask saucily, "Ok that's your gift. What's your news?"

Justine looks craftily from one to the other. "I just came from a visit at father's. And guess what I saw?"

"The painting!" Jonah erupts.

"Yes! And that's not all." And she goes on to describe the copy.

Sandra is amazed that her father, who had declined any previous involvement with Helena and Olas, was now with them hand and glove. "But why a copy?" she asks.

"I'm not sure. Apparently, Helena is hatching a plot that she's keeping to herself."

Sandra looks questioningly to Jonah as he speculates. "Helena is a rare person who sees possibilities where others see impracticality. She's a *bricoleur*, inventing as she goes along. That's why she'll always be steps ahead of Zaron. He can only see what's in front of him."

Justine has more news. "Russell has returned to the fold." Her eyes become translucent globes as she tells of Russell and Olas' break-in at Zaron's office. Sandra wonders how the daring Russell Justine described could be the same career-focused, risk-adverse man she knows. Apparently, there was a man underneath those layers of caution. Justine's eyes shade as she tells the rest: Russell and Olas have fallen in love. At first, Sandra is shocked. Russell has become someone else. But then, so has she.

The three discussed all this and more while eating dinner. Afterward they waited for their other guest to arrive. At eight sharp the bell rang.

Bartram entered as suspicious as a man could be who expected to find his lover in the arms of another. His invitation was Justine's idea. She intended to show him that his jealousy of Jonah was unfounded. He was icy at first as he observed the couple, so obviously in love, though he did try to disguise it. Justine read this as a sign that something really was wrong. She had never seen him as he was now: uncomfortable and distant.

He had more to be disgruntled about than Justine knew. If he was no longer jealous of Jonah because of *her*, he was jealous of him because of Sandra. He had always preferred Sandra's aloof beauty to Justine's waif-like prettiness and half-convinced himself that she secretly admired him. In this too he was deluded. Sandra couldn't stand him because of the way he treated Justine. Now Bartram's jealousy has in its sights Jonah as the object of both women's admiration. He had secretly gloated when Victoria left Jonah for Zaron. But that Jonah should no sooner lose one beautiful partner than gain another equally beautiful was an assault.

So it took a while for him to accept Jonah and Sandra as lovers without personal offense. He didn't miss the aura of happiness between them as they served coffee and dessert or the way it generously included him as guest. As the evening moved on, he visibly relaxed and accepted the inevitable. The conversation moved naturally and easily onto music. While the two men discussed the finer details of the score something amazing happened. Caught up in his love for music, Bartram entirely lost the excess consciousness he carried as a weight, revealing a knowledge of music that was deep, passionate, and eloquently spoken. In fact, he so lost himself that

Sandra couldn't believe he was the same person she had always known.

Eventually the lovers made an excuse, discreetly left him and Justine alone, and went upstairs.

She, who never missed an alteration in mood, and had seen the change in him tonight, brought up the Rothko prints again. He stared long and hard admiring them. Finally he said, "They appropriately suit the new life of Sandra and Jonah."

Justine nodded her head in wonder. There was not a tinge of jealousy in his language or demeanor. She had seated herself on the floor to study the pictures lined against the wall and he sat down beside her. With arms about her knees and feet tucked under her long skirt she was like a flower whose petals had folded into itself. A wave of sadness came over her, as if what she experienced with him tonight, what she had so longed for, would never really be. She, who joyfully embraced change, was afraid of a new-found happiness.

Bartram did not miss the change. He leaned tenderly toward her. "Justine, what's wrong?"

"Nothing." She shook her head slowly, solemnly.

"Let me help," he implored softly.

"You can't," she repeated, but with a grace that took the sting out.

He felt her sadness as a greater wound. And taking her hand, held it tightly, restoring them to one other.

20

In agreeing to care for the two paintings, original and copy, Regie had rallied to a cause. Secretly, he enjoyed having Olas with him again, not as servant this time but as artist. He even warmed to people he once disdained—Finny, his former brother-in-law, and Russell. Both came to the condo in Buckhead every few days and for different reasons to observe the progress and stayed to talk about art. Imagine, Finny McGinley talking about art! In fact, all four, Regie, Finny, Russell, and Olas often talked over drinks into the wee hours of the morning when tongues were loosened and what was said was not remembered. All for one and one for all, they had made a pact to protect the secret hidden in Regie's condo. However diverse their perspectives, the work in progress had turned four individuals into a fraternity. It was a strange twist of fate then, when of all people who could conceivably show up in their midst, it should be Zaron's mistress!

It happened like this: One evening Helena arrived at Regie's and was greeted by the four men grinning like hyenas. When she saw the mellow state they were in, she tactfully suggested that Olas, Finny, and Russell go out to eat so she and Regie could have a good gossip.

They had just settled down in the living room when the unaccountable happened. The doorbell rang! Mysterious, since only those on a security roster were permitted to use the elevator to the penthouse. Though the painting and its copy were now hidden in a gallery room Regie kept locked, caution was essential. "I'll go into the bedroom while you get rid of the caller," Helena whispered. "Rap on the door when it's all clear."

She waited, expecting Regie to dispatch the visitor in a minute or two. Minutes passed and still no knock. Then voices in the living room. A female! Helena cautiously cracked the door and peeked out. The woman, whose back was turned, was elegantly dressed in heels, designer cape, and hat. Whoever she was, her effect on Regie was dramatic. His eyes blinked rapidly and he appeared flustered. When the guest turned to look around the room, Helena understood why. Victoria Vargas, Jonah's ex-wife and Zaron's lover! She strained to hear what they were saying.

"I'm honored that such a famous artist should pay me a call," Regie intoned. "You must be extremely busy with a performance coming up at the ASO."

Victoria's back stiffened as she answered coldly, "I have withdrawn from the *Passion*." He seemed surprised and amused, so she added with an edge of annoyance, "It would be awkward, don't you agree, to be singing for my ex-husband?"

He appeared not to understand, and so convincingly that Helena wondered if he were the only person who didn't know that the celebrated diva was divorcing her famous husband. But when he threw a deadpan look in the direction of the bedroom, she saw that the pretense was for *her* benefit. "Ah yes, forgive me, I did hear something," he apologized loudly.

"Do you mind if I sit down," Victoria inquired haughtily, and without waiting for an answer, removed her cape and sat down on a low chair, her back to the bedroom. From behind Helena could only see the collar of a filmy white blouse, but she caught the effect in the widening of Regie's eyes and assumed there was much less of the blouse in front.

"Please do," Regie said breathlessly as he seated himself across from her.

"I won't take much of your time. I have little to spare," she sang in a note of soprano disdain.

"Certainly. I'm at your service," he said with an ironic grimace.

"Now that I've corrected your lapse in memory about my ex-husband, you may perhaps recall who my partner is?"

He cleared his throat but said nothing.

"I'm here on *his* behalf," she said loftily.

Regie's eyes widened, astonished at her presumption, then narrowed in distrust.

"Dr. Zaron wonders if you have any information on the whereabouts of Dr. Russell Baramore. You can appreciate that when Dr. Zaron employs someone, he likes to have that person available at all times." The insistence on titles continued. "Dr. Baramore seems to be out of touch lately and Dr. Zaron thought perhaps you might know why."

"And this is important to me how?"

She added accusingly, "I am assured by Dr. Zaron, that Dr. Baramore has spent time here with you."

Regie's tiny hazel eyes expanded into pale greenish globes as they looked first at Victoria's blouse then in the direction of the bedroom. "Mr. Baramore has been to see me occasionally in the past," he tendered guardedly. "But as he is no longer with my daughter, I have no idea of his whereabouts. I'm not in the habit of accounting for people with whom I have only a peripheral acquaintance." The last remark shut the door to further questions.

"Bravo Regie," Helena whispered under her breath, "a British freeze out." But his cool response did not appear to ruffle the diva, for she made no move to get up. At the expense of missing a response to this delicious rejoinder, Helena retreated to the bathroom and sent "Dr. Baramore" a text saying, "Trouble. Stay away from R's."

When she returned to her vigil, Victoria had moved to another topic and her lovely soprano had a riper sound. ". . . And as *my* face will foster *all* the arts, he wants *my* face associated with the new museum alongside his. He thinks my picture will bring people from around the world to see his collection." Then adopting a false tone of confidentiality, she added, "He would never have just anyone represent the museum. He said it has to be someone as beautiful as any work in the collection."

With a solemn smile and mock-deferential nods, Regie seemed to be encouraging this paean to herself. Either this was vintage Regie or part of the act for her, Helena's, benefit. Victoria appeared to have forgotten she was in a rush and inquired in a creamy voice, "Well, Sir Reginald, aren't you going to show me some of your famous collection?"

Alarm rose in a wave over Regie's face as he hemmed and hawed, "You'll have to excuse me, Madame Vargas. I'd be delighted to show you some of my pictures, but I have a guest who requires my time and attention."

Her back immediately stiffened. "Oh, I see," Her voice dropped an octave to a cooler register. "You should have said something." Then rising from her chair like Botticelli's Venus from her shell, she resumed her favorite topic. "I hope your 'friend' will forgive me." Her head lifted proudly. "But really, Sir Reginald, you should have said something." With a bow, Regie proffered his hand and kissed hers, which seemed to restore her mood. Deliberately turning in the direction of the bedrooms with a knowing smile, she revealed what had attracted Regie's attention. Exposed above the low-cut blouse were the two half-moons of her breasts and between them hung a gorgeous pearl necklace that disappeared into the ruffles of the cleavage. With the practiced motions of the theater, Victoria slowly put on her cape, shook her mane of black hair becomingly, and smiled like the beauty that she was.

No surprise then that Regie had succumbed to a figure and face so perfect, eyes so dark and flashing, lips so beautifully molded. Not for the first time, Helena thought of Jonah, one of the most reflective human beings she knew who had been blinded by such beauty. Victoria's flawlessness might make one gasp, but now he was with Sandra. Everyone took her for beautiful too. If not on this theatrical scale, with a beauty of mind to complement her appearance.

After the diva left, Helena returned to the living room where Regie was still hyperventilating. "Are you coherent enough to know what she really wanted? Do you think Zaron sent her or she came on her own?"

When Regie recovered from the erotic miasma and answered, it was with the *harrumph* of put-upon innocence. "Coherent enough? I beg your pardon."

Ignoring this, she thought aloud, "If she came on her own she may have overreached herself."

"Is that your impression?" Regie quibbled, not wishing to extend his neck to the blade before testing its sharpness.

"You mean of her as a person or her reason for coming?"

He winced, then said loftily, "Whether Zaron asked her to come or not, her interest was genuine."

"Genuine as in candid and unaffected, or genuine as in authentically false?"

His eyes lifted heavenward in exaggerated protest. "Really, Helena! I thought she played her little game rather sincerely."

"Sincerity is one of the worst self-blinding vices. It's like the murderer who says, 'I sincerely didn't mean to kill her.' Victoria Vargas wouldn't be able to differentiate between sincerity and veniality." Then yielding ever so little added, "However, I agree with you. Her so-called sincere self-interest made her want to help Zaron in all sincerity."

As he held back, she read his thought before he thought it and knowingly lifted an eyebrow. Was it not strange, she mused silently, that a man so acquainted with the world should topple like a tree before a seductive woman flirting with him? She had once seen him tear up when his greyhound died, yet not shed a tear when his wife did. How then might he have responded to Madame Vargas, if *she*, Helena, hadn't been in the next room?

To neutralize an uncomfortable topic, he shifted gears. "I really must say something to security about letting strangers to my door."

"Indeed. Victoria Vargas' ability to get in means others might. She wanted to know about Russell. How often do you see him up here?"

A trace of recognition passed across his features but did not filter into his answer. "He comes here from time to time," he sniffed, "to see the progress of the copy."

"The copy, or Olas?"

"What can you mean, or Olas?" His face went blank. He would not understand what he didn't want to accept, nor accept what he could not approve.

"I won't deny Russell is interested in the painting, but he's even more interested in our fair young artist. And I think the fair young artist is interested in him."

"You seem to forget, Helena," he cautioned primly, "that Russell was Sandra's partner." Whatever he may have remembered from British Public School was not a topic he wished to discuss.

She gave him a look of argent incredulity. "You are either the most innocent man alive or the most sublimely oblivious."

The rusted gears meshed and the unoiled pistons groaned. Whatever his mental machinery revealed he refused to accept it and, smarting like one who had missed a double entendre in a joke, changed the subject. "I need a drink. Will you have one?"

Helena, who understood that her intensity sometimes exhausted others, agreed. "Yes. Let's celebrate the success of our little eavesdropping behind-the-screen. But first, if you don't mind, I'd like to see the two paintings."

He unlocked the door and turned on the light. She had seen Olas' copy just a week ago when it was not fully there. Today it had found its place as a tribute to the original. For a long time she simply stared at the two works side by side, wondering at the miracle that often occurs at the last stroke of the brush. How is it that a painting is not finished until that mysterious moment, when like the travail of childbirth, the painting cuts itself free to become a separate being? She continued to gaze with Regie alongside, until she asked, "Can you tell the difference between the two?"

With a hand on his chin, he looked again at the copy, then the original. "I've been asking myself the same question for several days. The copy is amazing, almost a twin of the original. Not *exactly* alike. Rothko used a medium that is impossible to duplicate. Still, Olas has done something noteworthy. At a first glance, I'm not sure I'd be able to say—except for the difference in size—which was which. Using an aged canvas, and painting M. Rothko on one of the original stretcher bars will make it look genuine."

"Finding the stretcher bars from the dumpster was fortunate. And you're right," she half-accepted, half-qualified, his view, "Rothko paints a membrane so thin, so multi-layered, only an expert would be able to see a difference. It's not Olas' skill that is in question though. It's something else."

Perplexed, he looked at her for an answer.

"Olas Lindgard, for all his ability, intelligence, and sensitivity, is young. He has only experienced a little of the rejection, bitterness, and discrimination suffered by the sixty-seven-year-old Jew: foreigner, recluse, thinker, and sojourner in the world. All *his* experience is distilled in each brush stroke. That takes the humility to put himself and his suffering aside and find the human itself." She paused a moment looking for the right words for herself and for Regie. "In understanding the power of light to do opposite things, to both illuminate and extinguish, Rothko grasped the formless *outside* creation, but did *not* try to paint that. That would have been representation or worse. You could even say he paints the empty bed of an absent love. That loving emptiness is the essence of all his greatest works, especially the dark paintings that bear the weight of forbidden glory."

"Forbidden glory?" He echoed, puzzled, but reaching for the insight eluding him.

"Some things are 'visible' only invisibly. The black and mauve paintings in the Houston chapel reveal the magisterial glory of the nothing, the empty void. They speak the divine by not naming it and reducing it to a thing. It's the lack of a name or an image that opens a place for the divine to appear. That's the weight that Olas' painting cannot bear. Every painting has its own inner light. Olas' is of the world *after* creation. It is light. But it is Olas' light."

"I don't quite catch your meaning. Are you just saying that his copy is inferior?"

"Not at all! It's perfect." She looked up at it again and her thought took a leap inconsistent with what she had just said. "In fact, it's more than a copy, it's almost . . ." She hesitated, unwilling to speak the word. She tried again. "Olas has been inspired to do something remarkable. Do you remember Rubens' copy of Leonardo's lost *Battle of Anghiari*? As great as the Rubens is on its own, it still bears the indefinable signature of the hand that originally wrought it."

Whenever Helena talked like this Regie inwardly rolled his eyes. This time however something in her manner lifted him to her side. He studied the two paintings again trying to see what she saw. As his usual aesthetic consciousness—the critic's judgment of beauty and taste—began to wane, something odd happened. In the briefest of moments, the dark blue and silver-grey of both paintings loomed so large it filled the room like the night sky. Then it disappeared.

Exhausted by the event and Helena's inexhaustible energy, he asked quietly, even humbly, "Should we have that drink now?"

"Yes!" The sparkle of her answer made him want to gather her in his arms had inbred reticence not prevented. Instead, he held the door open and with a gallant gesture ushered her back into the living room.

While he opened a bottle of champagne, she rustled up some hors d'oeuvres in the kitchen. Then they settled down to enjoy the Atlanta nightscape from fifty stories up. "Don't put the lights on," she requested softly, "let's be illuminated from without." By the time they had finished a second bottle, the beautifully polished shell that encased Regie had opened a little. He talked, mainly about art and a nostalgic English past that never was, while Helena, who never tired of human analysis, observed what she called "the working of the obstructed subject."

It usually took the form of an enclosed rationality limited to the kind of knowledge found in an encyclopedia—useful, efficient, repeatable—and utterly useless in dealing with affect. Regie's was a particular case: a connoisseur who brought vast knowledge about artist, history, and technique, but without being captured by the singularity of any work itself. There was a barrier between him and the work like the glass between this room and the night sky. For him Art—always with a capital A—was a protective container rather like his manner. He had been molded by disappointments that were more characteristic of the man than his aristocratic appearance.

As his tongue loosened, she heard the rare, melancholy song of desire. He was making a gift of it, sending it out into the universe, the song beyond the self. The line in Whitman came to mind: "I am larger, better than I thought; I did not know I held so much goodness." As she let him talk and empty his soul to the dregs, she supplied the empty place of the analyst.

Realizing that he had been doing all the talking, he murmured wistfully as from a deep hollow, "Helena, I'm glad we're friends again. You seem to understand this Englishman like no one else."

Understand? Yes, she thought, it was her calling as a Morellian—to discover in people as she did in art, the real in the little things. Regie was filled with longing, and though his overall demeanor often said the opposite, he revealed that longing in a thousand different ways through gesture, expression, even sighs.

Still in a confessional mode, he added, "I see what you have been saying about the two paintings."

She replied in a voice that took on soft lustrous tones whenever she found a meeting of minds, "The authentic painter paints what is given to him. It is a gift . . . of love. Augustine says, 'For what I am I love, since I have put in this place all that I am.'"

In the darkness she felt Regie's eyes embracing her as this came softly from his lips, "You know, Helena, you are still a very beautiful woman."

What she thought was, "Eros flows like water wherever there's a low spot." What she said was, "You're not going to fall in love with me are you, Regie?" He had once been her suitor! It happened after Kate died. He had been divorced for several years and pretended not to be touched, yet was secretly wounded. But he had lost more. Even his daughters had deserted him. So he had retreated into his polished shell like a nautilus and sealed the valves to its chambers. Their brief love affair had drawn him out and caused her to wonder if that's why she yielded. The only ostensible reason at the time had been that she loved his pictures. Now this evening had evoked things she wanted to forget. Abruptly snapping on a lamp, she exposed the lost, crestfallenness of a human face asking for love.

21

Helena got off the elevator on the lower level of the Museum. Here, as everywhere in the building, light welcomed both the faraway and close at hand. Tall African effigies and totems were reflected dramatically through a glass wall into the trees, buildings, and people outside while an exhibition of drawings invited a quiet intimacy. Though pressed for time, Helena couldn't resist looking at a favorite line drawing by Ellsworth Kelly. She loved the way, with a single, continuous pencil stroke against a clear white ground, he was able to invoke a full world. Turning away reluctantly, she continued a reflective walk to the glass conference room. Inside, giving a lie to the transparency of glass, a cloud of grey pinstripes hung thick around Zaron. Lawyers! What was supposed to be a private consultation had become juridical.

As she reached for the glass door, the anonymous faces looked at her with bland curiosity. Among the phallic neck ties was the single bow tie of Arthur Sadlowe, art consultant of dubious reputation. Not a crook exactly, but someone who could be persuaded, or could persuade himself, to err on the side of self-interest. Art experts were reluctant to commit themselves in cases where there might be a long legal battle. There is always the chance of being sued for *not* claiming as genuine something that turns out to be. By aligning himself with Zaron, Sadlowe was proclaiming himself in advance on the side of a lie.

She had requested a private meeting in the vain hope of forestalling a court challenge. Surprisingly Zaron had agreed—provided a member of the board presided. Helena accepted, confident that the spineless Felicity Hardcastle would pose no real challenge. But the presence of the lawyers altered everything. In a pretense of transparency, Zaron would depend upon legal obfuscation to camouflage a false receipt and a false claim. She might have been amused at the carnival side show had the stakes not been so high and the consequences so far reaching.

Seeing this much in one glance through the looking glass, Helena strode confidently through the door and sat down at the long conference table. Zaron, having observed her, parted the cloud of lawyers and sat directly across. Following this cue, the lawyers aligned themselves on his side, leaving a single chair beside Zaron empty. With the blunt instincts of a predator, he scrutinized Helena for signs of weakness. Ignoring him, she motioned through the door to Regie, distinguished by well-tailored aloofness, to sit beside her. Whatever might happen, Regie would help her make their deception, the copy in his condo, work.

Several days before the meeting, he had been coached on how to act. "Regie darling, your face is an open book in that you hide everything. To an American it looks suspicious."

He had turned a watery pink at the word "American" and sputtered, "I'm not accustomed to laying out every little fiber of my soul in the dim light of public scrutiny."

"That's my point. At the meeting, be even more yourself than usual. Remote, unapproachable, condescending. We want to intimidate the other side." He did not miss the irony in asking him to *act* rather than *be* the aristocrat. The message on his face said, "I don't know why I put up with you."

And her reply was, "You wonder why you put up with me. It's because I say things you'd like to say but can't."

He blinked several times and frowned. The directness he admired when she practiced it on others exasperated him.

"Regie dear, if I didn't exasperate you, you'd have far less to feel righteous about."

He cast about for a rejoinder. "Really Helena, you can be so vulgar."

"Yes, and you love it."

A sigh said it was true but that he'd prefer not to be reminded. Having caught the meaning, he refused to acknowledge it. "Really Helena," he exclaimed, repeating his favored form of exasperation, "you act as if you're directing a player on the stage."

"I am. Our meeting with Zaron will be high theatre, Stygian drama with a comic subplot. If our scheme works, Zaron and his lot will be confounded. If not, we will accept defeat gracefully and hand over the painting."

Now, in the conference room, she was reminded of that conversation. The presence of the lawyers proclaimed that the meeting was not about a painting but about money and power. If she and Regie were to win, they must not be distracted.

Last to arrive was Felicity Hardcastle, the supposed mediator who had obtained the conference room as neutral ground between contested borders. With an expression of pinched nerves, she looked about puzzled, until Zaron beckoned her to a place beside him. Flushed at how compromising this looked, she gave Helena and Regie a wan smile of apology.

The meeting was ready to begin at last when Zaron got up abruptly, prompting several lawyers to do the same. While everyone waited, they conferred in a corner with whispering and vigorous shakings of the head. After they returned to their seats, one of the lawyers opened the proceedings with a long speech claiming that the painting held by Mr. Phineas McGinley rightfully belonged to his client. Helena listened, darkly contemplative, as the voice droned on in tortuous double-speak that flayed words of their sense. When he ran out of hot air, another voice described "exhibit A," a receipt included in the Sverdlov collection, "proving conclusively that Mr. Phineas McGinley has no legal right to the painting." Helena looked at her watch. Already an hour had passed in false contention and boredom.

She and Regie listened silently for another hour as the lawyers, one by one pontificated, threatened, and cited obscure legal precedents. When it was Arthur Sadlowe's turn to speak, he did so with a prissiness that purported to explain why the painting was *not* genuine. "The quality is not sufficiently high to indicate it is the Rothko. It does not have the nihilistic darkness of the Chapel paintings that expresses the artist's depressive state of mind." His psychological analysis was another subterfuge. Zaron didn't care about authenticity, only supremacy. He was using legalisms to fragment and delegitimize every proof.

Now, as if on cue, a burly-looking lawyer rose to full six feet plus of height and towered over the table menacingly. If the first two hours were a macabre version of *carrot*, he was the *stick*. He addressed Helena in a hostile voice that implied "I'll get you," arguing that the University, Helena's employer, "ought to have known the painting owned by Phineas McGinley belonged to Dr. Zaron and therefore it may be an accessory to a crime." He finished by insinuating, "Dr. Zaron may be entitled to damages." Then with a flourish he handed Zaron a paper. Expecting that the painting would be handed over summarily, he had already drawn up a contract.

The paper lay on the table conspicuously as the meeting droned on. Finally, Felicity spoke: "Dr. Gandolfi and Sir Reginald, perhaps it's time to present *your* case." Zaron leaned back in his chair, arms folded in all his glory. As for the lawyers—wing-tips shuffled, throats cleared, papers gathered, briefcases opened and shut—as though their cause was won.

Helena and Regie did not stir. They opened no brief cases, shuffled no papers, laid out no pens. It took a full minute for the other side to realize that the two had come unarmed and without paper bullets.

"Let the fine doctor speak," Zaron snarled, leering open-mouthed at Helena.

With an actor's sense of timing, she smiled at each face across the table until they were all visibly uncomfortable, then began. "I requested an *informal* meeting to resolve a question of ownership without lawyers and the shadow of litigation." She stared pointedly at Felicity, who flushed grey. "But my request wasn't heeded." Felicity looked away; Zaron chuckled soundlessly; Sadlowe sneered.

"The painting is genuine," Helena declared. "Dr. Zaron's receipt is a forgery. And I can prove it in any court of law. I will not waste more time proving it here, but all legal challenges will fail. Mr. McGinley does not want the claim of ownership to drag on needlessly. He hasn't the funds or the time for a court case. Nor does he want to see a legal procedure grind on while the painting remains out of public view in a vault."

Zaron interrupted. "You expect me to give up my claim just because McGinley doesn't want to go to court?" He laughed heartily at the absurdity. The laughter registered as grimaces on the lawyers' faces and rigidity on Felicity's. They reminded Helena of a painting by Bosch, *Christ before Pontius Pilate.* In it the accusers are arranged claustrophobically around Christ, their features revealing their inner ugliness.

"I think you're getting ahead of yourself, Dr. Gandolfi. Show us your proof!"

"I didn't come here to prove anything," she answered scornfully. "Your receipt is a sham and so is your claim. Mr. McGinley has the genuine receipt, signed and dated by the Sverdlovs with whom he had forty years of friendly relations."

"And you expect me to take this at your word? Really Dr. Gandolfi, you amaze me."

Refusing to stoop to his level, she did not reply.

Felicity interrupted in an unsteady voice. "Perhaps Dr. Gandolfi should be invited to explain why she thinks the case does not have to go court."

"Then she should get on with it. I'm a busy surgeon and my people"—Zaron gestured toward his hired operatives—"are busy people." Slamming both hands on the table dramatically to cut off further comment, he charged, "State your case now Dr. Gandolfi, or this meeting is over."

The lawyers who had hijacked the meeting resumed their foot-shuffling and paper-shifting. Helena and Regie, hands folded on the table, did not move. Only when the sound had dwindled to the buzz of florescent lights, did she go on. "Since you've already wasted three hours, we will be brief."

Then Regie rose majestically to his feet. "This meeting is a ploy," he glared at Felicity and she winced. "It is a crude ploy; it is a deceitful ploy; and it shall not stand. Dr. Zaron has no claim. The painting is his means to another end: Money. When in the end he loses, he will still have gained what he wants most—notoriety." Leaning across the table his hands gripped tightly on the edge, he declared in a commanding voice, "I have offered to buy the painting from Mr. McGinley. If he should change his mind and agree, I will fight you with every resource I have."

There was a visible stir at this announcement. Sir Reginald's money and clout would be a *real* challenge. The mood in the room was in flux. The fog had lifted and a space cleared for something new to emerge.

It was into this openness that Helena spoke. "Mr. McGinley offers a solution," she said calmly. "He will give you the painting." This caused consternation. She continued: "With two provisos: First, the painting is not to be sold, and second, it must be hung in your new museum for the public to see—whether you think it's a Rothko or not."

No one was prepared for what did not belong in the system of exchange. There was no place, no legal concept—even in the excessive giving called potlatch—for a gift that could not be bartered, amortized, or reimbursed. Zaron was the first to recover. "Do I understand you to say that Mr. McGinley will simply *give* me the painting—as a gift? Without any compensation whatsoever?"

"That's correct. He'd rather *give* the painting away than see it sold or remain hidden."

"I don't understand. Does he know how much the painting would be worth if it *should* prove to be the real thing?" His face said that he would have to—he must—it was imperative that he undo the "gift."

"He would prefer, since it was given to him as a gift, it should be passed on as a gift." This too, like everything Helena said that had a ring of truth, was received with silent contempt. Except for the burly lawyer whose mouth opened wide in a hollow guffaw.

"And all I have to do is agree to hang it in my new museum and not sell it?" Zaron shook his head incredulous.

"Correct." She watched him struggle, contradiction stamped on his face. He couldn't know that her gift was not what it seemed but, schooled in deceit, he was suspicious. If he agreed, he'd have his painting. But there *would* be a cost: Nothing comes for nothing.

Like a fly that can't focus light clearly, he jumped to what was nearest. "Must I attribute the painting to McGinley publicly?"

"If you drop your claim, certainly. Since it would be giving the painting to you as a gift."

"What? Not even give in to some preposterous demand that my claim is false?" The cynicism usually etched on his face was supplanted by disbelief. He and his minions had brushed up against the incomprehensible and were looking for traps. An intellectual like Helena didn't understand money. It permeates all, like the air one breathes. Zaron had the money, ergo the power. She, absent money, had none. He picked up the contract and made a show of handing to her. "Then you'll need to sign this."

"That won't be necessary. All you need is a receipt." She pushed the contract back across the table, drew a signed receipt from her purse, and passed it to him. He swept it up like the winnings in poker. "When do you plan to *return* my painting to me?"

"We'll *give* you the painting at your convenience."

"You know of course I don't think it's a Rothko."

"Dismiss your people and I'll answer that."

He made a gesture with one hand and his entourage filed out like a line of obedient ants. "Well?"

"Rothko has signed and dated a stretcher bar on the verso."

"So, you kept that back did you? Just in case I'd give up my claim?" He did not miss the point that if there were stretcher bars, Helena must have gotten them from the Sverdlov dumpster.

Her response was more qualified. "We never thought you'd give up your claim." He looked surprised, as if his crude portrait of her had revealed the shadowy traces of an intimidating pentimento. He soon recovered and adopted the false position he wanted to be true. Wasn't he, after all, getting what he most desired?

22

"What have you done, Helena? You gave it to Zaron! Just gave it to him." This accusation greeted Helena when she opened her front door. An insistent banging roused her from a solitary dinner minding her discouragement. It was Justine, whose outburst was unanswerable—at least in the open doorway.

"I guess you should come in," Helena remarked wryly and went into the living room with Justine like a snapping dog at her heels.

"Now," Helena declared firmly after seating herself in a chair. "Sit down," she pointed to the sofa, "and tell me exactly what you heard."

Justine, sitting tensely on the sofa edge, complained, "You . . . you gave up the painting without a fight. You and my father of all people let such a man have it. How could you betray us?" Then, momentarily running out of verbal steam, she looked around distractedly.

"If you need more time to vent," Helena said coolly, "I'll just finish my supper."

Justine spread delicate hands over her face and several sobs escaped through her fingers. "Listen!" Helena's command was like a slap across the face. Slowly the hands lowered and a pair of wild, soulful eyes peeked out. "I deliberately kept you in the dark. To pay for a court battle, we would have been forced to sell the painting. By then it would have been worth so much on the open market even your father couldn't have afforded it."

"What was your plan for the copy then? You never told me."

"It was an excellent copy, but not enough to fool experts. If we had gone to court, we would have been guilty of forgery and fraud."

Justine's face crumpled in response. But Helena knew her too well. Something else was bothering her. Justine sighed deeply, blinked back tears, then wailed, "I've been fired."

"What?" Helena was stunned.

"Two days ago. Just before Zaron made his announcement."

"Ah, I see," she understood. "Perfect timing."

Mistaking Helena's drift, Justine gave an earnest account of the firing that missed the jiggery-pokery of corporate double speak. "So you see," she concluded, "they felt they had no choice."

"Take it not for what it isn't but for what it is."

"I don't understand?" She asked wide-eyed and confused.

"Perfect timing. It doesn't matter what their excuse was," she declared coldly. "Zaron got to them first. He somehow arranged to have you fired just before the meeting."

"Arranged?" She echoed.

"To demoralize you . . . and me. And if I had known you had been fired he might have succeeded."

They fell into a brooding silence as Zaron hovered between them like a wasp whose sting they had to avoid. He had made a mockery of the gift in the media. In his mouth, Finny's gift was a Trojan Horse. The small vestibule on the lower level of the Museum had been crammed with cameras and reporters, all askew like rumpled clothes on bent hangers. The clamor had only been silenced when a triumphant lawyer raised a fat hand against questions. When there was a modicum of silence, he motioned to someone. Shouts sprouted up like noisome weeds then died away as Zaron emerged dramatically from the gallery wearing a smile as wide as triumph could paint on a face.

Twitching like dung beetles around carrion, all eyes including the unseeing eye of the video cameras were on him as he announced that "Mark Rothko's last and perhaps greatest work is to take pride of place among the other great works in my collection."

"No questions," an anonymous lawyer said, quelling a tempest of shouts. Zaron continued. "The painting, I'm delighted to say against my own doubts, has proven unequivocally to be the real thing. Furthermore, *rightful* ownership has been amicably established. As you know, Mr. Phineas McGinley had *claimed* it was a gift from the Sverdlov sisters." There was a long pause to allow the misrepresentation to take hold. Then the cry of victory. "This painting is a gift, not just to me. It is a gift to the world!"

Now, after a chastened Justine left, and with Zaron's words still echoing in her mind, Helena returned to her supper, grown cold as her courage. As she toyed with her food, her thoughts wandered to other worries. "How fight a world where art is a commodity? Where art dealers fly around on private planes? Where "in" artists are stalked like celebrities and heads of auction houses meet secretly to set prices? Where revolutionary ideas get drowned in a sea of opinion? Why resist?" She recalled a chorale from the *Matthew Passion*. "*Come ye daughters, help me lament . . . Behold his patience, / Behold! . . . our guilt.*" She encouraged herself. They could not, they must not, they would not yield to despair!

"How could he be so brazen?" Sandra protested to herself. She wanted to tear up the invitation in her hand but decided to consult Helena first.

The voice on the phone was as charged as polished silver. "You must go. And you must take Jonah."

Sandra was shocked. "Take Jonah? To see Zaron flaunt his success? With Victoria Vargas at his side?" She wanted to shout, "What good will it do? He's beaten us and he knows it. We'll only be attending the wake of our defeat." But she didn't shout. She couldn't. Even in defeat, Helena would find a reason to hope.

"Yes, take Jonah. Just as I am going, and so is Regie. Finny I've let off the hook. He would be like a coney before a pack of hounds."

"But why should we go?"

"To take the edge off, to make him uncomfortable."

"It will certainly make Jonah and me uncomfortable."

"To act courageously we must put personal feelings aside." Her tone of finality brooked no further comment on an event that had the attention of local art enthusiasts.

This is what happened. As soon as the painting was in Zaron's hands he had arranged a banquet to celebrate the acquisition. It was to take place at the Midtown Four Seasons—until Arthur Sadlowe reminded him that the Rothko series in the Tate had been commissioned and angrily withdrawn from that very same hotel in New York. "Rothko," he had said, "hated the idea of his work hanging in the tony restaurant and intended the paintings to give the customers indigestion." As an alternative, Sadlowe suggested the Piedmont Driving Club at the western edge of the Park. Only the most select of Atlanta's elite would find their names on the gold-embossed invitations. A few handpicked members of the press would be invited, not to eat of course, but to salivate over the grand painting and the even more grand personalities.

When Sandra broached the invitation to Jonah, he surprised her by agreeing with Helena. "We must attend. To honor the painting."

"Honor? How will it be honored in being displayed like a war trophy. It will be vulgarized."

"Even in war, the work of art is undiminished, an exception to economy. We'll be there to testify to that." The anxiety on Sandra's face made him take her in his arms, kiss her on the forehead, and mock tenderly, "There, there, little one."

She accepted the consolation laughing, then kissed him back with passion. Afterward, lying curled up in bed, he nuzzled her face. "We'll be a formidable couple at that banquet. Lovers are immune to petty ego games."

"Fine words my love," she said softly, "but *we* don't have the painting—*he* does!"

"He has the physical object, but he can't possess it. Its power can't be possessed."

"Too bad," she joked, "otherwise we could terrorize him. Steal it from the banquet."

"Oh, so now we're terrorists," he laughed. "I think there may a streak of that in you. You weren't afraid to threaten to expose Zaron in his hospital den."

"And what about you, taking on Victoria in his lair?"

"That was terrifying enough." They laughed together. A few weeks had moved these two from a declaration of love to a marriage of minds. "We must not let ourselves be defeated," he mused. "Look what happens to the characters in the *Passion*. They encounter hindrances, they retreat, they suffer defeat, they endure, and finally gain the peace they've been searching for. That's what the music is about. We carry on even unto the cross and death—or its modern equivalent."

"You mean, I suppose, that *we* are to carry on by watching Zaron swagger?"

"Even by watching Zaron swagger! When Jesus is falsely accused, Bach uses an eighth-note rest between each tone to indicate His silence. He uses musical dissonance to express the dramatic color. It's a musical substitution that lifts an otherwise horrifying event into sublimity."

"Then we'll silently defy him!"

"But that would put the emphasis on *him*. He's only a petty tyrant expanding his empire. We'll show that indifference is the greater passion."

"Indifference?"

"Not in the sense of evasiveness but keeping faith with powers he doesn't understand. Giving ourselves as witnesses, exposing ourselves without protection. It's not about what *we* want or what *he* wants. It's about receiving."

"Receiving? What? From whom?" Only love kept her from

slipping into doubt. Still she wondered, why do something that can have no consequences?

"From the painting, from art. In the same way we *receive* from Bach's *Passion* by witnessing it." He qualified, "Witness in the sense of testifying silently to its power. So we'll attend his celebration of power and remain distant from it."

"Attend, yet remain distant? I hate paradoxes!"

"Only in the sense that what seems absurd and contradictory can in reality be true."

"Ah, then we will silently defy him."

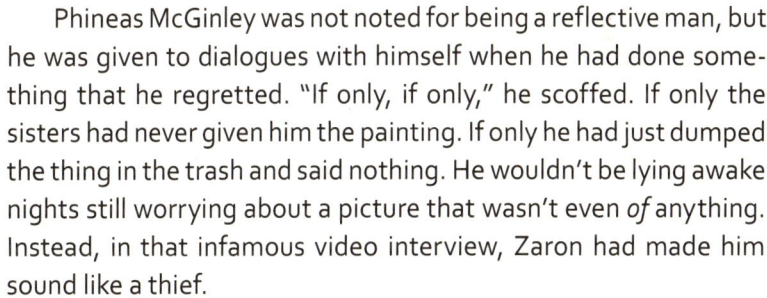

Phineas McGinley was not noted for being a reflective man, but he was given to dialogues with himself when he had done something that he regretted. "If only, if only," he scoffed. If only the sisters had never given him the painting. If only he had just dumped the thing in the trash and said nothing. He wouldn't be lying awake nights still worrying about a picture that wasn't even *of* anything. Instead, in that infamous video interview, Zaron had made him sound like a thief.

"How could you be such a chump?" he asked himself. Then he adjusted his tie and set off to meet a client. At the end of the day showing properties in Ansley Park, he decided on a whim to visit Helena. The impulse was contradictory. She inevitably talked him into something he didn't want to do. He couldn't resist. Somehow afterwards he always felt more alive. So in a mixture of trepidation and excitement, he rang the bell at her door and was disappointed when Bartram answered instead.

"She's not at home," he grinned ironically. He always found Finny a comic figure. "She's at Sandra's. They're off to the great surgeon's bragging party."

"Bragging party?" Finny asked incredulous.

"Yes. Didn't you know? Mother and Sandra's presence are

required when Zaron crows to the aping mob about his acquisition of *your* painting!" Bartram gave him one of his wryly-smug looks and rolled his eyes.

"My painting?"

"Yes, *your* painting. Or should I say the painting you stole from him that will now grace the halls of his new museum. It will be on display at the banquet. The spoils of war."

"On display?" He repeated like a stuck needle.

Bartram frowned drolly. "Do you always repeat what other people say?"

"Does Justine know about this?"

"I don't think she was invited."

"Helena and Sandra were *invited*?"

"*Commanded.* With gold-embossed invitations delivered on a silver platter by a footman and six white horses." Bartram dropped the irony. "I told mother she was insane to go. Of course, she shrugged my objection aside and said she *wanted* to go."

"Wanted?" Finny echoed in dismay. The words sent his thoughts galloping off wildly in a thousand different directions. Vainly he tried to rein them in. "What time?"

"Time?" Bartram repeated, poking fun at Finny's annoying habit. "It's 5:45 p.m. Eastern Standard Time."

"Not the time *now*. What time does the banquet begin?"

Raising his eyebrow. "Oh, that time. Eight o'clock I believe. Cocktails and asslicking at seven. Why?"

He answered evasively, "Just wondered." What he thought was, "I've got to get in touch with Justine. Now." Bartram put his hand on the door impatiently and Finny turned away. "Thanks," he mumbled, looking at his watch. "Gotta run." The door closed but he didn't move. He was thinking of that chap Meleager that Helena talked about. He had looked him up on the web. Meleager killed his uncles when they tried to wrest the boar's head from that goddess. Then adding insult to injury, Meleager's own mother threw a brand representing his life into the fire, and *he* died. History was repeating itself. Helena had given in to the mob. Now *he* was the useless brand thrown on the fire. He sighed heavily and called Justine.

"Uncle Finny," she answered. "How marvelous to hear from you. What..."

He interrupted. "What do you know about this banquet tonight?"

"What banquet? What are you talking about?"

He explained in one long anxious wheeze.

"Oh, no," she gasped. Then moaned, "Who told you?"

"Bartram. Listen, can you meet me somewhere for supper."

"I can't. I don't have a car."

"What about the company car?"

"I don't have one. I've been fired."

"Fired?" He parroted.

"Never mind that. We can't let Zaron get away with this."

"What can we do? There's nothing to be done."

"There *is* something we can do," Justine insisted. "We *must* find out what's happened to the copy."

"It's too late for that."

"No, it's not too late! Pick me up," she commanded. "We're going to my father's condo." The unusual authority in his niece checked his objection.

Three quarters of an hour later in the lobby of Regie's high rise they hit a snag. Justine was not on the concierge's list and he refused to let her go up.

"My name is Justine Foxcroft. I am Sir Reginald's daughter," she said with a hauteur that surprised Finny and rattled the concierge. "Of course, my name is on the list." Then she offered him one of the smiles that could shrink a glacier and he melted.

In the elevator Finny asked curiously, "Why wasn't your name on the list?"

"I had it removed. I didn't want my name associated with my father or Olas," she answered matter-of-factly. "It might have connected them with the painting." He marveled at her foresightedness. Was this the little niece-waif he had always worried about?

The door opened on the fiftieth floor and they were greeted not by her father but by Olas and Russell. The former looked blank for a second, then threw his arms about them both wildly. Apparently they—or Olas at least—had been dousing his troubles in alcohol.

"Come in and drink with us," he shouted jubilantly.

She would have none of it. "Where is your copy of the painting?"

No charming Justine here. This one shouted orders and expected to be obeyed. A fierce intelligence gleamed on her face and her body vibrated with resolve.

Olas' golden eyes widened into ash-colored disks. "I don't know. Helena says she's keeping it safe, but she won't tell me where."

Justine hadn't counted on this development. "Did she say why she didn't give the copy to Zaron instead of the original?" She knew Helena's answer but didn't know whether he knew.

The fair pale face lost its inner light. "She said that my copy, even though it was perfect, wouldn't pass the experts. So she had to give Zaron the real thing."

"Never mind," she answered unsympathetically. "We'll think of something else."

Puzzled by the cryptic remark, he invited them to sit down and renewed the offer of a drink. Finny readily accepted as Justine remained standing, folded in thought.

Olas handed Finny a whiskey. "When I heard what Zaron said about you on TV," he looked at Finny sympathetically, "I felt like going to the pre*ssh*," he slurred the word and corrected himself, "the press, and telling them what a, a, *blaggard*—is that how you say it? —he is."

Justine interrupted sternly, "Do you know where Helena is tonight?"

They didn't reply, not even Finny, who knew the answer. He observed her covertly. She stood like a warrior, hands on hips, legs slightly apart. His bleary eyes widened in a shock of recognition.

She looked like . . . like . . . that goddess in the picture Helena had shown him! Helena had even said she would!

Justine answered her own question: "Helena's attending a banquet tonight. Zaron is throwing it to celebrate his prize Rothko!"

"What?" Olas and Russell exploded in unison. Then she told them what Finny had heard from Bartram.

At this, Olas lost what little he had of his Nordic coolness, "How can Helena let him do that?" He started pacing excitedly around the living room. "The idea that my copy might have hung in his museum was bad enough, but that *Rothko* should hang there is terrible! A travesty. What's worse is for Zaron to dangle it before a bunch of ignorant culture vultures like a hunk of raw meat. It's barbaric!" He poured himself another drink, downed it in one gulp and continued his raving: "I can just see what will happen. There will be boxes of Zaron Detergent distributed to the guests with the painting on it. Later he can market it on rolls of Zaron Toilet Paper for his gift shop. Or maybe Zaron hospital can drape its surgical patients in canvas copies." His eyes narrowed to gold pellets. "I won't let him! I won't let him do that! I'm going to crash that party. I'm going to expose him for the fraud he is."

Finny, who had hastily downed another large whiskey, interjected. "Expose him for what?"

Olas looked at him in surprise as if he were unaware. "Why, for giving bribes to unscrupulous art dealers and curators. For writing off donations that he never made to every art museum in the country, for . . ." he was going to say, "hiring thugs to do his dirty work," but remembered in the nick of time his own role in Justine's apartment.

She completed his idea, "For making the true false."

"They'll never believe you," Finny asserted morosely. "Believe me, I know."

"What *they* believe isn't important," Justine declared. "But how do you intend to get in? It's a private club." In raising the objection she was already exploring the idea.

Russell had remained on the sidelines till now. "I assume it's black tie. If you dress the part, you might succeed."

Olas seized on the idea. "Sir Reginald has several tuxes. Let's look." He loped off in the direction of the bedroom with the others following. There was indeed another tux in Regie's wardrobe. He tried it on—too long in the sleeves and trousers.

"Maybe we can just roll up the sleeves and pants legs," Finny offered.

"It will still be too long in the waist and crotch," Russell countered.

Olas, euphoric from alcohol and the thought of seeing Zaron's party in ruins, "I'll wear his kilt instead. Or I'll just cut out the crotch." He simpered at Russell, "Or maybe I'll borrow one of Helena's ball gowns." Russell flushed and said nothing.

"There's no time to waste on frivolity," Justine dismissed impatiently. "It's seven twenty-five and the dinner starts at eight. We have to find a way." They stood silently looking down at the floor of the bedroom as if the answer were there. They weren't aware, though Helena, had she been there, might have reminded them, that in yielding their separate interests to a collective thought they were already acting. No one there would have said it was throwing a bolt in the machine, but that's what it was—creating a rupture in the status quo without regard for the consequences.

"I see what to do!" Justine started, her face ablaze with purpose, as if everything in life were at stake. "Bartram! He's your size, Olas. We'll borrow his orchestra tails. You'll be better dressed than any man there."

"Will he let me?" Olas asked hopefully.

"Certainly!" She flashed it at him with assurance and began walking back and forth. If it is possible to see thought made visible they saw it now. "We won't give him a choice," she announced. Olas, who saw Justine as a heroine ever since she bashed him with an art tube, cheered her on in mime, saluting, loading a rifle, shooting. "Well, what are we waiting for? Let's go!"

They scrambled into the elevator, flew through the lobby, and squeezed into Finny's car, their excitement at fever pitch.

"Take Piedmont," Olas suggested. "It's the shortest."

"No Peachtree," Russell offered. "Less traffic."

"Finny's the driver," Justine insisted, shutting down further suggestions.

Finny, with a noble, forbearing look on his face, shot off like a race car driver on a route only a veteran real estate agent could know, zigging and zagging through neighborhoods on his way to Ansley Park. While he drove, Olas' wit alternated between singing martial songs and naming ever more outlandish items Zaron might sell in his shop.

At Helena's house, an astonished Bartram opened the door and Justine barged inside with the others in tow. She explained the situation with such firmness, that Bartram could only yield. He led Olas upstairs and they returned some minutes later with Olas in tails looking like a figure from Raphael, body animating the clothes. Only his shoes gave him away, for in the rush to leave the condo he had forgotten to change his sneakers.

Justine was the first to notice the mistake, which Bartram corroborated. "My shoes are too big for him."

Torn between admiration and a need for sartorial correctness, Russell agreed. "Even like that, how will he get through the doorman at the Club?"

Inspired, Bartram had an idea. "Carry my flute case and pretend you're hired to play for the banquet." Caught up in the animated mood of the group, he added, "I think I should go with him. I have another set of tails. If we both carry instruments it will be more believable."

"Yes, go, go Bartram, hurry," Justine prodded, "It's twenty past eight now. They should finish the dinner around nine. We need to be there before the speeches end." While Bartram was changing, the others rehearsed their plan. Justine and Finny would wait in the getaway car at the Club entrance. If there was a problem, Russell would say at the door he was a doctor called to attend someone who had taken ill.

Russell raised the question to Olas that no one had thought to ask. "What exactly do you plan to do once you've crashed the party? And how, after accusing Zaron, do you plan to escape?"

"I don't plan to escape! I'm going to stay until they arrest me or throw me out." The alcoholic fog had long since dissipated, replaced by a militant haze. "I'm going to denounce him in front of everyone."

"Then we're with you!" Justine said. It was a question of doing the impossible and rejecting any idea of difficulty.

Some minutes later Bartram returned dressed in his tails and carrying two flute cases. He handed one to Olas. "Be careful with this—it's irreplaceable."

The lofty look on Bartram's face made Olas reject any idea he had had of using the flute as a weapon. At last, at 8:50 they were ready to take on the world.

23

"In Babylon Belshazzar the king made a great feast. He commanded to bring the gold and silver vessels, which his father Nebuchadnezzar had taken out of the temple in Jerusalem that he, his princes, his wives, and concubines might drink from them."

The modern banquet recalls the ancient civic feast in honor of men and the gods. The timeless rule of hospitality, *xenia*, was a sacrosanct relation of obligation more than friendship. *Xenos* meant many things: guest, host, stranger, friend and foreigner, and was protected by Zeus Xenios himself. Once a guest entered the host's house—whether as a humble stranger or as an enemy—he was offered hospitality, shelter, food, and gifts. Reciprocation took the form of respect, courtesy, and gratitude. The whole code was sanctioned by the possibility that divinity might appear at a feast in disguise.

There would have been no sacred relation of course without its profanation. Profanation as when Penelope's unwelcome suitors demanded nightly feasts of wine and entertainment, or when, at a banquet, Atreus, father of Agamemnon, served his brother the flesh of his own sons. Belshazzar too. He drank from the sacred vessels of Jerusalem at his feast, violating the rule that a king treat the objects of another religion with respect. In retribution, a mysterious handwriting appeared on the wall cursing the king and foretelling the fall of Babylon. And so, to this day, *xenia* is the fugitive hidden at every banquet like an unknown stowaway secretly sharing in its rituals and evoking its rule.

This evening a banquet is taking place at a private club on the western edge of Piedmont Park. A discreet exterior of native stone marks the entrance to the otherwise fortress-like building. All grandeur is reserved for the inside with an abundance of marble, ornament, and gold leaf culminating in a majestic banquet hall. The hall is designed as a basilica, (from the Greek, *basileus*, or royal) with central nave, columned aisles, and climactic semi-circular apse, as in centuries of Christian churches.

Enthroned in the apse once reserved for the altar are Zaron and his Diva. Behind, like a cloth of honor in paintings of the Virgin, a monumental blue and grey painting. It's soft-edged rectangles shimmer as if they had been breathed on the canvas, whose outer edges cast a shadow behind the dark lord and his lady. To either side of the work creating a triptych traditionally associated with altar pieces are flashy renderings of the Zaron museum. They lend a vulgar commercial aspect to the painting. Two long rows of tables dressed in the trappings of spectacle—flowing cloths, sparkling plate, glittering candelabra, floral arrays—extend from the apse to the rear of the hall. It is an hierarchical arrangement the host with cold hospitality has ordained. The richest and most important are seated next to him and the rest in descending order of importance to the rear. A mere 10 feet from the dais, four places have been reserved for Helena, Regie, Jonah, and Sandra, who raises the question, "Why are *we* seated *here*?"

Helena, silver above the peopled dross in a shiny beaded gown, has a ready answer. "He wants to watch us while he gloats."

"Then we'll gloat back," retorts Regie, staring haughtily at Victoria Vargas, swathed in shimmering red satin, as she leans devotedly against her master's side, calculating every gesture for attention. From time to time she glances triumphantly in the direction of her ex-husband with a smile that says, "See what you lost." He however has eyes only for Sandra, who in a strapless black gown, trailing white scarf, and long white gloves attracts admiring glances.

The center of attention, however, is reserved for the dark lord himself, a figure of splendor in all the accouterments of wealth and power. He wears conquest effortlessly, his handsome face triumphant, as his dark eyes shoot wounding darts at those he commends as friends but thinks are fools.

Earlier during cocktails, he had circulated among the guests with Victoria fastened to him like Velcro. While he pawed over his diva, clasping her in a way to raise envy, he searched the room for Sandra Foxcroft. As he dealt out flatteries to guests, barbs to enemies, and leers at cleavages, he maintained a princely exterior. But now, during the dinner, a strained tone has replaced the fawning sociality of cocktails. Hospitality has been superseded by discomfort, for no one with any sense wants to be here.

When, at last, the interminable courses and after-dinner drinks are over, and cigars are lit against club rules, it is a signal for Zaron to stand and gloat. Lifting a chalice in his hands like a priest, he offers a toast celebrating the painting and swallows in one gulp. The guests obediently lift glasses and drink to their own vanquishment. Then at tiresome length he describes his perseverance in the search for the painting, the clues that led him to it, the cost in multiple zeros of its authentication. All this is chaff to the kernel he's aiming for: the proposed Zaron museum.

During this charade, Helena stares mournfully at the painting. That it should be profaned by such mockery. "*If the tears upon my cheeks can / Naught accomplish, / Oh, then take my heart away!*" So this is what has come of her clever scheme! The question draws an answer that mirrors the whole effect. "No one here wants to see, no one wants to hear, no one wants to know anything."

Meanwhile, a man dressed in tie and tails has quietly entered the back of the hall. He stares with far-seeing eyes at the apse and catches only snatches of what is being said. "*My* finest philanthropic enterprise," "capstone of *my* collection," "*my* proposed museum," "my . . . my . . . my." Slowly the figure advances ceremonially up the aisle like one taking part in a procession. His noble bearing and hypnotic look catch eyes that have been focused on the dais.

Midway down the center aisle he pauses, staring straight ahead, a pause that heightens the drama. Suddenly he shouts, "Stop! Stop this farce! Now!" The words ricochet through the hall like gun shots. The room falls silent, all eyes riveted on the tall, fair intruder with glowing hair, eyes of amber and face of an angel. Pointing an accusing finger at Zaron, he declares in prophetic voice. "This man is a fraud and a crook! He is guilty of bribes and corruption." He gestures toward heaven as though invoking divine judgment. "He hired *me* to steal the Rothko. Now he falsely claims it's his."

Zaron stiffens, his darkening face like an angry storm cloud, and mutters, "Baseless lies."

"Throw him out," Victoria cries in an operatic soprano, pointing toward those trapped at the tables. The cry goes unheeded. Helena is taken as much by surprise as the rest. She watches Olas anxiously, worried he's about to do something reckless and ruin her plan. Let him continue? Intervene? Try to shut him up?

Olas again processes like a priest toward the altar, then stops dead in his tracks. He stares open-mouthed at the painting. It's pervaded by an inner glow, almost alive. The colors and form shimmer before his eyes like a shadowy blue cloud. His eyes widen in amazement: It isn't the Rothko! It's, he gasps in disbelief, it's *his* painting! And yet . . . not his!

Helena sees what he sees. The painting not as the copy but a *new* work of art. She had almost seen it herself in Regie's condo. The unexpected guest in disguise, like the divine handwriting on the wall. It exposes the sham banquet and turns it into dust.

"This painting is *not* Rothko's," Olas shouts. "It's mine!" Like Moses descending from the mountaintop, Olas is transfigured, his face lit with a strange light. Then a shadow crosses it. Glancing around anxiously, he snatches a knife from a table, and dashes madly toward the painting with upraised blade.

Instantly Helena sees and divines the intent. "Stop him!" Her voice cuts through the room like shattering glass. Jonah, seated on the aisle closest to Olas, jumps up and grabs the knife from his hand just as he reaches the dais. The reporters, who have been corralled like cattle in the back of the room, run toward the front shouting questions. "Who is this man?" "Is it a copy?" "Did he say it's a fake?" "Where's the real Rothko?"

The banquet hall is reduced to a shocked spectacle. Security officers arrive and take Olas into custody as a reporter yells, "Were you hired to steal the painting?"

"Yes!" Olas answers, as he is dragged from the room handcuffed. "Zaron can't tell a copy from the real!"

Laughs, jubilation and the eruption of chatter: "fraud," "fake," "Who is he?" "Is it really a copy?" Felicity Hardcastle replies to someone in her high-pitched whine, "Of course it's genuine. I would recognize it anywhere." Stranger yet, somewhere a flute is playing a galloping tune from Grieg's *In the Hall of the Mountain King*—mock-heroic commentary on the host and his courtier trolls. Unnoticed in all the commotion, the painting has been spirited away and Zaron and his consort have vanished. Left behind, forgotten on their easels, are the tawdry posters of the Zaron museum.

Helena looks at the empty hall, filled with dirty plates, soiled linen, and half-emptied glasses. It reminds her of El Greco's *Christ Cleansing the Temple.* Jesus, whip in hand, scatters money changers, merchants, animals, beggars, and prostitutes with the force of a whirlwind, flinging them against the outer edges of the picture plane. Tonight something has burst forth, displacing the best and worst plans. No one has initiated, produced or provoked it. Neither Helena, the most perspicacious, nor Olas, the most reckless, nor Zaron the most calculating will be able take credit for its happening. And yet, somehow, it will count for what will have been when all the future has been decided.

24

Then came the aftermath. Aftermath: Originally, the mowing down of a second crop of grass after the first harvest. Later, an event, particularly one of a disastrous nature, like the aftershocks of an earthquake.

In the aftermath of the banquet, everything was leveled to means and ends. To the practical. Is the painting a copy? Are the accusations true? What will happen to the young intruder? And where is the Rothko now?

Later that night, Helena lay awake. "What have I done? I had Olas make a copy of the real thing only to find that the copy is also real. I've turned his true work into a fake, like those imitators who press an original into lifelessness. Saved the Rothko at the cost of consigning the Lindgard to darkness! The irony of it. Now there are two works to save. I must make Zaron give up his claim of the Rothko *and* return the Lindgard. Impossible . . . unless I gamble again and risk both."

The next morning, a Sunday, Bartram was surprised when he came downstairs to find his mother dressed and about to leave. "Where are you going?"

"I have to see a man about a painting," was all she said, though the sparkle had returned to her grey eyes.

Twenty-five minutes later, she pulled up to Zaron's mansion in Tuxedo Hills. Despite the heat, a thick yellowish fog lay on the ground, as if the aftermath of the banquet had spread a miasma over the city. Opening the car door, Helena wrinkled her nose at an acrid smell of burning trash and stepped out. Before she reached the mansion, the door opened and an unshaven Zaron appeared, looking shrunken and haggard, with hollow, sleep-deprived eyes and rangy expression.

Without a word, he ushered her down a long corridor with large side rooms. When he reached a darkly paneled office, he went inside expecting her to follow. Instead she remained at the threshold observing as he seated himself behind an ornately carved desk. The heavy wood furnishings were made bleak by an unlit fireplace and rays of faded light dimed by the window. Readied for battle, she went in and, without invitation, took the chair opposite him.

"I don't suppose you've come to apologize for that little stunt last night," he said with a sneer. His narrow, unshaven face had a foxlike-look wary of its prey.

"Believe me or not, I was as surprised as you by what happened."

"Oh, so you didn't arrange to have my partner's ex-husband conveniently grab that demented young man, when he was about to attack me?"

"*You* weren't the target. The painting was."

He dismissed the explanation with a wave of his hand. "What did you come here for?"

"I've come for that painting. It doesn't belong to you. It belongs to Olas Lindgard. He painted it."

"What do you mean? What are you talking about?" It was like the Doppler effect; her words faded into insignificance as they went past.

"It's a copy, *his* copy. When Olas recognized it, he wanted to destroy it."

He scoffed, shaking his head in refusal. "And how exactly can that be?" The handsome face and nose lengthened as the curved mouth pulled downwards.

Instead of answering, she asked, "Are you going to press charges against Olas?"

"I haven't decided." He dangled the option like a lure. "And if I do, why should I tell you?"

"Because that's what he wants. He refuses to be released on bond. He's hoping the publicity will destroy you."

He guffawed as if this were nothing. "Why would someone want to be convicted for a crime? Unless he's demented."

"I've tried to tell him that you'll quash the accusations rather than let him tarnish your reputation." He looked surprised. "But," she added, "he won't listen."

His stony eyes flickered, though he kept up a bluff by staring. A drive to be right and inflict wounds reflected on his face. "As I told those reporters and I'm telling you, *I* have the genuine Rothko. It's been authenticated, if you remember, by *you*. The *M. Rothko* on the stretcher bars!"

"Olas forged that signature." She dropped it softly. Then added in an upbeat voice, "The bars are original however."

His shocked eyes traveled around the room looking for a place to rest anywhere but on her face. "What if I said that I displayed a copy last night because the real painting is far too valuable?"

"Say anything you like. *I* have the original."

Stunned again, he dropped the self-assured mask for a moment, then resumed it. "If it is a copy—mind you I'm not saying it is—then you have to give me back the original as we agreed."

She leaned forward in her chair and stared into his eyes. This was the moment that would count for everything. "I can prove that I have the original Rothko, and that you have been duped by a copy. When I do, you'll look like a fool. No one will want anything to do with your museum. You'll be the laughing stock of the art world."

He had maintained the stoic face of a chess player until now. A disdainful expression grew on his face, lips pressed tight to prevent an outburst. Self-control rescued him. "Why did you offer me the painting then, unless its authenticity was in question?" He leaned back in his chair, arms outstretched and hands spread atop the desk.

"There is no question of authenticity." She dropped this as an anchor in his sea of denial.

Still he persisted. "How do I know that the one you say you have *is* a Rothko and mine isn't?"

"The *genuine* signature, *M. Rothko, 1970*, is on a stretcher bar."

This would have been a setback for a person with less hubris, but he appeared unconvinced.

"Rothko's fingerprints have been verified on both the verso and the tacking margins. I have the signed declaration of the Rothko estate." She passed him copies.

He swept them across his desk without looking at them and laughed sardonically. "So what is it you want from me?"

With grey eyes sparkling, she gave him the slightest of smiles. "I'm offering you the chance to salvage your reputation as a philanthropist."

"What's the catch?" He stared at her suspiciously.

"None," she said, still and grave. "It's an offer you'd be a fool to refuse."

His head snapped back. "Do I have a choice?"

She didn't answer immediately. Apparently he had taken the bait and was not going to press charges against her. As long as he had the copy he might succeed. A bait and switch, he could say in court. Her reputation and career would be destroyed and her disgrace, at least in the eyes of the world, would be irrevocable.

"Your only choice is the following." She counted them out on her fingers without taking her eyes off his face. "You will pretend the real painting in my possession is yours and give it as a gift to the High Museum. You will return the copy to us. You will stipulate that the painting must be on permanent display, free and open to the public." Her voice rose in emphasis. "This is the one absolute condition Mr. Phineas McGinley, the rightful owner of the painting, insists on." Having made her point, she continued in a lower register. "Finally, you will provide the museum with sufficient funds to maintain the painting for open viewing."

He chuckled silently as if to say, "Why would I do that?"

The grey eyes turned flinty. "You will do it because I have copies of the excessive deductions you took for art donations during the period 2012-13 to fund your museum." She passed him a copy. "I also have in your handwriting a copy of bribes given to dealers and experts to acquire particular works. That, or I go to the IRS."

His face contorted in anger and for the first time he lost control. "So I'm to let you blackmail me over a thing I'm entitled to? By announcing that I've been made a fool?"

He turned in his chair for a moment and stared out the window readying a response. On turning back, he said, "I may charge libel and fraud against you, McGinley, and Lindgard for passing off a copy as genuine. You gave me a receipt for a fake."

But she was ahead of him. "How can a *gift* be fraudulent? *You* assumed the painting was the real thing and broadcast it to the world. Any charge will work against *you*, not Olas Lindgard or Mr. McGinley. You'll not only appear a fool, you'll be labeled a thief."

He shifted uncomfortably in his chair. There were two apples here, one wormy. Which should he take? If he accepted her offer, he might still present himself as a benevolent philanthropist. He gestured menacingly at her to make a point. "What guarantee would I have that the IRS wouldn't get wind of these charges if I accede to your demands?"

"None," she said sharply. "What I can guarantee is that no one will ever know that the painting you hold now is a copy and that we have the original." She paused to let this take hold. "Accept our conditions and you can salvage your name from the dumpster."

Again, he dodged. With time and distance, the glare of his misdeeds might go away. "And who is this 'we' and 'our' you're talking about?"

"'We' are a small group of like-minded citizens who care deeply about saving the Rothko for posterity."

"For posterity. My how lofty that sounds. And what do you

think I'm doing with my new museum if not preserving art for posterity?"

She had an answer—"What are you doing? Building a monument to yourself. Adding to the world-wide plunder and commercialization of art." Then she returned to the subject at hand. "Olas Lindgard recognized the painting last night. He knows, but no one else."

"How is that?" He looked puzzled, as if he had been overthrown.

"I said I had to give it to you."

His face was like a storm cloud pushing against her sun. He had accepted the copy as a gift to gain this advantage. Twisting now in the wind, all he could do was yield. "I see. You had to give it to me or you would have ended up with a painting worth a lot less because its authenticity was in question." He laughed bitterly as the implications became clearer.

"The fingerprints and DNA resolve all that now."

He stared at her hard. "So you have worked against me from the start."

"No, your way started with the apple in Eden."

He refused to acknowledge a comment that didn't fit his world of facts. "And I suppose you have some figure in mind?"

"I have." She handed him a paper. This time he did not cast it aside. "The exact amount you cheated on your income tax." He snorted, the irony not lost on him.

"And what about Mr. Lindgard. Won't he blab?"

"Not if he knows you'll give the painting to the High. But he wants his copy back."

"I'll have to think about it," he stalled, the last ditch in his retreat.

She rose from her chair, threw back her head, and fixed a metallic gaze on him. The fog had lifted and light streamed through the window, shimmering like a halo on her head. "Think as much as you like. But either agree now or I go to the media and IRS as soon as I leave this house."

After so much drama, Helena was reluctant to go home. She whiled away the time eating without appetite a solitary lunch in a nearby Buckhead restaurant. Staring off into space over a second cup of coffee she didn't want, she wondered why she felt so defeated. She had won. Zaron had acceded to all her demands. She ought to be happy. Why then, did everything seem so devoid of meaning? Eight months of her life gone. All her energy, intelligence, and will, given over to a nigh impossible task. In the process, she had resorted to cajolery, subterfuge, misrepresentations and blackmail, not just to her enemy, but even to her closest friends. And for her pains she had been burglarized, had her office ransacked, her career and reputation put at risk. Now it was over. Worn threadbare, she was too exhausted to feel anything. All she wanted was not to have to think, not to have to explain, even to Justine or Finny.

She got in her car and escaped from the city, driving for miles deep into the north Georgia hills. At a roadside picnic area overlooking a deep, forested hollow, she stopped and parked. Too tired to get out of the car, she leaned back against the headrest and closed her eyes. Exhaustion caught up to her and she fell soundly asleep. Sometime later she woke not refreshed, but groggy and leaden.

With nowhere else to go and no one she wanted to see, she drove home and parked in the driveway without going inside. The park was only two blocks from her house, though she could not remember the last time she had been there. She locked the car in a rush and walked rapidly until she reached the park entrance.

In the early evening light, the park appeared not beautiful but abandoned and ugly, like a shabby khaki gash against a grey jungle of dead buildings. Some event had taken place earlier, leaving behind a kitchen midden of trash—cans filled to overflowing and paper littering the ground. It was a dreary commentary on her day. A gust of sadness engulfed her. She missed her husband Carter; missed Kate.

As she looked across the grassy expanse, a flock of starlings eating grains tossed on the ground suddenly took flight. Forming and reforming in a pulsating dance, they arced and swooped, twisted and swirled, shifting speed and position, no longer individual birds but a single organism. One of the starlings suddenly dropped down on the grass next to her to pick up a piece of grain. Close-up it wasn't a generalized black but singularly speckled and multi-colored, with a brown and white outline on the edges of its wings. It cocked its head and looked at her with eyes of polished jet. She looked back seeing herself reflected in its eye. The bird flew off again and joined the others overhead. In the distance, it was indistinguishable from the flock, smudged and suffused in the greying light. Come alive, like the painting, its shadows veiling the lighter layers below of grass, air, and water.

She was one with them, a tiny part of a greater whole—sky, water, birds, light. Even Zaron and the spirit of the city, its possibility, they, too, were forces of nature. Thankfulness was on her lips. Atalanta may no longer roam virgin wildernesses or run through forested splendor, but her spirit is there in her absence. She was the unforeseeable. Not thing, or object. Only footsteps visible after she had passed.

25

The modern glass building asserts, sometimes ostentatiously asserts, its openness and transparency. But there's more. The glass façade may be a deceptive mask. In pretending to tell all, it tells little. Directness, illumination and transparency are contradictions in the institutions that resist clarity. A building made of glass can be as impenetrable as stone. The less transparent High Museum is an exception, an example of pulling back the veil and revealing things as they are. Patterns of light and great clear spaces welcome the eye and lift the spirit.

Designed by Richard Meier, disciple of light, the High's white concrete and glass quadrants curve through space and bend with the light like gravity made visible. The opaque exterior doesn't try to force transparency but to transmit it in clear lines that yield to light. Inside, ribboned glazing, clerestory strips, and panel perforations create an openness where the light circulates.

Renzo Piano's addition to the Meier building forms a gracious piazza and Pavilion, white, wave-tipped, and paneled, with vertical thrusts and scoops that filter light inside from above, enhancing circulation. Here too, transparency doesn't need to be literal, for this is architecture that doesn't hide a secret wish to intimidate behind glass. Instead it transmits a sheltering permeability.

One autumn day at dusk, Justine and Finny are on their way to the Museum just after closing. As the last two owners of the Rothko, they have been invited to see the new installation before it opens. "Look, Uncle Finny," Justine gestures in her new authoritative manner, "a real public square surrounded by streets and a loggia. A gathering place like in the old cities of Europe."

Finny looks and sees only aluminum and glass. A long "hmm," is followed by a grunt of surprise. He had looked at piazzas in Florence, though looking-at is not seeing. Why did he never notice this before?

They pass under the canopied entrance into the glass lobby of the Wieland Pavilion, where the white aluminum cladding complements Meier's circular atrium. They enter a small, softly-lit sanctuary, a former cloak room now transformed into an intimate home for the 6 x 5 foot Rothko. It hangs low on the wall opposite the open doorway, its blue-grey colors dominating the space, as if one walked directly into evening shadows.

Justine points to the attribution plaque on the wall with Finny's name on it. "See. You're properly listed."

He looks, reads, and is non-committal. Though he is named as a former owner, the plaque is given over to praise of Dr. Ouruk Zaron. That irks him. Once he would have glanced at that canvas and said, "My kid could paint this. 150 million for that blob?" But he has tasted awe and his life has changed.

Because no one else is there, they sit down on the bench facing the painting and fall silent. At first Finny sees nothing but shadow and darkness. Expecting nothing from nothing, he is surprised when slowly a light emerges and grows, as it had the night in Justine's apartment. Now he doesn't resist, he surrenders. No longer assumes that, recognizing nothing, nothing is there. Gradually the colors take on different shapes, then fade again into obscurity. Now he sees there are many colors, not just two, even a ghostly white he would have sworn wasn't there before. Something stirs in him.

He looks over and sees Justine weeping quietly.

Though embarrassed by the softening that her tears inspire, Finny too yields and stares glassy-eyed.

"It gives us more to see than we can think," she murmurs softly.

Finny mumbles a flat, "Uh-huh," not because he doesn't agree but because he doesn't know what to say.

She returns to an earlier thought. "Did you notice how the light seems to rise out of the darkness?"

His eyes sharpen with recognition. "I do. It's eerie."

"Rothko paints light where nothing can be. Isn't it *won-derful*?"

He is jolted. She has given words to something he vaguely feels. "It *is* wonderful," he says in surprise as a last resistance crumbles. Each time he's seen the painting it's been different. The first time, disappointment. The second time, terror. The times at Regie's, indifference, puzzlement, curiosity. But nothing like this!

For months an unlikely group has fought for and suffered over a painting. It is fortuitous that at the climax of their struggle, the ASO and chorus should be performing Bach's iconic work, the *St. Matthew Passion*. For the art fellowship the concert provides a mythic background and commentary on their battle for a work of art and the city. Just as the resonances of ancient culture, both pagan and Christian, took the measure of Zaron's sordid scheme at his banquet, so the divine allegory of the *Passion* summarizes the experience of the fellowship.

Mark Rothko, in an address to the Pratt Institute, had said, "my paintings are concerned . . . with the human drama . . . in which one participates in a direct way." All human suffering and death is in those paintings, and the *Great Passion* is another such transformative experience, a paradigmatic story of human being in the face of suffering and death. For six members of the audience the music recapitulates the sacrifice that must be endured to save the work of art from exploitation. Tonight the narrative retells from a distance their story.

The fully staged oratorio—choirs, instrumentalists, and singers acting as well as singing and playing—begins with a grand *Agnus*

Dei that plunges the listeners into the action. The evangelist, seated at one side of the stage, broods while the chorus gathers in a circle lamenting Christ's imminent death. At first the tenor Matthew is shocked by Christ's announcement of his crucifixion, but by the time he describes Christ's anguish in Gethsemane and Judas' kiss of betrayal, the evangelist is the one in anguish, the one betrayed.

The deeper the singers move into the musical narrative, the more they and the audience identify with Christ. The music chatters, gossips, and reviles as the chorus in visible discord enacts the angry crowd; laments when they lament, moans when they moan. At one moment a calming, melodic flute accompanies the Alto; at another a shimmering halo of strings accompanies the chorus. Instruments slither up and down like serpents when the Soprano cries out against Judas and they become the wrack and ruin of nature during the tumult of Christ's capture. The layers of sound leap ahead and behind, engulfing singers, instrumentalists, and audience alike.

Then during the famous *Aus Liebe,* "*For love my Savior now is dying,*" the musical ground drops away and the flute alone sustains the structure, weaving everyone into a harmonic tapestry. Just when the participants think they can bear no more, the great chorale of rest and contemplation interrupts. "O Sacred Head Now Wounded" is repeated in a variety of moods, harmonies, and keys. Death is not the end. In tones of repose, chorus and soloists sing the aftermath, burial and entombment. At last, during an operatic finale, the halo of strings rises above the peaceful sad resignation of, "*My Jesus, good night.... The weary soul finds rest. / Sleep in peace, sleep Thou in the Father's breast.*" And the distinction between audience, performers, and world is annulled.

The performance over, the audience lingers in the long, charged silence that follows the music, framing before and after. Like the spectrum of colors in painting, the overlapping rhythms and harmonies of the music shatter meaning and set in motion instinctual responses beyond the words of the libretto. At the end the conductor keeps his hands raised, holding the audience in silence. Slowly he lowers his hands and releases thunderous applause. Audience and performers transformed into the potentiality of a coming community

During this extraordinary evening attended by Justine, Sandra, Helena, and Regie, an idea has formed in Justine's mind. In the inspired moment she gives it words. Pulling Helena aside, she says softly, "Bartram played the *Aus Liebe* like compassion itself." Before Helena can respond, Justine grasps her by the wrist and whispers solemnly in her ear, "If he's ever to be who he was tonight you must throw him out."

She stops short of naming Helena's maternal complicity in his self-absorption. She might have said this and more, but out of love—*Aus Liebe*—she doesn't.

Helena sees as much. She had observed her son as he played his solo and recognized something new—a resemblance to her late husband. Like a star that bends light away from a more remote galaxy, his narcissism had prevented her seeing Carter in him until tonight. Now, challenged to love her son's welfare more than her own sentiment, she answers humbly, "You are right. I will tell him. He must go."

When all six leave the hall in the highest of spirits and walk with a happy crowd from the Woodruff Center toward Peachtree, Justine catches, or thinks she does, a glimpse of a young woman running west on 15th under the Athena elms. She is dressed in a short tunic, her long hair flying in streamers behind her—unremarkable—except that she seems to be carrying a spear in one hand. But when Justine looks again the girl has disappeared.

26

A festival. From the colorful eight-foot letters spelling the name **M-I-D-T-O-W-N** at Colony Square to the lobby of the High Museum, people celebrate. They amble, dance, promenade, and mill to the sounds of reggae in the Piazza and jazz on the green. Streaming into the Wieland Pavilion where the ASO chamber orchestra plays, they celebrate a painting.

The final work of Mark Rothko, like a monolith to some forgotten god, has been moved into the lobby to accommodate the many viewers. Absent from public view for five decades, it finds a permanent dwelling place in the museum and city that welcomes it home. The place restores the word "mid" to its original meaning. Not a measurable halfway point, or an area passed through to get somewhere else, but "mid," as in assembling and meeting in conjunction with others beyond calculation, work, and commerce.

One notable person is missing: Dr. Ouruk Zaron. A defeated and damaged man, he has resigned from the hospital, dropped his plans for a new museum, and taken his money and collection elsewhere.

In the crowded lobby eight friends gather. Helena Gandolfi and Sir Reginald Foxcroft together, one to give a speech, the other to give the event an aristocratic air. Next are Phineas McGinley and Justine Foxcroft, last to possess the painting. Off to the side are Jonah Hartman and Sandra Foxcroft, he to sing, she to listen. Russell Baramore and Olas Lindgard, together, on their way to New

Joanne Cutting-Gray

York because of *another* work of art. All stare silently at the painting displayed like a cenotaph above the crowd.

Several days earlier, Regie and Helena had invited the couple to his condo for an announcement. "Tonight," Regie had said to them proudly, "if both of you agree, I will be the owner of an original Olas Lindgard." He had paused dramatically to let the surprise register. Then with great ceremony handed Olas a check. "Olas created not a copy but a Lindgard original." Helena and Regie agreed that the painting *was* a true work of art and deserved to have that reflected in the offer.

Now, as the eight friends celebrate a new beginning for a work of art and the end of their fellowship, a member of the museum staff informs them that the opening ceremony is about to begin. After remarks from various city officials and the modern and contemporary curator, Jonah is introduced. Accompanied by the orchestra, he sings an aria from *Andrea Chenier* that captures the artist's role in shaping the spirit of a people. There is a respectful silence when he finishes, then enthusiastic applause.

The tone has been set to acknowledge the gift to the city. After being introduced by the director as the painting's guardian angel, Helena speaks with shining face and argent expression: "We are gathered here in the spiritual heart of the city to celebrate this," she gestures around the lobby, "the place of myth and imagination."

"We could say much today about the artist Mark Rothko, his life, his hope and his despair, his successes and failures, the history of his work and his place in history. We could tell the story of how the painting came to Atlanta, of why it was lost, of the mishaps along its passage from private hands to public ownership. We could describe the methods for its authentication, how it is assessed, recorded, and preserved. We could do all that . . . but we will not." A pause.

"Instead look at this," she gestures to the work suspended behind her, "what do you see? Two blue and grey floating rectangles with smudged edges. 'That's all?' some might ask. 'Why does it tell us so little? How are we to look at it? How are we to *see* it?'

No one stirs as she continues. "Mark Rothko would sit in front of his easel and stare for hours meditating, waiting to receive what an empty canvas would give him. And that's how we should see *this*, waiting expectantly to let the not-yet-visible come to light. Waiting for what at first glance has so little to tell. If we subtract the human form from the great work of art, say Rembrandt's, *Supper at Emmaus*, we have what this artist painted. By taking the human form away, he gives us more of the human. With that in mind, let us take to heart what Rothko said of his own work, 'There is more power in telling little than in telling all.'"

"Practical men do not study the eternal, but what is relative in the present."

Aristotle

When Babylon falls, the merchants, traders, and shipmasters raise a song of lament (*Revelation*)— "Where is the life that late I led? 'Tis gone. 'Tis gone" (Shakespeare).

Atlanta a few years later. Boomtown: Celebration of sky cranes, backhoes, jack hammers, forklifts, diggers, bulldozers, graders, scrapers and hard hats. In dust and din, downtown to Buckhead, they are knocking down, dredging, excavating, hauling, stock piling, fabricating, forming and erecting. Commerce in a profusion of tongues and towers. Retail centers, residential units, corporate headquarters, banks, hotels, theaters, office complexes, and streetscapes. The old, semi-old, and relatively new levelled to make way for the all-new. Awash in projects, the city, host designate of a new heaven and earth, invites the mainly young, technologically savvy, college-educated, capital rich and entrepreneurial in triumphal march toward paradise.

Gone: Vacant lots, scarred and trash-filled, anonymous detritus of constructions past in neighborhoods abandoned to drugs, crime, and the poor. In its place a posse of smart new apartments, condos, and townhouses that the former residents cannot afford. Gone, the old-fashioned boarding houses, decrepit motels, down-at-the-heels parking lots, offices and inns dated and unfashionable. Gone, too, modest apartment houses and homes, humble shops and businesses.

In all these planned erections to glory, the arts still have a place. Foremost, architecture, the most material, least ephemeral art of the twenty-first century. Glass blades, fractals and crystals, forms free and random, curvilinear and hyperboloid, minimal surfaces with zero curvature. Sacred pillars on retail pedestals. To the south, a gleaming, faceted-glass metal sports arena with a retractable roof; to the north, sumptuous hotels and trading posts for the wealthy; to the west, retooled warehouses for trendy galleries and the decorative arts; to the east, conurbations of town, suburb and walkable venues.

In the middle of it all: Midtown. Where once eight-foot high, parti-colored letters gave a meeting place beyond commerce and an orientation for nondescript bedroom communities—a new Colony Square. The Bau Haus complex of the 70s worn at the edges, reimagined and rebuilt. Where once a running girl with a spear graced its paths, an expanded Piedmont Park and beltline trail. The spirit of Atalanta, hunter-goddess and remnant of ancient myth, protectress of the sacred—that past forgot. Prohibited and enclosed in receptacles, containers, coffers and casks—corks to repress lost meaning.

Once upon a time open spaces allowed reflection, memory, and experience. Then a chain of effects to enhance "the quality of life": management, economy, efficiency, speed. Blind faith in progress. All evident today in Renzo Piano's gracious piazza at the

High Museum, that once allowed for a fluid circulation of light and energy to complement Richard Meier's curvilinear white concrete and glass quadrants. Now a mountain of excavated earth beside a hole. A billboard-sized sign foretells what will fill it—the new Zaron-High Museum addition—a five story diamond-shaped, glass pyramid with a faceted cladding entered via an underground tunnel. The pedestrian path that once swept diagonally up to the sculptural forms of Meier's entrance with satisfying geometry—testimony to the mathematical infinite—to be replaced by a protective wall of bricks and mortar.

There is a small sign for the architecturally curious in the window of the Wieland Pavilion: "The reimagined Zaron-High Museum is a diamond, the hardest and most translucent of gemstones and symbol of purity in truth. It signifies the museum's commitment to the highest value for all the arts and their technical fulfillment." — Felicity Hardcastle, Director.

It was not always so. Mark Rothko once sat before his easel and stared for hours meditating, waiting to receive what an empty canvas would give him, waiting expectantly to let the not-yet-visible come to light. Waiting for what at first glance had little to tell. The practice prompted a question. Was he a mystic? "Not a mystic," he said of himself. "A prophet perhaps—but I don't prophesy woes to come. . . I paint the woes already here. . . . This is a problem of reticence. Some artists want to tell all like at a confessional. I as a craftsman prefer to tell little."

So to show the human he subtracted the human: "There is more power in telling little than in telling all."

Printed and bound by PG in the USA